Night Shade

Night Shade

Pauline Knaeble Williams

40

PRESS

Cover Design: Catherine Knaeble
Author Photo: Annmarie Boyan

Forty Press, LLC
427 Van Buren Street
Anoka, MN 55303
www.fortypress.com

ISBN 978-1-938473-29-6

To those who dedicated their lives to the abolitionist movement. To those whose names we remember, William Still, Margaretta Forten, Robert Purvis, Lucretia Mott, Abigail Goodwin, Peter and Elizabeth Mott. They appear in this book in a peripheral fashion, as a tribute to the brave work they did in and around the city of Philadelphia during the mid 1800s. The more central, fictitious characters in this novel represent the individuals who contributed to the struggle for freedom and equality, but whose names did not reach the history books.

"I received my freedom from Heaven, and with it came the command to defend my title to it. I don't respect this law - I don't fear it - I wont obey it! It outlaws me, and I outlaw it and the men who attempt to enforce it on me."

—Rev. Jermain Wesley Loguen,
(abolitionist, Syracuse NY)

1850

Chapter 1

Above the boy, hidden somewhere amongst the leaves, a bird sent forth a long, last note into the coming night. The cry broke against the balm of slumber and the boy sat up from where he had dozed in the forked arms of an old butternut tree. He waited, hoping the bird might call again, but the only sound that came was the one he'd been fleeing for the past three days.

He untied the rope that had lashed him to the branch, dropped soundlessly to the ground, and darted in the direction he knew to be north. The bird, too, flew off, but the pounding of the boy's heart left no room to imagine how a meadowlark might soar up through a placid sky.

He had been instructed to keep the river on his left, proceed until the deciduous forest gave way to the evergreens and then, when the ground began to climb, turn hard for the water's edge, mount the boat hidden along the shore and paddle in a line for the other side. He knew the number of miles he needed to cover, but hunger, weariness and a steady pain from where his foot had been torn by a sharp *rock clouded his mind. His eyes strained to find a clear path in the failing light.*

When the undergrowth thinned, he moved faster, allowing his feet to touch the ground only briefly. Behind him, the wailing of the hounds rose up along the tree trunks and hovered beneath the canopy of leaves before stretching insidiously across the narrowing distance between the search party and the fleeing boy. Feeling a stab of panic at the notion that they would soon spot him, he steamed forward. Then oddly, his mind landed back on the bird, as if it needed to latch on to something besides dread. He wondered why a meadowlark, whose sweet lazy songs had played like a flute while he toiled in the fields, had left the meadows for the wooded tree tops? How easy, he thought, for it to hide in the tall grass or perch upon a fence post and reveal its yellow belly. He envied, not its ability to do either, but the freedom to choose between the two.

He pressed on a bit longer, then stopped to scoop up a handful of earth. From the decaying leaves, rose the sharp scent of pine. He was almost there. He set off again, hurdling a fallen log and dodging a stretch of bramble before he wove more easily between the trees. Just when he thought his legs would give out, he felt the hill rise up to meet his step, he cut left and within minutes reached the shoreline. He searched for the rotting tree, backtracking to find it. The dogs were close; their barking, the snap of trampled brush, an intermittent shout.

Using the tip of the paddle, he pushed the boat out onto the surface of the water and climbed in. He could feel the pull of the current but the strength in his arms was more than enough to keep the boat aimed for the opposite side, each stroke issuing a soft swish that swirled up toward the moonless sky. Night had swallowed up the trees along the bank and settled low against the water on all sides. It closed in and the world behind him vanished. He was alone, at last, under the cover of the shade of night.

He paused to catch his breath. High above, beyond the veil of clouds, the tiny stars began to laugh. As if he could hear them, his gaze lifted. Then, he dipped the paddle back into the water and pressed on.

The Trossen dwelling relied on Penny McGinty for the up-keep of the four-story home on Pine Street in Philadelphia, in the center of the city. For the past ten years, Penny prepared the meals, lugged the firewood, scrubbed the floors, beat the rugs, laundered the garments, planted the gardens and performed the countless other duties needed to maintain a clean house and ensure the inhabitants were well-fed, properly dressed and reasonably comfortable. Mr. Trossen traveled often, residing in the home only periodically, but there was still much to do for Mrs. Trossen and the young niece, Miss Agnes, who had arrived a few years earlier for a visit that now seemed to have no end in sight. Penny sometimes wondered how long a temporary arrangement could persist and still be referred to as temporary. Despite her natural inclination, she kept her opinions to herself. She often needed to remind herself that she was just another Irish immigrant deemed to bang about in a hot kitchen and sleep alone in a narrow bed.

She would have groaned over a kitchen in the basement, like those found in so many other homes. There were already more than enough stairs to climb, and although her kitchen was often stifling during summer months, she was grateful for windows and an outlet to the back garden. Most pleasing was that through the pantry a door led to a little room that she could call her own, just wide enough to hold her bed and a small wardrobe, with a high window to let in light.

One June morning as Penny lifted a bowl of batter over the hot fry pan, her thoughts grazing through the strange and elongated courtship of Miss Agnes and her beau Mr. Hommes, she was interrupted by a rapping against the back door.

Startled, her hand jerked and the batter lurched for the rim of the bowl, a drop falling, with a hiss, into the skillet below. The sound hardened into the smallest cake she had ever made. She grinned, poured in the remaining batter and stepped to the door. Opening it, she expected a delivery of some kind not a weary, dark-eyed stranger rooted on the step.

"I've come, mam," was all the young woman said.

Penny paused. Puzzled she began to untie her flour-dusted apron, just to give her hands something to do. Then immediately she re-tied it, releasing a puff of white powder that snowed upon the tops of her shoes. "I beg yer pardon?" she said at last. "And perhaps I'll beg it twice, for I don't believe once will do the trick. What did you say yer needin'?"

She could not understand the matted nature of the girl's hair, nor the soiled look of her clothes. Her dress seemed to have taken on the exact color of dust and her face struck Penny in such an odd way. Her features seemed to waiver in an exaggerated manner, suggesting someplace long ago and far away. Then in the next moment, she resembled any scrawny and down on her luck girl, from just around the way.

The young woman had stood before the door for sometime, before knocking. Long enough to spy a lone window in the garret and to let herself imagine a real mattress upon which to sleep, not just a pallet on a floor or a bed of pine needles. She had also gazed out over the garden. From a distance the plants blended together into a sea of vegetation, yet, she deciphered the bee balm by its pink blossoms spreading in a multitude of directions, and the white fuzzy heads of fruiting dandelions and the leaning stalks of rough hawkweed all indicating how the garden was in need of attention. As she turned to face the door, she loosened the string from around a purple charm bag tied to a loop of her skirt. Removing a pinch of salt from the velvet pouch, she tossed the salt upon the step to ward off anything that needed warding off. Then the soft bag, with its D stitched in silver thread, disappeared, within the folds of her dress and she tapped at the door.

"I come to offer my help, figuring you could use it by the size of the house. I know all there is to working hard. If there is a room in the garret, that would do fine. And meals, of course. I shall be needing for nourishment."

Penny once again remained silent, finding herself feeling strangely adrift by the words uttered. The meaning—an offer of assistance—weighed as much as a burlap sack of dried beans, and yet the cadence of the girl's voice caused Penny to float slowly toward someplace she had never been, but could now vaguely imagine. Water, not the wide, salty ocean, but a narrow, snaking path more green than blue, more reeds and bank than a clear current, trickled through her mind.

She forced her attention back to the girl in front of her. Based on appearance, she wanted to spin the girl around and send her back into the thicket from which she had crept, except that Penny had never had anyone knock on the door asking to help with even the smallest task, even though, she had long held the opinion that the size of the house, with its countless stairs to scale, hearths to attend and dust mites to tame could not be properly kept by one poor soul, no matter how hard she labored.

"Where is it you say you come from, then?"

"Yonder."

"Yonder?" Penny yelped. "'Tis just the place I claim to have sprouted from myself. But I don't suppose we're talkin' o' the very same yonder, given' yer manner o' speakin' don't carry all the charm as my own." She chuckled.

She would not have been surprised if the young traveler possessed an Irish accent, as so many from Ireland were pouring into the city just as she had. But the girl's voice held a southern quality that reminded Penny of a licorice twist.

"Suppose not, mam," said the young woman as she folded her hands together to hide the dirt lodged under her

nails. Suddenly, Penny was convinced that too many questions were often more wearisome than their worth, especially on a day sailing by without the chamber pots emptied
nor the herring's head severed for the broth. She indulged
in the lovely possibility of having someone else help shoulder the household burdens, and, harboring a momentary
wish to lower onto a stool to listen to the girl recite a poem
with many stanzas, she was not overly concerned with her
origins, yet merely thought taking on a new maid should
require a certain amount of inquiry to ensure the seriousness
of the matter. She rather enjoyed pretending the decision
was hers to make.

Penny waved her in, mumbling, "Come on then, I'm certain we can sort it out proper but no more o' that "mam" talk.
That's what I called my own mother and I won't have you
draggin' me through sweet thoughts of her when I'm needin'
to tend to the business o' keepin' house."

The girl entered. Knotted on a string and hidden under
the buttons of her dress hung a key, cool against her skin.
She had come upon it years ago, when she was a child, as
she bent to pick watercress growing wild along a stream. She
now brought her hand to it as she crossed the threshold and
stepped inside the house. While in need of a good sweeping
and scrubbing, the kitchen's wide floorboards were a far cry
from the dirt floors of those she had been in previously. But
what caught her full attention was the cookstove parked like
a boxcar in the middle of the room, for she had never seen
one before, and through the grated door she could see the
flames of the fire feeding the four burners being put to use by
a kettle, a smoking skillet and two bubbling pots.

"Mother Mary," groaned Penny, "look what I've done!
Serves me right standin' around like there's naught to do but
look dainty." She wrapped her apron around the handle of
the pan and moved it from the burner to the shelf below.
The bottom crust of the shortbread had burned adding an

unpleasant odor to the hot room. Penny pushed opened the shutters of the window and saw the bewildered look on the girl's face. "Starin' at the fry pan, as if you've never laid eyes on one before?"

"It's not the frying pan, but that," the girl pointed at the stove. "I only know how to make do with an open fire."

"No kiddin', eh? I've not had to labor over a flame for many a years." Penny reached for a spoon to scrape the burnt pan. "Yonder it must be, then, if you've yet to bump against a cookstove." She toppled the shortbread onto a plate, noticing the girl's eyes had fixed on the food.

"Help yerself, then. I can't serve the likes o' that or it'll ruin my reputation for certain. The kitchen gives me no trouble a'tall, 'tis the rest of the house seems I can't keep under my thumb. I've been tellin' Mrs. Trossen how in need I am of help, but she's like a jar o' molasses when it comes to such matters," Penny sighed. "If you can work hard as you say, with a bit o' my charm, I'll bet I can see to you stayin' round for a stretch. But not dressed like that, pardon me sayin'."

She then lifted the kettle, poured warm water into an enamel basin, and handed over a thin bar of soap.

"Freshen up a bit. The dirt will come out from under those nails after I set you upon the pots. Believe it I would, had you claimed to have dug yer way here." She took another long look at the girl, feeling as if she was missing a most obvious sign. "Now where to find you a proper dress!" She shook her head at her own silliness as she marched through the pantry into her small rear bedroom, remembering an old dress she had relinquished due to its tapered fit.

The young woman rinsed her face and patted it dry, she then broke off a chunk of the burnt shortbread and ate it quickly, while peering again at the stove. She followed the blackened stovepipe as it ran up to the ceiling and disappeared through the roof. Along the ceiling beams she noticed bundles of herbs drying over the table. She spotted a cluster of sage, bound by a thin piece of twine.

Penny returned with the dress, another slice of shortcake and a cup of milk. The Trossen women had ventured to Camden to visit friends and wouldn't return until tomorrow. If they could make the house shine before their return, how could such a sparkling idea be refused? She guided the girl to the pots and baking bowls stacked about the sink.

"And the floor will be needin' a nudge with the broom. I'll see to the rooms above." She pointed a finger upwards. "'Tis three more floors, I'm afraid. For every ten steps the landin' turns, and with every landin' comes another set o' rooms cryin' for attention." She gathered her pail and rags and headed up.

With a fish broth simmering and the house empty, she could attend to the tasks of dusting fireplace mantles and brushing down bed linens. These would be some of the chores she would eventually give to the girl, along with the daily ones of emptying chamber pots and winding clocks. With two parlors on the first floor, a drawing room and study on the second and the bedrooms spread across the third, there seemed always a pressing reason to ascend the formal staircase at the front of the house or descend along the narrow one in the back. Each room required perpetual attention, including airing out in the hot months, or when the cold arrived, a constant feeding of the six fireplaces scattered throughout the house.

Penny began on the third floor. She moved about the bedrooms; dusting, sweeping and tidying. She adjusted the height of the lamp wicks, fluffed the pillows, and shook the dust from the draperies. She ran her rag over the high, solid baseboards and the deep window sills. She carefully weaved around the furniture so as not to knick the wood of the polished bureaus, nor knock the lamps from the bedside tables. On the second floor, in the drawing room that Agnes used each afternoon, she replaced the top to the ink jar and straightened the stack of stationary upon the desk. She noticed a small drawer left ajar. Reaching to close it, her eye caught upon a leather-bound journal. With one finger, she inched the drawer out until she could discern an A for Agnes embossed across the cover. Her heart quickened at the temptation to reach in and pluck up the book. Easily, she could leaf through a page or two and no one would be the wiser. A silent moment passed. She sighed and with her hip nudged the drawer closed. Her mam had taught her better than to snoop. Easy as it would have been, she did not want the burden of knowing what filled the pages, while having to carry on as if she didn't. She collected her pail of soiled rags and tottered down the back staircase.

When she entered the kitchen, she set her bucket down with a plunk. Not only did the dark wood of the floor glow like a roasted chestnut, but the stove appeared polished and the grime upon the window panes had been wiped away. The pots were scrubbed and the bowls stacked. For a moment the kitchen's tidy appearance distracted Penny from the scent of smoldering sage, but when her nose filled with the earthy smell, she looked up to find the young woman standing tip-toe upon a chair, waving a smoking bundle of herbs toward a high corner of the room.

Before Penny could voice her dismay, a familiar clattering sound rose from the front of the house. She turned at once and marched toward it. The new maid followed tentatively. Upon reaching the front hall, they found a set of Mr. Trossen's trunks and the door left wide open. The bustling activity of the street outside ran up the steps and wrapped around their skirts, as if binding them to their spot.

Mr. Trossen was not expected until later in the month, but it was not unusual that he arrive or depart in a rhythm-less fashion. He could be absent for months, arrive home and within days request that his bags be repacked for another jour-ney. Penny didn't mind much, as he had a benign disposition and was content with any plate of food she set before him, but it was not always so easy to get his clothes laundered and his belongings aired before he was turning around to leave again. And now, she would need to run to the market for a proper cut of meat, as she could no longer indulge in the meandering thoughts an empty house allowed but at once needed to formulate plans, as fish broth was fine for a maid's meal but would never suffice for the head of the house.

A dark figure, silhouetted by the bright day behind him, mounted the steps and entered the house. But it was not Mr. Trossen. Penny recognized him even before her eyes adjusted to the light. The silhouette was tall and lean, not barrel-chested with a generous waistline and a pigeon-toed stance.

"Good day," he said touching his hat.

"O' course, Mr. Clemons." Why she had failed to expect him to be handling the heavy trunks and the two bags he now set near the bench, she didn't know. The day seemed to have acquired an aberrant quality since the girl's knock on the kitchen door.

"Not like you to burn a thing, Miss Penny." He inhaled deeply. "Though it don't smell like something belonging in a kitchen." He closed his eyes for a minute. "Reminds me a old folks."

"Ah, Mr. Clemons," she grinned, "what would you be knowin' about old folks?" His hair was showing the first signs of gray in the front where it sprung up away from his forehead. It reminded her of the one fellow, the ex-slave, who went about speaking on the issue of slavery. Frederick something? She didn't know precisely what his speeches addressed although, she thought, who could argue that such a thing wasn't wrong?

"I had a mother once," he began, putting his hat back on. Silas Clemons had learned to let his guard down around the Trossen's cook. "Told me I was gonna live to be a hundred years and then some. Since I ain't yet close to halfway, that puts me near about the age of, let's see, well the age of a spring chicken."

It was then he noticed the other woman standing in the

shadow of the large grandfather clock. She seemed poised to step backward into the next room and yet she had a curious look upon her face. He held her in his glance long enough for him to see what the cook had not.

"You ready for him now, Miss Penny?" he asked, turning away from the girl and back to the task at hand. Calling out over his shoulder, "He's more tired than hungry from what I can tell. If you got the bed turned down, you all set."

Penny wondered if Mr. Clemons had another fare waiting or perhaps had consumed a bit of turned buttermilk that morning and needed to attend to his bowels. Ordinarily he tended to tarry, seeming to enjoy letting Mr. Trossen, who liked his belongings to precede him into the house, wait in the coach awhile. Today's sense of deliberateness on Mr. Clemons's part, only added to the oddity of the morning. But there was no time to dwell on strange developments or peculiar foreboding; there were pressing matters that needed to be addressed.

She spun around to the girl. "Hear me now, off you go. Best to keep you out from under foot. 'Tis not the mister's nose that should be pokin' about in the affairs o' the kitchen. That's best left for the lady o' the house. There's a heap more to do, but not before you see to that mop on yer head." She offered a hairbrush, then shooed the girl down the hall, whispering, "Without loosin' all the bristles, eh?" just as the men's voices rolled up from the street.

Chapter 2

Wobbling as he stood up, the boy slipped into the shallow water of a small inlet, its weak current wrapping around his ankles. Hoisting the tip of the boat up the bank, he then stood for a moment, allowing the cool water to soothe his stinging feet as the blades of grass, high as his head, twitched all around him. *I am safe here*, he thought; *I could stand here forever and no one would find me.* Just then a hand appeared at his side and yanked the skiff further in. A shot of panic surged through the boy, but the hand, rough and worn, reached for his elbow and guided him up the bank. The man drew a finger to his lips as the cattails whispered good-bye and the sawing of the frogs started up again. As they began to walk away from the riverbed, darkness seeped in so tight that the boy could barely make out the man in front of him, only that he moved with a stooped gait, and smelled of fish.

When they paused beside a tree whose trunk stretched wider than the two of them put together, the old man took a moment to catch his breath.

"What name they call you?" came a voice so low the boy could not be certain anything was said at all. The river murmured while the man gave a little grunt to prove he had asked a question.

"Zeb," he said in a rusty voice, just as the moon, rising low and heavy on the horizon, broke through the clouds.

"All right then, Zeb. Follow me." But he didn't move, just remained standing with his eyes latched firmly upon the boy. "You ain't near grown yet, is you?"

"No, sir." The man reached over and rubbed the boy's head, just once. Under the slender glow of the round moon, the boy's eyes gleamed with tears. He had not been on the receiving end of kindness in a long time. The two walked in silence and the boy imagined that they had known each other for a long time. Half a mile into the woods, in a small candle-lit cabin, two plates of food sat on a table waiting for them.

The Trossen women returned the next day to stumble over Mathias's house slippers parked in the front hall and then, as they trudged toward the back of the house in search of a refreshment, they were surprised to spot a complete stranger pruning weeds in the garden. Penny tried to explain, then called the girl in, motioning her to straighten her cap.

"Tell the Mistress yer proper name, now, and where 'tis you come from. Better for you to say it clearly, than me to mix it half up," insisted Penny not wanting to admit she knew neither.

The traveler stood before the ladies of the house, hair now combed and oiled, fingernails clipped. She opened her mouth, closed it, opened it again. She had no intention of revealing the truth or inventing a lie, either of which might entangle her later. She strung together whatever bits and pieces she could salvage from stories overheard at the fireside or from songs sung to keep the sun moving across the sky. The slippery tale had no beginning nor end, slithering back and forth, tangling days into nights, twisting people into places and comings into goings. Soon all that filled the room was the rhythm of her voice, the words having fallen apart. Upon finishing, a forlorn sense of bewilderment hung about, leaving nothing but a few lingering words like footbridge and moss peal, and the phrase "Jimmy crack corn."

Josephine cleared her throat and looked as if she was to say something of great importance, but merely asked for a tall glass of water and a place to sit.

Her niece, Agnes, closed one eye and tried to remember if the girl had mentioned a name by which she could be addressed. While Agnes had lived her entire life in Pennsylvania, her parents had been born in the Netherlands and had recently made the decision to return to their homeland. They had agreed to allow Agnes to stay on for a time with her aunt and uncle in Philadelphia.

"And what did you say we should call you, lass?" Penny placed a glass of water for Josephine upon the table.

"Larkspur."

The name landed awkwardly upon the ears of the listeners, but off the tongue from which it was issued it opened like a first bloom.

"Well, there we have it," chimed Penny and instructed the girl to fetch greens from the garden for dinner.

As Larkspur slipped through the backdoor, Penny reported that Mr. Trossen had gone out for the afternoon, yet they should be aware of his intentions to have the Blairs and the Spiedlers invited to dinner next week. She added how his enthusiasm to enjoy the neighbors' company and host a perfect evening seemed exceptionally high. Of course, the help of the girl would be vital.

Mrs. Trossen, already fatigued from traveling after a poor night's sleep, had not the patience to point out the tradition of past dinner parties succeeding without the use of extra help. Nor did she have the fortitude to face any decision-making in such a wearied state. "I shall need to rest now," was all Josephine could muster. She had made little sense out of the story rattled off by the young girl, but if Penny needed help for another of Mathias's nettlesome socials, what did it matter?

She could let the girl go at the end of the week. She shuffled out of the kitchen. The drink of water had helped to clear her head, but her feet pinched in her slender boots.

Agnes, tired as well, was just turning the first landing of the front staircase when she heard the trill of the lever being turned at the front door. She waited for Penny to attend to the visitor and winced when she heard Bernhart's voice. She was in no condition to receive him; her dress musty, hair uncombed, and eyes puffy. Crossing her fingers, she was relieved when the heavy front door closed and the house grew quiet, save for one set of footsteps.

From the bottom of the stairs came a loud whisper, "I sent the poor lad off, knowing the state of yer appearance, Miss. He left his visiting card, with the corner turned down, o' course. Shall I climb up now or can I send the young sprite up when things have settled a bit?"

"In a bit then, Penny," she answered, smiling over the fact that Bernhart had missed her. She was thankful for Penny's good judgement.

In her room, the curtains were drawn to keep out the afternoon heat. Removing her dress and stiff petticoat, and loosening the ties of her corset, she then lowered onto the bed. Earlier she had anticipated the moment she could recline in the dim solitude of her room.

She had imagined it while dismounting the ferry that had carried them back to Philadelphia, and while trudging up the path leading to the cobblestone streets of the bustling, malodorous city. They had needed to dodge the scuttling wagons, the piles of horse dung and the peddlers shouting out the marvels of their wares. Finally, they succeeded in flagging down a coach to bring them across the last, brief leg of the journey. While the driver arranged their luggage, she noticed two stray dogs begging at the door of a meat shop, until the butcher, in his stained apron, raised his broom to shoo them away. And as they bumped along the cobbled street, she watched out the window as they passed the row of farmers' wagons parked against the curb of the open market house, glimpsing the shoppers weaving amidst the wide and voluminous array of goods for sale.

These images and the remnants of the pungent smells and the distinct sounds now drifted beyond the edge of her thoughts and fell with her into sleep. Her breath lengthened. Her limbs melded into the soft mattress. Tucked into the dream, too, was Bernhart. Calling from another carriage, his arm stretched out towards hers and yet the space between them widened, as she was swept along in the opposite direction, until she could no longer decipher him from the crowd.

༄

The date for the dinner party was put off from one week to the next. To Penny's frustration, the delay allowed for an excess of frivolous planning, with preparations seesawing back and forth for no better reason than there was time for idle suggestions, sudden cravings and change of hearts. Yet she had no reason to complain, hoping the longer Larkspur stayed in the house, under any pretext, including drawn out dinner arrangements, the harder it would be to send her off. The end of the month of June neared before a day was finally set and the invited parties confirmed.

During this time Mr. Trossen occupied himself with business appointments and Mrs. Trossen spent her afternoons at her sewing club, while Agnes and Bernhart found occasions to spend time together. There were walks along the riverfront, strolls through Washington Square, an occasional dinner outing and countless afternoons when the two would merely visit in the front parlor over tea, Bernhart invariably spilling upon his lapel and Agnes politely ignoring his clumsiness.

On the afternoon before the date of the dinner party, as

Bernhart finished his second cup of tea and latched upon the topic of the medicinal benefits of mugwort, Agnes interrupted. "Bernhart, is mugwort that tall, scratchy looking weed that makes one sneeze when tromping about the countryside?"

"Why yes, it is prone to irritate the sinuses, and yet I have only just read that it is a help with cardiac complaints and general malaise."

"Are you suffering from bouts of general malaise?"

"No, no of course not," he grinned.

"And yet do you recall what happened when we last visited Bartram's Garden? How can you be so enthralled with the mugwort plant when it caused you to sneeze all afternoon?" She frowned and Bernhart was uncertain as to whether she was becoming genuinely agitated or, on the contrary, enjoying the dual.

"Dearest Agnes, while what you say may be true, you forget how we Germans stuff our Christmas goose with a sprig of mugwort and proclaim it 'goosed'." At this, he raised his teaspoon and let out a bellow, which brought Penny from the back of the house worried an opossum had come down the chimney again.

"Bernhart, you must promise me," Agnes began, "that when you come tomorrow night you will attempt to refrain from bellowing or speaking of anything pertaining to sinus irritations or heart failure. While such subjects can be intriguing, you must admit a dinner party may not be the proper stage. And I do so want you to continue making a fine impression upon my aunt and uncle. Yes?"

He assured her he would remain a mannerly and reserved guest throughout the night.

෨

Bernhart dressed for dinner. After trimming his beard, he looped a tie around the high collar of his linen shirt, then slipped into his evening coat. Before reaching for his top hat, he picked up the daily paper from where it had sat folded on his desk. He began to scour the headlines, knowing that when dining with the Trossens political discussions invariably accompanied the meal's courses. He did not want to appear as an uneducated citizen, even though the task of staying abreast of the day's current issues was less intriguing than spending time with a thick volume of Egyptian alchemy, or at a work-table studying the cross-section of a root, and afterward de-scribing it all to Agnes. Within the hour, he arrived at the Trossen home and was soon standing in the front parlor with the other guests, as he waited for Agnes to make her appear-ance.

Outside the light had begun to drain from the deepen-ing sky, so the new maid went about the room lighting the lamps. Bernhart noticed, as she passed the open windows, a gust of air blew the summer curtains so that they billowed out and nearly enveloped her in their lacey arms. Momen-tarily surprised, she halted and glancing up caught his gaze. As the curtains fluttered back to their place against the wall like sullen and apologetic children, she quickly looked away and returned with diligence to her task. At the same moment, Mathias Trossen's voice jumped out in Bernhart's direction.

"No man could argue the impact of the invention of the cotton gin," Mathias said, grinning at Bernhart while hold-ing the elbow of Mr. Blair, "yet so many fail to see how it has entirely boosted our position in the world market."

At this Mr. Blair raised his finger, poised to respond, but Mathias continued on, guiding his guest toward the stoppered bottles of liquor kept upon a tray on the sofa table. "Samuel you must realize, full well, how much cotton we export yearly. An enormous amount that could never have been imagined before the gin's invention, just fifty odd years ago."

Then to enlarge his audience, with his glass refilled, he turned to Bernhart only to find him fully distracted by Agnes just entering the room in a low-neck evening gown the color of grated lemon peel over an icy sorbet.

Bernhart watched as she set about greeting each guest, carrying herself with a steady grace. Her dress, its wide skirt contrasting with the narrow-fitting waist, accentuated the elegant way in which she engaged her full torso for both her slight and grand movements. He thought this a splendid revelation and so different from how his own stiff actions began and ended in the shoulders. He would need to study himself in the mirror when he got home. Perhaps there was an explanation for his clumsiness after all. Suddenly, Agnes stood before him, and while the rest of the room continued with its tinkering exchanges, the two found themselves alone in a private moment.

"Agnes, my dear," he said reaching for her hand.

"Bernhart," she replied.

They stood looking at each other, her hand left to rest gently in his palm, until they realized the guests were being summoned for dinner. Offering his arm, she tucked her hand within it as they headed to the back parlor where the table was set with more pieces of silver than one could take the time to count, white china with gilded rims and a bouquet of hydrangeas poised at the center.

All present knew that Mathias Trossen was a keen businessman, always at the forefront of investment opportunities. His past financial success and his willingness, no, exuberance to travel allowed him ample opportunity to find the most promising markets in which to entrust his money, as well as the money of others. Having benefited from the cotton boom for decades, he was always willing to credit Eli Whitney for this simple, yet transforming, invention.

Mr. Blair struck up the conversation where it had left off. "Mathias we are well aware of your fondness for the cotton engine and your opinion that it has created a revolutionary change to the country, but this is not news. Surely, for the past few years we have all been enjoying our increased economic position in the world market, but let us not forget the other grand technical innovations. There is the railroad system, the steam engine, the telegraph and the less touted, reaper. Why, they say McCormick's mechanical reaper will allow the wheat of the midwest prairies to emerge as the great crop of exchange; paying debts, purchasing goods and land, and allowing farmers to trade amongst themselves."

Mathias smiled. "Good and well, but I shall keep my money on cotton, as it has proved the reason behind our nation becoming nothing less than an agricultural powerhouse," Mathias brought his palm to the table to emphasize his point. "For our textile mills here in the northern cities can now clothe the backs of all of Britain, not to mention our own. Look at my lovely niece in her yellow gown. It must have taken fifty pounds of cotton to stitch a dress with such an unending number of folds and flounces. I thank Eli for that." In actuality, Mathias knew only a few pounds of cotton was required for a dress even as elaborate as the one Agnes wore, but he could not resist embellishment to charm a slightly intoxicated audience. He raised his glass, to which the rest of the table joined in.

As Larkspur lowered a bowl of consomme in front of Agnes, its watery contents surged dangerously toward the rim of the bowl. Agnes was surprised at the new maid's carelessness. She looked up to find her expression impassive, giving no indication of what might be hampering the girl's ability to focus on the proper etiquette needed to serve a formal dinner. Agnes glanced at her Aunt to see if she had noticed. The older woman, with her lovely white hair drawn back softly from her face and her lips pressed together, had her eyes set upon a painting just above her husband's head.

Bernhart was attending to a stuffed button mushroom skirting about on his plate, wondering if an inappropriate use of his butter pick might draw scrutiny from Agnes, when he cleared his throat. "While I know very little about trends of fashion, nor the purpose of folds, nor the advantage of flounces, I would argue it is Agnes herself who gives the dress its appeal. Nonetheless, I suppose Elijah should be given due credit for his invention."

Agnes hid her smile with a spoonful of soup.

"I believe the name is merely Eli," corrected Mathias, then charged forward. "Most are not aware, the machine itself merely performs the time-consuming task of separating the seeds from the cotton fibers. It can process fifty times what a person working by hand can do in a day. But the actual making of the fabric, the combing and carding, weaving and dying, that is much beyond the humble machine's capabilities. That is accomplished in the mills up here in the north." He paused to sigh, balancing his spoon upon a saucer. "But of course, it is what occurs prior to the cotton reaching the gin that has the country torn asunder."

Agnes was eager to find a way to participate in the discussion. "What must transpire to supply the cotton gin with so much cotton, Uncle?"

"Why, my dear, it must be planted and picked. A most backbreaking task that only a slave is equipped to endure. Infact, I would argue that only a slave is designed to endure, given his high tolerance for physical labor and his decreased capabilities to assess his own miserable lot in life. He can work all day with only the crack of an occasional whip to keep him on his toes and he'll rise the next day, eager to begin again as the toil of the day before is but a lost memory. Although, I should not say he, I have heard that it is often the females who can outpick the strapping males. Either way, sunup to sundown, such buoyant labor is what keeps us all in high fashion."

"Dreadful," Agnes murmured. She tried to imagine working in a field all day. "It is good to know it is left to slaves who do not suffer from it." But once verbalized she couldn't deny that such a theory seemed debatable, if not rather preposterous.

"Surely the invention of new machinery, like the cotton gin and the reaper, will help to limit such laborious tasks," offered Bernhart, rejoining the conversation.

"Perhaps you will invent one soon, sir," suggested Mr. Blair. "But some inventions, like that of the cotton gin, have served only to dramatically increase the need to send more and more slaves into the fields. Would you not, Mathias, credit your wonderful machine for the birth of the internal slave trade? Why I believe, slavery was a dying business until it came along."

"I would level it was dying along with the tobacco industry," Mathias said, "and then nearly stomped to death when Congress banned the importation of any new slaves into the country back in '08. But we have learned to make do with what we have." Mrs. Blair, sitting to the left of her husband, hummed in agreement, placing a knife upon her bread plate.

Finally, Mr. Spiedler cleared his throat. "You well know where I stand upon the issue of slavery. The internal slave trade, sending slaves from the border states to the deep south to work the fields, is no less abhorrent than shipping them from across the ocean. Although they may not yet be on par, in many respects, with those of us of European blood, I cannot condone how they are moved about as if nothing more than cattle. I certainly wish, but most severely doubt, that Mr. Hommes can invent something that would put a halt to such trafficking. And now, with Congress in a stalemate and the talk of strengthening the fugitive slave law, I only hope that the Negro can naturally endure more than the rest of us, for that is precisely what he will be required to continue to do."

Larkspur returned to remove the soup bowls, while Penny plated the next course in the kitchen. The sunchoke gravy was to be spooned over the mutton any moment, so Larkspur needed to be quick about it, yet she couldn't help but linger over the comments coming from the thin, furrow-browed Mr. Spiedler.

"Ha," Mathias chuckled, keeping his voice feathery as he leveled his next remark. "You have many hopes and wishes Charles, and one may include joining the ranks of the reckless abolitionists, yet still you sit before me in your finely-tailored attire, failing to enjoy how you benefit from all that you despise."

Here was the point at which Josephine could endure no more of her husband's self-assured antics. She could see how Mrs. Blair and even Mrs. Spiedler leaned forward when he spoke as if to prove his wit and knowledge were not going unappreciated. She was certain he could go on forever attempting to display his immeasurable store of charm, but she required a well-deserved respite.

"At last, the main course," she announced as Larkspur and Penny came forward. "Let us savor our meal, dear husband, before we embark upon what shall become of the California territory or the compromises of Congress. Anna and Elizabeth, tell me of your summer plans?"

Most at the table were happy for the turn in conversation. The topics of weather and travel, specifically the unpredictability of the railways, spun their way around the table. Bernhart took the opportunity to catch the eye of Agnes, but she had her gaze cast toward the work of her knife and fork upon her plate, her thoughts still entangled in the previous conversation. She felt a surge of adrenaline at the possibilities of all there was to consider when it came to making the world go round. It was both dreadful and exciting. She looked to Bernhart, hoping to find upon his face a sign that they shared this tide of interest, but he was now engaged with the other women at the table, insisting that their summer would not be complete without a visit to Bartram's Botanical Garden, just west of the city along the banks of the Schuylkill river. When Mrs. Blair frowned at the possibility of encountering insects as well as poison sumac all in one day, it took great effort for him to hold fast to his pledge to Agnes not to bellow in dismay.

The remainder of the evening proceeded as expected. After the pudding was served and finger-bowls of lemon water were offered each guest to signal the end of the meal, the women repaired to the upstairs drawing room for tea and coffee, while the men lingered around the table, indulging in a glass of port before joining the women. Josephine, more than once, envisioned her talkative husband as a sack of flour that she might punch, while Agnes expected Bernhart to work for her attention despite not feeling entirely capable of returning it. Bernhart was satisfied to spend the mild summer evening, the air from outside floating in through the open windows to weave about the ends of coattails and blouse sleeves, observing Agnes's graceful torso. Adjusting his own movements, ever so slightly, to absorb some of hers.

∽

Silas Clemons jiggled the latch to inform Mercy Tubbs the day was dawning. When the stable door swung open and daylight flooded toward her stall, the particles of dust, hay, cobwebs and love shimmered in the path between the man and horse.

"Yeah, a course, old girl, I came back. Just like yesterday and day before that. A promise is a promise. Ain't that so, Mercy Tubbs? Something a man can keep, is his word. Not too much a nothin' else, though." The horse lifted her head into his hand as he petted her.

"Yep, you the one," he murmured, "and spoiled rotten." He petted her soft coat that he had brushed through the night before. He set a bucket of oats in front of the horse, who snorted so that Silas drew a handful and held it to her mouth. She ate slowly, licking his hand purposefully as she gathered the grain upon her tongue. Patiently, he hummed a sorrowful tune they both favored.

When his hand was empty, he said, "Even the queen got to feed herself, Mercy Tubbs. Get at that bucket, girl, I got my own business to tend to."

A wheel on the carriage needed attention. He set to work sanding out a dent. The streets were crude and unpredictable so that damage to the wheels was common. Silas was capable of handling most of the repairs without needing to bother his employer, Mr. Spiedler, to call for the wheelwright. Sitting down on a stool with his tools, he was soon singing a song of maypoles and yellow baskets, happy to be holding something of wood even if less interesting than the sticks lying about the yard that he often whittled into a mermaid or a porpoise.

So many years had rolled away, that he could scarcely recall how white oak, pine or even cherry felt under his palm. For a long time, back in Virginia, he labored as a carpenter, crafting furniture from which the man who owned him profited nicely. Skilled with his spokeshave and adept in carving dovetails, the drawers of his dressing tables glided in and out, the doors of his cabinets swung open without a creak. He modeled his pieces in the style of the time, sensible and functional, with only a decorative flair added to the wooden knobs.

His admired craftwork prevented him from suffering the hardship of plantation life, although he lived under a constant threat of being sold off to endure just such misery. The continued demand for his work kept him bound to the same man for years, until the two traveled to the city of Philadelphia where the fate of each took a sharp turn.

Not long after he had gained his freedom, thanks to an unusual facet of Pennsylvania law, and unable to gain employment as a carpenter, due to the singular condition of his skin color, Silas agreed to a paid position with Charles Spiedler. He resigned himself to the task of driver, transporting the

Spiedler family and others in the neighborhood who found it easier and more frugal to use a coach-for-hire than to own and care for one's own horse. Silas procured an occasional tip offered by a gentleman, and more so, utilized his mobility to his carefully measured advantage.

The morning eased along, the shadows shortening and the air warming. The Spiedlers, still recovering from the previous night's dinner engagement at the Trossens, had yet to require transportation, so Silas kept busy with chores around the yard. By late morning he was back on his stool near Mercy Tubbs. It was then when he heard voices from over the wall. The carriage house was located at the remote end of the yard and opened to a narrow lane that linked into the wider, cobblestone street. When the gate was closed, the back end of the yard offered a sense of seclusion. It offered, under the shade of two old Sycamores, a space in which Silas felt at home. On the other side of the gate and just across the grassy lane, was a stone wall surrounding the Trossen courtyard. On a calm day, when sounds could linger in the air before evaporating, it was possible to hear, if one had ceased humming while whittling with one's pocket knife, strange conversations between two young women hanging the linens.

Every other Monday, dubbed by Penny as affliction day, was set aside for the tackling of the wash. The copper was filled and set to boil, the lye soap added, the musty garments stirred and prodded with the dolly stick, rubbed against the washboard, rinsed in another cauldron and finally sent through the mangle. Afterward, the heap of it was left in a basket near the kitchen door for Larkspur to hang. While both maids knew that the Trossens expected to move about in tidy, pressed attire, with clean detachable collars and cuffs, spotless handkerchiefs, and a fresh change of undergarments at least once a week, neither woman suspected that the family members gave any thought whatsoever to the likes of soap cakes, raw knuckles, and washboards.

Agnes had awoken in an agitated state. She rose from her bed determined to shift her mood and so had spent a focused amount of energy smoothing the wrinkles from the bed covers, removing the stitching from the previous day's needlepoint and pacing the floorboards of the drawing room while she waited for lunch to be served. Still the discontent lingered so that she suddenly found herself marching out the back door into the yard to help with the laundry, telling herself not to worry if the new servant found her odd. Her only concern was to shed the disconcerting feeling she'd acquired since the dinner party the night before, and she thought the challenge of an unfamiliar activity might clear her thoughts.

She began imitating Larkspur's movements; bending, snapping, pinning. For a fleeting moment, surrounded by the green garden and humming insects, she brightened. But it was not long before her arms ached, sweat dotted her forehead and she began wondering how a person could persuade herself to return to such a grim task having tried it once. Dropping her arms to her sides with a huff, she waited, hoping the girl might speak or pose a question. But the new maid remained silent, moving gracefully between the basket and the clothesline with a rhythm that resembled the carrying out of a dance rather than a chore.

Finally, to keep herself from sinking to the ground in a heap, Agnes blurted, "Have you no mercy? Must I beg you to remind me of your name once again?"

Slow to offer a reply, a bird overhead warbled to fill the silence. At last the girl said, "A name is a hallowed thing."

"And so please, can you not spit it out?" Agnes was depleted of patience. It was not that she was particularly interested in the information she sought, but merely harbored a vague sense of wanting something, a foothold of some kind.

"Larkspur," offered the maid, raising her voice at the end to suggest that even she might not altogether be certain of the name she possessed.

Agnes eyed her for the longest time awaiting an explanation to the question mark hovering between them. The girl's dark hair seemed to grow fuller, a curl slipping out from under her cap. Her eyes were like wet stones.

"You can call me Larkspur," she added more confidently, pinning the last dish towel to the line.

"Larkspur is a very unusual name. I can't recall having heard it before. Brings to mind something purple and noxious." Met with silence, Agnes charged gallantly into the fog that had clouded her thoughts since she awoke, triggered by the events of the night before, not only the dinner conversation that exposed the complexity of the world at large, but more so the distance she felt between herself and Bernhart that only seemed to be filling with confounding emotions. She yearned to sort it all out and without a clear path of where they might land, the words began tumbling forth.

"What I find most puzzling is why a man can move through the day at his tasks, say pounding dry seeds with a pestle or filling glass beakers with liquids, and then arrive into evening with the liberty to relay such activities in as much or little detail as suits his mood. The listener, no matter if she fancies the speaker with his odd and agreeable nature and finds most of what he says entertaining, is expected to regard it as sufficient to fill that which the rest of her day has lacked. Although, it is safe to project that I shall never clamor to return to the tasks I have attempted today, I do sometimes wonder if that which gives a maid's day purpose and structure does also serve as a buffer against a certain kind of madness."

By the look on Larkspur's face, Agnes feared she may have said too much, despite knowing she had conveyed very little of what weighed upon her mind. She could not explain how on some days she felt flat, as if her lungs had been sent out of the room so that her heart could wallow in the growing realization that her life was lacking some indiscernible substance. On such days, she struggled to look ahead with enthusiasm to the honorable role of wife and mother.

Larkspur, struck by the indulgent notion of searching for a purpose in life, realized Agnes was waiting for a reply. "Work is just work, I never seen a way around it. And going mad, well that can find a way of sneaking up on just about anybody."

There was something in the maid's tone that did not sit well with Agnes. Or perhaps it was the words themselves. How would the woman, roughly her same age, have acquired more wisdom than she had found in all her books and years of tutoring? It was pathetic enough, in this moment of weakness, to envy a maid her role, but now to covet her acumen was too much for Agnes to shoulder. Spinning on her heel, she dashed through the yard, struggled with the door and finally slipped in. Ignoring Penny at the table, she made her way through the house, and arriving at the foot of the front stairs paused. She had a strange and sudden urge to take them two at a time, but of course, the unwieldy length of her dress and the bothersome petticoat underneath, rustling an admonishment, warned her to proceed with her customary reserve.

Chapter 3

*Z*eb stayed with the old man and his wife through the night and into the next morning. When the sun rose in a still, blue sky, the woman roused the boy to clean the gash in his foot and wrap it in a poultice of comfrey leaves. She had argued that he should stay a while to let the wound heal properly, but her husband shook his head no. The sooner he traveled on, the better for all of them.

"Once we get you some shoes, you got to be going. Nothin' but trouble comes from stragglin' in one spot too long. Them peoples you running from might figure out you crossed over and get themselves they own boat. You should a done been gone 'cept you can't get nowhere barefooted. Sure sign of a runaway."

"How you two get to be free?" asked the boy.

The couple chuckled. "We ain't free boy, it's just Sunday," she explained. "We so old they let us stay out in this here cabin away from the others, since ain't no room in the quarters noways." She patted her thighs a few times. Neither the woman nor the man had reached the age of fifty, but their bodies were worn out from unending days of labor, beatings and never enough food to fully regain the proper energy and strength necessary to get up each morning and start again.

They were old compared to the others. Most didn't live past thirty.

"But we still young enough to get the lash if we don't see to our tasks daily," her husband added in a light voice that didn't match the creases around his eyes. "'Cept Sunday." He lifted his gaze beyond the clearing in front of them and latched onto the solemn trunks of the trees.

"Hmmpf," she murmured. Her skin was papery so that Zeb wanted to reach out and touch it. "Can't see no sense to why these white folks think feigning Christian-like one day from seven gonna save their souls from going straight to the hell fire. Still leaves six to count for. Everybody be knowin a time comes you gotta pay the piper, no way 'round it. Ain't that so, husband?"

The three sat on the step of the small cabin, looking out over a small clearing surrounded by woods. The boy watched a pair of bumblebees hover above the flowering henbit, the sun growing strong as it stretched toward the treetops. A kerchief of food for the journey sat at the boy's hip. They had told him to wait in the cabin, to be safe, but he had found it so gloomy, he had come out to the step after a while.

"Look at him," she nodded toward her husband, who had dozed off, "suppose to be on the lookout post. Make no sense puttin' your fate in an old-timey sleep on the job. But lord knows," she smiled, "you take what you can get. It's a small miracle to get to keep a husband for longer than it takes a cat to wink it's eye." She stared at him for awhile, then looked at the boy. "And now you listen here, you gonna need a little help along the ways. Gets tricky figurin' who to trust and who ain't nothin but the devil. Watch out for the ones whose smile don't match the look in the eyes. Ain't only the whites who might do you in." She raised a finger in the air. "Only thing you can count on is an inkling. You get a hunch, you pay it some mind."

A figure emerged from a path leading out of the woods.

Zeb jumped up in alarm but the woman whispered, "Only James." She nudged her husband. James placed the shoes on a stump and kept moving.

The man jerked awake. "Only James with the shoes," he said, "Come on boy, it's time to take out."

Although in poor condition with the stitching frayed near the toes, the boy was grateful to put the shoes on over a pair of socks. They nearly fit. The old man explained he should follow the path James had come along. When it split in two, veer to the right. It was no more than a few miles before he would come across a large poplar tree, hollowed out at the base, in which he could hide until nightfall.

"Always move at dark and find you a good spot to hide by day. I know you ain't no wild animal but you got to move like one. Know which way you is heading by watching the sky. The food you got should last till Richmond. It ain't but three days, if you go steady. You want a man goes by Captain B." Then the old man patted the boy's shoulder and pushed him off. "Be quick getting to that poplar."

His wife was tempted to call after the boy, who seemed to her no more than a baby, but the whole endeavor was so tenuous she didn't want her words to shatter the fragile air. When he disappeared into the woods, the warm day settled down in the small clearing where she and her husband stood. The sound of the insects rose to fill the void left by the departed young boy, a boy too much like the five she had birthed only to have been taken from her before they were grown. The world felt to her like a lonely, god-forsaken place.

The days moved up and down, as summer days do; the early mornings docile, the afternoons heavy and humid, the lush sounds of evening calling the curious from their homes to stroll along the cobblestone streets, pausing in the park squares to absorb the deepening hues of twilight. A single day stretched long and each part of it seemed different from the other so that those in the Trossen household seemed to swim along, sometimes up current and sometimes down. Aunt Josephine confused one day for two and then two for four, so that after awhile it seemed the new girl had been with them far too long to bother considering if she should stay or go.

If anyone were to notice, the house shown brighter and the garden flourished. Penny, although hesitant to part with ingredients she used for her soup broth, had agreed to give Larkspur a portion of the kitchen scraps to compost for garden soil. Larkspur pruned the bee balm and the sage, discovered comfrey and lavender thriving amidst a bed of creeping buttercups, and put in an array of root vegetables so that by fall they would have a harvest to store in the cellar.

Over breakfast on the first morning of July, Mathias announced that next week he would be called away on business for an indefinite amount of time, traveling to the bottom states. Agnes had joined her Aunt and Uncle and the three were now concluding the meal with raspberries and sweetened cream.

"Louisiana?" asked Josephine. "Is there anything beyond alligators and panthers in such a swampland?"

"On the contrary. The city of New Orleans is now the fourth largest in all the nation and is deemed a magnificent sight to behold. I don't suppose I shall find an alligator along any of its streets." He laughed affably. "And if all goes well, I will travel part of the way by steamboat."

"But Uncle, you forget that your stomach does not fare well on boats," Agnes reminded him.

"My darling, when it comes to important business matters, I shall brave the challenge. There is forever more to learn and I'm happy for the chance at it. The trading season begins in September, therefore I have much to observe in order to prepare myself before autumn arrives."

"It will be miserably hot this time of year," Josephine

noted, trying not to reveal in her voice the relief she felt over her husband's plans of departure.

"The trading season of what?" asked Agnes.

He hesitated. "Why, the slave trading season, if you must know. Such questions! It seems you have procured a sudden interest in affairs of great magnitude. Perhaps a step beyond your reach, beyond the focus of your own schooling? No doubt the years of tutoring, arranged by your caring parents, were to see that you arrive into adulthood as a fine lady, able to draw the attention of a gentleman like Bernhart without appearing as an empty vessel." She poked at the last raspberry in her bowl while her uncle continued, "I have always encouraged you to ask questions, but Agnes, be careful that you mind your curiosity outside these walls. A woman with too fervent a disposition can be like a potato salad with all too much vinegar." He laughed alone at his joke.

Agnes pressed on. "But you are a banker. What has that to do with slave trading?"

"I am in the business of financing, which requires one to consider a very vast landscape of possibilities," he said with assuredness. "It is that which transpires in the deep, fertile soil of our southern region that keeps us humble northerners prosperous."

His wife held her eyes closed while Mathias changed the subject without taking a breath. "Now, dear Wife, I plan to depart following the fourth of July holiday. Have we not received an invitation to celebrate the great occasion with friends or acquaintances, or are our admirers hoping we host yet another glorious event in our own home? I cannot stand to think we would consider a picnic along the river as we attempted some years back, with the mosquitoes outnumbering guests, and the mud, and the running short of beverages. Regardless, we must include Bernhart in whatever plans develop. I am growing rather fond of the fellow." He grinned at Agnes.

On a number of occasions, Josephine had raised the issue of the impropriety of lengthy courtships, suggesting that if an engagement proposal did not materialize soon, perhaps they should consider Agnes's chances for marriage back in Holland with her parents.

Mathias was still on the topic of Bernhart. "If only I can flush out more clearly his strengths, so as to steer his path toward a proper profession. He seems to be wavering between... well who knows what? Why he chose to forego a role in his father's factory, I've never understood. Although I suppose to the young, the thrill of city life surpasses that of staying in a small town to manufacture pillows and... is it buttons?"

"I beg to argue," Agnes countered, "He is following in the footsteps of his inventive father, who after all, built upon one of his own ideas to establish the pillow factory." She paused to fiddle with the handle of her tea cup, then charged, "Furthermore, Bernhart is on the verge of securing a number of innovations of which, one might wager, he needs no assistance at all."

Her uncle only smiled at this. It was the age of the patent. Manufacturers had come to utilize interchangeable parts for their machines, which were making many products that had only been constructed by hand in the past. He had just read a humorous piece in a penny paper on the flood of patents pouring into Washington for street sweeping machines, convertible beds, flytraps, and the like. And now there was a patent office on Walnut Street.

Her aunt sighed at the magnitude of Agnes's patience when it came to the crawling nature of her courtship to Bernhart. Finding the topic necessarily worrisome, but rather tedious to actually discuss, she decided to change the subject.

"As for the fourth of July, Penny has begun preparations for a day outdoors. It has scarcely rained this season so there is little to worry of mud and insects to ruin the celebration." She could not endure another house party.

"Darling," Mathias whined, "If it's not insects than it is the Quakers milling about along the banks of the river in their drab, peaceful manner ruining the remembrance, the bloody thrill and anguish, of the noblest war ever fought."

"Perhaps I shall ask Penny to prepare a potato salad for the picnic basket," declared Josephine.

"Light on the vinegar, Uncle?" added Agnes. Josephine smiled but Mathia's thoughts were already half-way to New Orleans.

◆

Penny stood at the door of the kitchen, popping raspberries into her mouth. She was relieved to overhear Mrs. Trossen heading off the possibility of hosting another dinner party. Preparing for a picnic would be much easier, and better yet, grant her an afternoon to herself with the family gone to the countryside. She sat down to season her skillets. Larkspur had scrubbed too vigorously at the cast iron so that now Penny had to dig two fingers into her jar of lard and rub the fat back into the heavy pans, front and back. While she worked, slow and methodically, she recognized a sense of unease within her. By the time she placed the ironware into the warm oven to lock in her work, she had identified the root. Mr. Trossen had involved himself in the business of trading slaves.

She could not decide if her surprise at the news was justified. She knew his endeavors kept him flitting about from one place to another, but the only thing she was certain of was his love for the cotton gin. One would think he had invented it himself, as he never wearied from discussing its merits. More than once, when the moral issue of slavery arose for discussion, only Mr. Spiedler voiced a strong position. While debates were as much a part of a dinner party as the white damask tablecloth and the soup tureen, and clearly Mr. Trossen reveled in the sound of his own voice, Penny now thought back on how he tended to cleverly diffuse most conversations before they became too heated.

Busy the rest of the day and asleep the moment her head touched its pillow, she awoke to find the light of the moon falling across her coverlet. She moved over so that her face was awash in the glow. Without the mistress in the sky, as she liked to call the moon, she had the sensation that she could lose track of all there was to track. Of course she could rely upon the seasons, paper calendars, the clock in the front hall, the clang of the church bells near Front Street, but she preferred the waning and waxing of the moon to remind her of the cyclical nature of things.

She had been looking to the moon since childhood, since her first tender years of womanhood when her mam had assured her that her own cycle would come and go like the moon. And in the beginning her menstrual flow followed its pattern, but that changed with the crossing of the ocean to arrive in a city where lamps dotted the streets and burned in every room. She sometimes wondered if it were better to let the dark be dark, than to fill it with so much light. She preferred to rise with the sun and sleep when it set; shuffling about most nights in her socks in the dark in-between, now and then lighting a candle to spark some distant memory. She now sat up in bed and looked out the high window in her room to find the neighboring rooftops awash in the milky moonlight.

Penny was born long ago and far away, or so it felt to her. She remembered a stone house with green shutters the color of the rolling hills behind it. It was a handsome dwelling with a gate encircling the yard and a bird that roosted on the fence post. Stepping gingerly along the muddy lane each day in her cracked boots, she pretended that her father would return from abroad to make such a house belong to them. Failing to understand that being lost at sea was a condition from which one was never found, she continued to imagine a house with stone walls and shutters, all the while huddled with her mother and grandparents in a shelter no more protective than that of a horse stable, and set on a small plot of land holding as many potatoes as could fit.

Her father had gone off to find seasonal work in Scotland, for nearly every cent the potatoes earned was handed over to the landlord. Journeying homeward, it was reported that the boat took water and went down. When Penny finally understood the meaning of his death, she thought of the coins in his pocket waiting at the bottom of the sea. She remembered his weathered hands and his blue eyes. It seemed that all he had left behind were the freckles that splayed across his daughter's cheeks and the color of her eyes.

Despite the condition in which Penny's family found themselves, there remained an optimism that each day could deliver a bit of happiness. Her granddad, for instance, had been denied the right to vote, to learn to read, to rent or own land, or acquire any profession beyond farming because he was born into a family of Catholic faith. Nonetheless, Penny could not recall any bitterness in his voice when they sat together in the yard watching for the sun to peek out from behind the low clouds. As he shared stories of long ago, he would trace letters in the dirt with his walking stick. She copied the shapes while she listened.

Sometimes, when he grew quiet, she would ask, "Grandad, how old are ye?"

"'Tis the very same thing ye asked me yesterday, lass," he replied, eyes squinting up at the brightening sky. "The very same thing. And what did I tell ye?"

"Ye said ..." She waited until he finished the sentence.

"I said, ask me tomorrow, not today," he sang out as if it belonged with a tune. He tapped his stick at the ground. "Now this one here is named the letter B for 'tis shaped after a baby's bottom."

"But today is tomorrow," Penny would protest, to no avail.

On other days, Penny would ask him why he didn't say his prayers at night, like Mam and Granny. Or attend mass on Sunday.

"'Tis the very thing ye asked me last time, lass," he'd cry in fake dismay. "And what did I tell ye?"

"'Tis slipped me mind," Penny said.

"I believe I told ye about the man I met strollin' down our lane."

"The man named Mr. Quaker?" The man had stayed on in the village for nearly a year. His name was Mr. Jimson and while they discussed religion only a few times, he had taken the time to teach her grandfather how to read.

"The very one," he answered. "And I called out to ask the fella where he was headed with such a cheerful step. And now, me Penny, ye must recollect where it was he claimed to be goin'?"

"About," she nearly shouted. "He said he was going about ... to find god in everyone."

He chuckled, tucking the stick under his bench. He stood up stiffly, then, "Yes, somethin' exactly like that," he winked at her, "or close there enough."

"But what is the meanin' o' that?" she pleaded.

He muttered as he hobbled off, "Ah, the devil if I know."

Years later, when she was a young lady set to sail across the ocean and her mother was seeing her off at the dock, it came up again. They had waited for the ship to be made ready, filling the early afternoon with conversation in order to blot out the nervous dread they each harbored. When it was time to board, Penny felt as if her legs were cast in stone. She could not imagine walking the narrow gangway without losing balance.

Her mother grabbed ahold of her shoulders and lowered her voice. "Listen to me good now, when ye get to the far shore, find yer way to the town called Philadelphia. If ye have to beg for directions, be sure 'tis a missus yer askin'. Don't be eyein' the menfolk."

"Why there, Mam?"

"William Penn, the Quaker, 'tis his city." She ran her hand

over the fabric of her daughter's dress as if brushing off sea salt she expected would soon accumulate there. She even clutched a handful of the skirt, shook it once before letting it fall still against the solemnity of the moment. She pulled the girl to her and pressed her ear against her cheek, then her neck, until she could detect a heartbeat, feel blood course like a river going somewhere fast. At last, she inhaled deeply the familiar scent of her child's skin and whispered, "Now off ye go my sweet, round, happy Penny. I shall think of ye at the top of every hour. Soon I shall hope to lay eyes on ye again. Until the day I do, be good! Shine and be good."

That was the last thing she had heard her mother say, "Be good."

Only when she had reached Philadelphia did she discover that William Penn had been dead for one hundred years. She laughed, wishing her mother were there to join in. Yet, because she had nowhere else to go, she settled in, putting the cooking her mam and granny had taught her to use.

As the moonlight stretched away from the bed, she found herself thinking about it all over again. Most times, Old Ireland seemed a lifetime away. She had been gone for over ten years and now there was no one left for her to return to see. Yet there were moments, like this one, that she could feel the soft rain against her cheek, the moss under her feet. She could hear her mother singing and her granddad's shillelagh tracing letters in the dirt. She could guess what he would have said about the buying and selling of humans.

∾

On the sticky morning of July Fourth, when the clock in the front hall chimed nine times, the first of the raindrops plucked against the flags of the garden path. By eleven, the steady downfall allowed Mathias to raise an arm and proclaim that the picnic would have to be postponed until next year. Josephine retired to her dressing room to attend to the possibility of an oncoming headache. Penny unpacked the picnic basket, thumping the contents onto the table and huffing about how unfairly a day of promise can be lost to a battalion of clouds. Larkspur peered out the window, watching the garden under the pounding rain. Agnes stood in the front hallway, deflated at the thought of a long day with nothing to do. She had been looking forward to a stroll with Bernhart along the riverbank.

Wandering through the house, beyond the wide staircase leading to the floors where her aunt rested and her uncle perused the newspaper in his study, Agnes stopped for awhile in the front parlor. Tapping her toe against the carved foot of the sofa, upholstered in a weave of rose blossoms, she felt boredom lodge within her like a helping of bland kidney beans. She moved from the room, only to wind up at the door leading to the kitchen, a crowded room extending out from the back of the house, with the cookstove on one side and the broad table for preparing meals on the other. The walls were lined with shelves to hold jars, tins, bowls and platters. The pots and pans hung from nails driven into a wooden strip running the length of one wall. Most of the foodstuffs were stored in the pantry or the cellar, but the washing board and laundry tubs cluttered the corner behind the stove.

"Yes, Miss Agnes, somethin' yer needin'?" The sound of the pelting rain upon the roof above, forced Penny to raise her voice to address Agnes standing in the doorframe.

"Tea, perhaps?"

"O' course, then. I'll bring it up to the drawing room, soon as it's ready." Penny thought it would be nothing short of a small miracle to go for an hour or two without a soul needing a cup of anything.

"I think I shall wait for it here." Agnes walked over to pull out a chair from the table, as a puzzled Penny continued chopping at her cutlery board.

Larkspur, who was watching the rain, turned from the

window. "I'll see after the tea," she offered. "Would chilled suit you, Miss Agnes?"

"Yes, thank you."

On the lip of the sink perched a red-handled pump. It drew from a pipe connected to the city's water supply. While the household drew from the rain barrel in the yard for the washing and cooking, they utilized the pump at the sink for drinking. Yesterday, Larkspur had tossed stinging nettles and thistle leaves into a large jar of water, before leaving it in the sunshine for the afternoon. She now opened the wooden ice-box, lined with iron on the inside, and chipped off ice from the the frozen block.

"What's good for the goose is surely good for the gander." Penny motioned for her to fill three glasses.

Before long, enough tea was consumed to lift the mood within the kitchen, despite the continued gloom outside. Penny's irritableness had burned off and Agnes found herself enlivened by the energy that swirled within the busy room. She observed the older woman's playful banter and the younger one's more guarded responses.

"Lass, the reason I keep you to tasks such as polishin' the napkin rings and dumpin' the ash pot is I'm rightly afraid of what you'll turn out in the pan," Penny said to Larkspur. "I never seen the likes o' so many things done with a bit o' cornmeal. What did you call the rough buggers you made yesterday?"

"They go by the name scratchback." Larkspur stacked a handful of serving bowls and placed them on a shelf. The sound of the rain upon the roof had lessened. "Then a dodger, that's different, if you fry it right."

"There's more ways to do the same thing, eh? Perhaps you're thinkin' I've a cravin' for more but let me set the story straight. 'Tis not a cravin' you sense," Penny teased, "but a panic. Variety is the spice o' life, I always say, and too much o' anything will cause yer ruin. I've had enough potatoes, for instance, to last 'til my end."

"Oh, I do so very much agree," Agnes jumped in, unable to remain silent. "Monotony is all together the most tiresome thing. I've had entirely enough of needle point."

Penny laughed but noticed Larkspur's face remain still like daybreak. The solemnity of the girl's expression made the truth sit down upon the older woman's heart. There does come a day, she knew, when things will no longer do, like the day she left her homeland. And the price that goes with it. The price of relinquishing even that which must be relinquished. She studied Larkspur for a moment longer, determining there was more to her than met the eye. Of course, when she thought about it, that was true of everyone.

"I have an idea," Agnes chirped. "What would you say to an apple pie? In this very moment I've been struck with a dire craving for it. Could we not make one?" Agnes beamed, impressed with her own spontaneity.

"A charmin' idea, t'were it apple season," replied Penny. "Now 'tis true the icebox cars do come along the rails bringin' fresh fruit from all sorts o' places I never heard the likes of, but there's still such a thing as a proper season. A good apple doesn't dare fall from the tree before autumn, while everyone knows that July is the month for berries, o' which we could fill a pie nicely. Are you thinkin' to tie on an apron, Miss Agnes, and learn how to roll out a proper crust?"

"Yes, indeed."

Larkspur left the two to cut the butter into a bowl of flour, while she cleared away the cups and saucers. Patting the moisture from the strained tea leaves, she spread them along the windowsill, next to the stinging nettle she had found growing wild along the back wall of the garden. Although Penny had suggested the prickly weed be pulled, Larkspur knew of its medicinal value, so had carefully contained it, utilizing garden gloves. She then selected a handful of leaves for the jug of tea. As to the used leaves upon the windowsill, they could be scattered over the rugs in the parlor to collect dust the next time they were due to be swept.

While rinsing the dishes, she reminded herself to be grateful for finding refuge in the Trossen home. A soft bed at night, more food than she had ever laid eyes upon, even ice in her drinks and a sense of freedom she had never known before. Despite her gratitude, she felt unsettled. Unease pressed into the bones of her shoulders, causing the muscles around them to ache. She stood at the sink drying her hands, deep in thought, when a pounding on the kitchen door startled everyone in the room.

"Goodness gracious …," said Penny stepping swiftly to pull at the door knob.

Under a dilapidated-looking hat drooped Bernhart Hommes, drenched from head to toe. Quickly ushered in and stationed on a small rug, Larkspur was sent to fetch towels. After a moment of wiping the rain from his eyes, he soon realized it was Agnes standing before him in a floured apron with a smear of blueberry across her cheek. The two stared, equally alarmed to be before each other in such a state.

"Why Agnes, I did not know you to be adept with a rolling pin," he said, shifting his weight from one foot to the other as his shoe made a strange sucking sound.

She set the heavy thing on the table, leaning it against a dish to prevent it from rolling. "And I would not have guessed that you consider a typhoon an inadequate reason to carry an umbrella. Does the bell at the front no longer sound?"

"Only when there is someone to hear it." He smiled, dispelling the tension between them. He looked down at the cluttered table. "Have I neglected to mention that blueberry streusel is a favorite of mine? My mother made it for me when I was just a knabe." He thought of what the woman who cooked at the boarding house he stayed at called it. "I believe Erzsebet refers to it as a cobbler."

"I believe Miss Agnes will call this one a pie, Mr. Hommes," interjected Penny. "Another round o' tea, then? 'Tis a holiday, after all."

More tea was served, this time with fresh lemon verbana thrown in, which allowed Bernhart the great delight of listing the latin terms for a variety of herbs found in the verbenaceae family. Larkspur listened attentively as she carried out her tasks at the sink.

"Such a fascinating color," Bernhart said, changing the topic. His eyes had fixed upon the blueberry juice, as it stained both Agnes's apron and fingers. At first, it struck him as wasteful for so much pigment to go unutilized, but soon it was Agnes's hands, and not the color of blueberries, that captured his full attention.

By the time the pie was ready for the oven, the rain had miraculously ceased and the sun broke into the room. Agnes agreed to go out to the garden while the pie baked. Before they had reached the stepping stones of the garden path, dark and slick, she had tucked her fingers into the palm of Bernhart's hand.

༄

Mathias opened the newspaper on the tenth of June to discover that President Zachary Taylor had died. It was speculated that a bowl of cherries and iced cream eaten at a July Fourth picnic had led to his tragic demise.

"How awful," he murmured. "How unfortunate." Yet after a few minutes of reflection, a small burst of relief arrived as he realized Millard Fillmore would now become the 13th president of the United States. Fillmore appeared a more definitive politician than Taylor, more likely to expedite the signing of the Compromise rather than continue to indulge in the moral and political arguments that sea-sawed back and forth in Washington around the issue of slavery. For Mathias, it was impossible to imagine slavery coming to an end, yet he was convinced that an alteration to the rules governing the institution could have a significant impact on the economy. For him to make sound business decisions, he needed to know what lay ahead. As he folded the newspaper and tossed it upon his desk, he felt optimistic that a change in the presidency might be good. He saw no reason to delay his travel plans to head south.

Silas arrived early with the coach and began packing the trunks while the family said their good-byes at the curb. It seemed to Silas that Mr. Trossen would be gone for an extended length of time, given the two heavy trunks and the animated lecture he delivered to his wife and niece, warning them of spoiled iced cream and water-borne cholera, the two conflicting hypotheses behind Taylor's death. As Silas helped Mr. Trossen up the rung and into the coach, a shout came from the doorway. Larkspur appeared with a basket in hand.

"Beg your pardon for hollering," she said, handing the basket to Silas who had come forward to get it, "but Penny fixed up Mr. Trossen's dinner. She doesn't figure a decent meal can be had upon a train."

He nodded and clutched the handle of the basket. It caught for a moment as the handle stayed hooked through Larkspur's arm. "Most likely right," Silas said, puzzled why the girl wasn't letting go of the basket.

Her voice carried a slow, somber melody as she slipped a folded note into his hand. "Hoping I might count on you."

"I'll see that he gets his basket," he answered, keeping the note hidden. Climbing up to grab the reins, he clucked his tongue to the roof of his mouth to let Mercy Tubbs know it was time to set off.

As he bumped along the cobblestones, he talked softly to the horse. "I should a guessed about that one, Mercy. Should a guessed something about that one right there."

ᷤ

No sooner had her husband departed, than an invitation arrived requesting Josephine join a friend on a reprieve at the oceanside. She quickly agreed to spend July and perhaps some of August, as she had in past years, at a small cottage along the New Jersey shore. She insisted that Agnes accompany her, as it would prove too hot and humid to remain in the city, not to mention the unseemliness of remaining alone without a guardian. Agnes, however, artfully convinced her aunt that she would not be alone, with Penny and Larkspur in the house, and that a month away would inhibit her ability to attend afternoon teas or receive an invitation to a garden party. How would she keep abreast of society's happenings from so far a place as Cape May? And then, she said with a sigh, since Bernhart tended to spend much of the summer at Bartram's Garden, she could seize the opportunity to apply herself to her needlepoint and penmanship. She might even draft a calling card, as her aunt had suggested time and again.

Josephine conceded, not because she envisioned Agnes exchanging calling cards and holding polite conversations under a garden trellis, but because she was tired of worrying about tiresome things. It was only recently that she had inherited the responsibility of molding a niece into a young lady. She leaned on this fact to convince herself that a short vacation, reclining under her parasol upon a beach chair, would replenish her patience and dedication for the task.

§

As it turned out, Agnes did not attend any afternoon teas, except those with Penny and Larkspur in the kitchen. She wasted no time on needlepoint, and while she sent off an occasional letter and attempted to keep at her practice of journaling, she began to spend an increasing amount of time sniffing through her uncle's books in his second-floor study. She stumbled upon the Greek philosophers and then grew enthralled by the writings of Lucretius of Rome and his idea that the universe was controlled by chance rather than divine intervention. After wondering at length, over how one's chances in life came about, she began to peruse the morning paper, a much better avenue than tea parties for staying abreast of news. And of course, she continued to spend time with Bernhart, escaping the heat by strolling through Fairmount Park or Laurel Hill Cemetery. Nearly once a week, they would venture the five miles west to Bartram's Garden, the air markedly cooler among the trees of the one-hundred-year-old botanical garden than along the fetid, urban streets.

One humid afternoon, as the sun slid between tufts of clouds and as Bernhart expounded on the theory of soil formation, Agnes pushed her hat off her head so that it hung from its ribbon around her neck. Ambling along a path near the Schuylkill River, a breeze rose up to cool her damp forehead. As the air brushed against her skin, she was reminded how, as of late, the measure of her happiness had swelled. She attributed her contentment to her newly gained autonomy, walks with Bernhart, relaxed meals in the kitchen with Penny and Larkspur, and chiefly, mornings spent in the study absorbing information on a myriad of topics.

While Bernhart prattled on, seeing how captivated she appeared by the habits of the earthworm, she struggled to envision what small miracle could emerge to allow such independence to continue. Upon their return, she was certain her aunt and uncle would disapprove of her studiousness, regardless of how she might argue that she felt perfectly suited to it. How could she resume a patience for letter writing and poetry reading? No doubt Bernhart would ask her to marry him, once he patented one of his concoctions, but what would marriage change? She peered at his endearing face, a dot of pollen on his nose. Oh, she was enamoured with him, but above all else? There seemed such a vast amount of so much more against which to compare him.

Seeing his eyebrows raised, she realized he was waiting for a response.

"Did you say loam?" she managed.

"Yes, it was the presence of loam where there once had lain cinders. Such a remarkably common thing and yet it has prodded Charles Darwin to explore the vital role of earthworms in producing a rich, fertile soil. Those viscous things, he claims, are amazingly instrumental." Agnes merely nodded. He continued, "Loamy soil, there is nothing quite like it and after reading Darwin's findings, I suddenly wonder if not all creatures are as purposeful and necessary as this invertebrate?"

She smiled at Bernhart, imagining the worms busily tunneling along and accomplishing so much without a moment of contemplation.

"I admit," she explained, "to knowing very little about this Darwin fellow and yet I believe a pang of envy has shot through my heart at the thought of the earthworm's ability to contribute so importantly to the transformation of cinders to dirt. And I'd imagine, they are void of dedicating an invariable amount of time lamenting over the meaning of such work. Although I can't say I would like to go about blindly burrowing underground the day long." She paused only to take a deep breath and then forged ahead, "I only wonder, how does one who is not an earthworm select which path to follow? A path void of sticks and stones, and … discouragement?"

Knowing that some thoughts are better left as thoughts rather than emitted as rambling sentences, Agnes found Bernhart eyeing her with a bemused look. Both stopped and turned towards each other with the sunlight stretching through the canopy above, landing in bright, scattered shapes upon their shoulders. Her hair had begun to loosen from its knot, while his face glistened with sweat.

"Agnes," he began, "at times your language possesses a wisdom I can only sense but not entirely comprehend. It reminds me of all that I am about to realize but, as yet, have not. I find it most difficultly hopeful. Like a box of lavender sprigs one would take to the apothecary to have pressed into oil."

He only now noticed that she had flipped back her hat, and that a strand of hair curved around her ear. He grasped it between two fingers, letting his eyes land in the hollow space where her collarbones nearly met. He loved this little pool with its delicate skin, holding the absence of something that had no name.

"Anges, I believe in this moment I should kiss you." Before seeking her opinion on the matter, but well after the instant she might have knit her brow or glanced toward her shoes, he tilted his head and with one arm drew her towards him. The kiss felt to Agnes as if the sun had set within her and then suddenly rose again.

With Bernhart's arm still around her, she whispered, "I believe one kiss is all that can be trusted."

Yet despite her words, they began to lean in once again until she drew a hand to his chest and pushed back gently. As they fell apart, like an apple cut in two, Bernhart drew a sigh.

She reached for her hat and fastened the ribbon so it sat properly upon her head. Turning up the slender path where the summer phlox stretched toward her skirt and the remnants of the kiss lingered in the sultry air, she found herself yearning for Bernhart, and yet, for something more. She fled up the path afraid that the something more would get swallowed up in her passion for him. So easily, in the wink of an eye, she could lose that which she had just begun to grasp, like water in a cupped hand.

Chapter 4

From where he hid in a dense thicket, a stone's throw from the roadside, Zeb could hear another wagon approach. The frequency at which they passed convinced him that he was not far from Richmond. For three days he had traveled by the cover of the forest, but the farms now were strung together and twice he was forced to cross a cleared field in order to stay in close proximity to the road. Traveling in the dark of night, his movement had alerted no one. Yet, he now troubled over how he would get through the city and arrive at the port.

It was dusk and a mosquito began to buzz close to his ear. Waiting for it to land upon his cheek, he then swatted it dead. Along his arms protruded red, oozing sores from previous bites that he had scratched raw. His belly growled but his kerchief, which he had rinsed in the stream to remove any scent of food that might attract an animal, had been empty since yesterday. Still damp, he spread it over one arm and then the other, hoping to sooth the small, itchy welts. He was anxious to get going. Besides creeping to the stream and back a few times, he had been in this same spot for most of the afternoon, still another hour would need to pass before the light would leave the sky and he could again move on.

He must have dozed while night descended. It was then he realized he had been jared from sleep by the clatter of an approaching wagon. It seemed odd to him that a traveler would still be upon the road at such an hour. Curious, he convinced himself to take a look, certain the darkness would protect him. He poked his head just above the line of brush behind which he was squatting.

The incremental way in which night can steal the day from under one's nose, caused the driver of the wagon to lean out over his horse, peering for ruts in the road without realizing how low darkness had sunk. It took an unforeseen branch to slap against his arm, for him to realize it was time to slow the horse, despite being a few miles from his destination.

Having loaded his wagon with produce destined for the market by sunrise, it was impossible to travel from his owner's plantation to the Richmond marketplace in less than two hours, so Levi was sent the evening before. As always, it was arranged for him to stay the night outside the city proper at the residence of the master's friend. He had gotten off to a late start and now the sun had abandoned him. Papers or not, it was not safe for a teamster to be out on the roads after dark.

Zeb felt a shot of fear streak through his body as he realized the wagon was slowing down directly in front of where he hid. In the dusk, he could just glimpse the face of the driver removing his hat to wipe his perspiring brow. As the horse clopped along, Zeb heard the driver talking to the animal. The boy panicked for a moment, a flood of indecision holding him to his spot, but then remembered the old woman telling him he would need help. He stepped from behind the shrubs and let out a quick, soft whistle.

Bernhart stood under a young mulberry tree as night eased in around him. A heathery hour, he both loved and lamented, that urged for the lighting of street lamps, the emergence of moths drawn to the light, and the arrival of nostalgia that lodged tight below the breastbone. He felt it now as he peered across the street at the Trossen home. The proper hour for a visit had passed and while he had hoped to see Agnes, at the moment he preferred the quiet loneliness of dusk over entering a well-lit parlor with its door jam rising up to catch his toe, or pastry cream diving for his lapel, or her fidgeting with the pleats of her skirt as though they held some great mystery.

He was thinking of moth wings, considering whether they were softer to the touch than even rose petals. It seemed to him that their texture was somehow attributed to the winking time between day and night. He closed his eyes and wondered if it was the sound of its wings in his ear or the image of the wings against the glass, that pricked the tiny sense of angst he had recently acquired when thinking of Agnes. The past two times he had visited, she had appeared distracted. And last week, had declined to accompany him to either Fairmount Park or Rittenhouse Square. If he remembered correctly, she had not seemed herself ever since the visit to the botanical garden in which they spoke of earthworms and shared the one lovely kiss.

Opening his eyes, he shook his head to sweep away the disquieting thoughts, then assured himself that his analysis of moth wings arose from scientific curiosity not the enchanting sentiments of twilight. As of late, Bernhart had latched onto the idea of crafting a well-scented dusting powder for a woman to use to compliment her delicate complexion. Would they or would they not, he needed to determine, be fitting if finely ground and added to a dusting powder? He spent a great deal of time tweaking the list of potential ingredients, both usual and unusual, that he hoped might procure the perfect texture and fragrance.

He shook his head once again, realizing the absurdity of standing alone on a darkened street contemplating the use of dead moth wings upon a cheekbone. Stepping out from under the tree and setting off toward home, soon he found himself passing Schuster's Saloon in a neighborhood filled with German immigrants. From the sidewalk, he could hear the voices of the men's singing group, rehearsing in the back of the hall. Joining in were the beer-drinking customers from the main room. The familiar lyrics and the desire for a glass of ale urged him to step inside, yet he hesitated for he knew he would face the customary questions regarding his efforts to find a German bride or why he rented from an Englishman when Herr Schuster could provide a room above the saloon for the same price.

So, he continued on through the shadowy streets until he reached the boarding house from which he rented his rooms. When he had climbed to the second floor, lit a lamp, wrestled off his waistcoat and loosened his shirt collar, he sat down to his writing table. Dabbing at the ink in the bottom of the jar, he began to write:

There seems such a vast amount of everything asking, no begging, for consideration. The never-ending avenues of which to explore, of which to focus my energy, often leave me little choice but to push on blindly in hopes a dose of clarity will suddenly appear amidst the clutter. Yesterday, for example, I spent half the morning watching a colony of ants parade to and from their hill. Entirely fascinating, and yet, how am I to attend to all that needs attending? My days' beginnings are filled with countless sortings and siftings, titrations and dilutions so that following my walk to the corner for the newspaper, I retreat to the back room for hours. Beakers to scrub, magnifiers to polish, glass slides to label. The lids matched to the jars, the jars to the lids, loosened with the left hand, tightened with the right. Then to record my observations! It is laborious, but of course, necessary to my professional betterment. And yet, I can hear most loudly the neighbor's bittersweet vine daring me to spend the entire

*day observing its climb up the painted trellis. I am entirely
convinced, with much determination and a bit of squinting,
I could detect its growth with my own eyes.*

Here he stopped, for he knew if he continued he would
begin to record his thoughts regarding Agnes and he preferred
not to wade in the murky bog of that topic at such a late hour.
He did make one final note.

*Come morning, dispose of the stash of figs in the desk
drawer. Certainly the rancid smell to the room is more than
the residual odor of last week's distillation attempt.*

Turning down the lamp, he then dropped onto the bed.
Stretching out onto his stomach, he was soon compelled to
roll over in hopes of catching a waft of air from the open
window. He waited, but only a firefly found its way in, bumping around the room to send off interval bursts of hope that
barely flickered against his closed eyes.

Bernhart was a vivid dreamer. While he slept, he was often
plunged back into childhood, his few years in Germany and
then later in the countryside of Pennsylvania. He was young
when he and his family crossed the Atlantic, yet his dreams
were often loyal to his earliest memories, walking him under
the beech trees of the Black Forest or daring him to peer over
the edge of the table to watch his mother prepare strudle.
Sometimes it was she who came to mind as he stood before
his worktable, the image of her stretching the dough with the
back of her knuckles and folding it without ever using her fingers, despite believing he had fashioned his vocation after his
father. It did not appeal to him to align himself with baking
pastries, despite his measurements and recipes. He thought of
himself as scientific and inventive, hoping one day to don the
title of inventor. He was determined that his father would not
be the only man in the family to perfect an idea.

Bernhart had been only five years old, his brother seven, when their father "slumped upon" the marvelous idea of using pheasant feathers to stuff the family's pillowcases. It happened one ashen morning amidst a hunting excursion in which Bernhart was allowed to participate for the first time. Erling had strutted about beforehand, bragging of his practiced marksmanship, but once the hunt began both boys were given the role of bagging the felled game. Bernhart spent the morning with an empty bag slung over his shoulder, hoping his father's aim would improve.

Weary from rising at dawn and marching through the muddy brush for hours without grounding but one bird, they climbed a dry berm and lowered to the ground for a short rest. While both boys' kopfs lay upon their scratchy coat sleeves, their father's head settled unintentionally upon the hardening bird. The morning slipped away, unnoticed by the sleeping threesome, until Bernherdi Hounnes awoke. When he discovered what had served so effectively as a pillow, he gave out a chortle of delight. Thanks to an improvement in his hunting skills and his wife's thread and needle, they soon had the village and the surrounding villages sleeping more comfortably. Eventually, they were able to save enough to move the family across the ocean, their name changing along with their location, to set up shop in Sullivan County, Pennsylvania.

When Bernhart rose the next morning he had no recollection of his dreams, yet he harbored a strong taste for something bready and sweet. When finished at the washstand, he slipped his clothes back on. He would ask Erzsebet if she might prepare a fruit pastry for his breakfast. And, feeling a swell of optimism, he promised himself he would keep his thoughts light and clear, as he tended to his jars and tins, musty books, small wooden crates and the contents therein. If Agnes appeared to need a bit of space, he could certainly oblige, for nothing had come between them to send him searching for a young fraulein or for her to suddenly prefer a blonde dutchman.

With the handkerchief of old figs in hand, he entered the basement kitchen to find Erzsebet at the cookstove. She motioned to toss the figs into her compost pot, then dumped a heap of coffee grounds on top to hide the smell. Having arrived early to begin her preparations, and already incorporating yesterday's extras into today's fare, she had no interest in receiving requests for the morning meal from any tenant unable to distinguish the mortar from the pestle, a parsnip from a rutabaga, or millet from barley. So when Bernhart suggested a fruit-filled pastry, she turned her palms up and pretended to look disappointed that she had prepared fritters, sizzling in the frying pan, by mistake.

"Oh," he remarked, trying to smile, "are those not the spirited morsels that kept me in the privy all morning last week?"

"Sir, there's no hot bakes for you today, but this," she began to scoop food out with a wooden spoon, "is what a man needs to fortify himself. 'Lest you aim to be the first to drop next time the plague comes through."

"I see," he uttered, deflated. While the woman seemed overly concerned with the chance of contracting cholera, he figured he should heed her warning since a bout of it had passed through the city last year. He sat down to the table.

While she fixed his plate she recalled, "My mama always said the thing she missed most was them peppers. Said they grew all over the island. But couldn't find 'em up here in these markets, so she got used to settling for the bland kind. If these ones put you in the outhouse, I can't hardly imagine what the island kind would do."

Next to a scramble of eggs and saltfish, she placed the fritters and set the plate before him. Erzsebet, finding it strange to have Bernhart eating in the kitchen with his elbows out and no one else present, busied herself over the stove, poking at the remaining food with a fork. While no other tenant would sit alone in the kitchen with her, Mr. Hommes was different, odd or too preoccupied with an immediate thought to consider what was expected behavior over what was practical. If he was hungry and a steaming plate of food was presented, he sat to eat it. If the only person in the room was a woman born enslaved and still regarded as not much more than that by some, it did not seem to deter him from asking questions.

"What is your opinion of moth wings, Erzsebet?"

Erzsebet kept her hair in short braids wrapped in a bright scarf of red or orange, or bright green, scarves that reminded her of the island she and her mother had left. When the master of the St. Lucian sugar plantation, on which the mother and small daughter toiled, died suddenly, followed by the mistress fleeing the island to escape the oppressive heat and the perpetual mold, a handful of house slaves were amazed to find themselves freed by a mistress overwhelmed at being in charge of other people's lives. The mother and child made their way slowly up the coast, first by water and then by land, stopping for extended stretches along the way, but finally reaching Philadelphia by the time Erzsebet had reached the age of ten.

"Since you're asking," she sprinkled a bit of cinnamon into her coffee, "wings ain't but for flying, Mr. Hommes."

৽

Agnes was standing in the center of the front parlor watching Larkspur rub away the patches of black soot left upon the walls from the kerosene lamps. Already it was hot and the August sun had yet to reach its height. With Aunt Josephine returning soon from the seashore, Agnes needed to attend to the tasks she had neglected, yet the binding corset around her middle and the cloying nature of her long skirts left her listless. There hung a silence in the room, penetrated by the birds and insects beyond the open windows.

"It seems unnatural to attempt an outing in such heat," said Agnes at last. "Perhaps tomorrow the weather will lift and I shall have the strength to take on the cobbler *and* the dressmaker."

Larkspur stepped down from the stool and swished her rag into the pail of water that had gone gray from the soot. Ringing out the rag and straightening, her dress was darkened under the arms and down the center of her back, perspiration trickled down her face and landed soundlessly upon her damp collar.

"Or perhaps I should go today," Agnes capitulated. "I shall need Penny to fetch my gloves and hat, and a parasol to shield off the sun."

Earlier Agnes had dressed in a chemise and stockings that stretched above the knee, held with garters. Penny had to tighten her corset and help her step into the wire crinoline. Next came the petticoat and finally her day dress. Because the wires of the corset pinched, she altered her breathing pattern, shallow inhales matched by quick exhales.

Now as she stood looking at the step stool and the pail of sooty water, the air around her thickened and grew fuzzy, like the skin of a peach. The silence began to vibrate against her temples.

"What is it, Miss Agnes?" Larkspur's voice swam toward her as the room began to darken and, lunging toward the sofa but getting nowhere near it, she crumbled to the floor before Larkspur could do anything but reach out an arm to slow the fall.

From the kitchen, Penny heard the commotion and came at once. Before the smelling salts could be gotten, Agnes was shaking her head and attempting to regain an upright position, yet the wires of her crinoline, a contraption meant to widen the appearance of a lady's skirt, made sitting up difficult. Penny knelt to pull at Agnes's left arm and then the right, but it was not easy to get her up despite much huffing and puffing and insistence by Agnes that she no longer wished to be on the floor. The futility of the act took a turn when Agnes, letting go of Penny's hand, rolled away only to come to a teetering stop facing the sofa.

It was Penny who first began to giggle. Then Agnes, lying on her side, joined in after spotting a lost button against the baseboard that seemed to be mocking her.

"I shall be wrecked now through, from all the laughin'," Penny said after she caught her breath. "And as yet, yer still not up?"

"Good news! I have spotted the button from my wool coat hiding under the sofa," Agnes announced and at that the two started all over again, while Larkspur indulged in a smile.

❧

When they had Agnes lying upon her bed, Larkspur parted the draperies while Penny fetched a glass of water.

"It must have been the capers from last night's meal. They seemed to disagree with me the moment I consumed them." Agnes's head was propped upon a pillow. "It's just that I have so much to do before Aunt Josephine returns. I have no time for fainting spells. There is the dress to have altered and the broken shoe. And I promised to draw up a calling card, so that I should hire Mr. Clemons to drive me to the printing house. Oh my ..." Agnes closed her eyes and sighed.

"It doesn't seem the day for any of that," Larkspur assured her in a soft tone. "Your color's not back yet and your breathing seems off."

"Well, how is one ever supposed to breathe fully in such heat with one's waist bound and the ribcage constricted and the lungs forced to remain in a space too small for their own good. As of late," she paused to catch her breath, "I have begun to wonder whether men actually care the least about the width of a woman's waist or rather prefer us to wear the horrible corset merely so they can enjoy the symbolism it represents. I can see them now, chuckling together over the genius of it. Not only do we do as told and mind our place but have agreed to keep our lungs in a certain dictated spot as well."

"How 'bout taking it off, miss?"

Agnes sighed, closing her eyes again. "As I've conceded to remaining home for the day, then it can be removed. If you knew the trouble Penny and I went through to lace it for my outing, you would know why I hesitate."

Larkspur conveyed her opinion of the corset by muttering, "I can't see why you fuss with it in the first place."

Agnes opened her eyes. Did the maid not understand that just because one perceived the absurdity of a societal norm, one couldn't go about carrying a banner deploring its use?

"There is a reason why we have two ears," Agnes began. "For there are proclamations we make to ourselves that must be cast only into the smallest canal of one ear so that not even the other may overhear it. But cast it we must, for the sake of sanity. Now if you shall help me up."

As Larkspur assisted her out of her many layers, finally untying the laces of the corset so it could be removed, Penny returned with a tray of cold boiled eggs, cucumber slices, and iced tea, of which she set upon the table before marching to the window to draw the curtains so the flies would not come in at the smell of food.

"How you go about all day cinched up like a saddled mare with no chance to move about in the pasture, I can't understand. 'Tis a near crime, I say. O' course, I move about the whole day, without the bother. Goes to even out the work o' the housekeeper compared to the hard tasks of letter writing and what not. If you don't mind me sayin'."

It required Agnes a moment to decide whether she did

mind. There was no point in arguing over the workload, but to be compared to a horse and then to suggest she did nothing but write letters? Well, it simply wasn't true. Was it? Before she could respond, Penny sped off to prepare the midday meal.

Larkspur returned to the window, parting the draperies once again. The room brightened despite a series of gray clouds that had amassed to blot out the noon sun. She watched them sweep closer toward the eaves of the houses, before turning back into the room to hang the petticoats inside the wardrobe. Agnes sat up to drink from the glass on the tray.

"I believe I shall declare exception to Penny's statement," Agnes said at last. "I cannot allow anyone to assume I do nothing but write letters all day, although I very well understand why she might reach such an erroneous conclusion. Until just recently, I had spent little time doing much of anything but pacing about this narrow room and tending to my pen and paper. But as of late, that has all changed."

"How so, miss?" Larkspur asked, her back to the room as she shook out the garments in the wardrobe to deter wrinkles and chase out moths. She was not yet accustomed to being spoken to as if she had an opinion.

"Why, I have discovered so much within the books of my uncle's library and even upon the nature walks with Bernhart, that I am inclined to believe that the world is a more intriguing place than I had ever supposed. Moreover, I can't help but surmise that it is inviting me to join it. How can I refuse, I ask myself? And how can I resolve myself to stroll along the cobbled streets in my long gloves when there is so much more to discover with bare hands? Yet, it is not decent. All this talk of abandoned corsets and calloused fingertips, traveling about to digest the entire scope of things, and yet, I fear I cannot move beyond the notion of it. I simply cannot."

Agnes had risen from the bed, circling the room in a milky dressing gown that waved about as she moved. Suddenly, she plopped upon the chaise and let out a short, clumsy laugh.

Here she was, rambling on again in the maid's presence when she knew such thoughts would be better placed within the hard bindings of her private journal.

"Miss Agnes, maybe those little pickled things *were* spoiled. That'd explain your head swimming in the middle of the day." Larkspur quickly realized, by the frown on Agnes's face, that her comment hadn't landed well. She added, "I'm only speaking of the reason behind the fainting spell."

She couldn't help but wonder, as she lowered her gaze, how someone intent on exploring the world could so easily have her feelings hurt. She doubted the woman could endure an hour of what Larkspur had witnessed in the past. Of course, that would not be the world revealed to someone like Miss Agnes, no matter where she traveled.

"I didn't mean any harm by it," Larkspur tried again. "In fact, a fermented thing can be just what the body needs, 'specially when your stomach's in a grip. 'Course, it's true that something sour's good for more than just that. It can shake things up when you got yourself stuck in one spot too long. Move you in a new direction."

Larkspur knew the benefits of consuming fermented food, but as she spoke she thought, given the upsetting nature of the day, she should be offering the woman something smooth and calming, like the stone stashed in her charm bag. Before she could weigh the risk of suggesting she hold it in her palm, Agnes surprised her by rising abruptly from where she sat.

"I think it best I have some quiet time to think." Agnes announced, opening the door to usher Larkspur out. She was suddenly convinced that a new direction, a change of course, was precisely what she needed.

☙

Yesterday's daily paper, which no one had yet read, sat folded on a low table in the study. Agnes fanned out the pages and began scanning through the articles. Had she paused for a moment, she would accept how illogical it was to search for one's future in yesterday's newspaper, yet she had come into the study still charged with the idea of finding a new path.

Near the bottom of one page she came upon a headline that sounded to her, when she closed her eyes on it, like a single water droplet striking the enamel of an empty basin. The sound, no doubt, of a remarkable idea. She studied the article beneath it, more convinced the further she read.

When she raised her head from the page, she said aloud, "Well, if Lucy Sessions can do such a thing, so most certainly can I!"

Her proclamation was met with a clap of thunder. Rain followed, blowing in through the windows and causing steam to rise from the street below. She inhaled deeply, as the wet smell of opportunity, of chance, filled the room. She had just read the inspirational story of Lucy Session, the first black woman to graduate from a college in the United States. She spoke again, "If she can do it, then why can't I."

The next day, Larkspur was instructed to prepare Mrs. Trossen's rooms for her return, while Penny escorted Agnes, in a more loosely-fastened corset, on her errands. Larkspur busied herself by dusting tables, sweeping floors and airing out bedspreads. Tasks made more pleasant by the cooler weather following yesterday's rainstorm. While working, she listened to Penny fuss over whether Agnes needed an umbrella for the outing.

Finally, Penny yelled up, "We're off then, shouldn't be long. In about an hour, be ready to wet the tea. I'll be needin' a cup the moment I return."

Larkspur heard the heavy door close, the glass rattle and then all go silent. The tall, slender house seemed to moan

once before falling silent. As of yet, she had not been left
alone in it for more than a few minutes. Neither had she gone
much beyond the backyard or the cellar door at the front of
the house. She was glad Penny liked to take the daily trip to
the market and adhere to the other occasional errands, rather
than sending her out.

Sweeping up the last pile of dirt, she then rolled up two
small rugs and tucked them under her arm. Down the back
staircase, she went out to the yard to hang them on the line.
After only a few whacks, she tossed the rug beater upon the
grass and decided to tend to the garden. The large tomatoes
were nearly ripe, but they needed weeding. Before she knelt,
she removed her shoes and stockings. At once she felt better,
having her feet touch the ground.

Working her way around the garden, slipping sprigs
of rosemary and thyme in her apron pocket, noticing the
growth of the radish tops, popping a few remaining garden
peas into her mouth, she stopped at the snap beans. In need
of picking, she began to pluck carefully and nimbly, filling
a tin pail in minutes. Then she moved over to the trellis she
had made out of sticks and strings where the purple pas-
sionflower vine snaked up towards the sky, the large flowers
calling to the bees.

Finally she stepped back into the shade of the two sycamore
trees from across the lane and closed her eyes. First she listened
for the sound of insects, waiting for the buzzing to collect, to
come together into a pattern, to rise and fall and blend. Within
the soaring runs of the cicadas she found it, her string of names.
A string of names given to her by a woman she had called Aunt
Celena. The names chanted in a rhythm, sometimes deep and
slow to the frogs' croaking, or quick and steady with the crick-
ets, until Larkspur knew the names by heart. She had come to
lean on the song when there was little else to lean on.

A pain shot through Larkspur at the thought of Aunt
Celena, but she did not let it diminish the sense of courage

and determination the names evoked. She opened her eyes. Not even on tip-toe, could she see over the fence and into the Spiedler's yard, so she searched for a second sound. After a few moments, her ear detected a faint, dull pounding. She walked over to the weed pile, tossing in a handful, then with the pail of beans in her other hand, left the yard and crossed the grassy lane.

It had been weeks since she had passed the note to Silas. He had either chosen to ignore it or been unable to gain an opportunity to respond, which struck her as unlikely, given their close proximity. Surely any free man could think of an excuse to pass through two gates. She now called softly through the slats.

"I brought you some beans," she said, lifting the pail when the gate creaked open. They looked at each other and then finally he nodded, reaching for the tin. "So?" she whispered, looking over her shoulder. When he didn't answer, "The note?"

He had avoided responding to the contents of the tattered note she had tucked in his hand. Worn at the creases, as if it had been forgotten for a century within a pocket, the paper had contained a mere four letters in a wobbly, unpracticed hand. He had tossed it into the flames of the stove, not know-ing what to make of it, deciding to be cautious rather than put himself, or anyone else, at risk. Yet, as he had drove about town, a jutting cobblestone jarring the wagon or a small child clinging to her mother's skirt reminded him that a request for *help* did not disappear merely because the paper it was written on had turned to ash. And now as the girl stood before him, he felt the measure of caution he had maintained shred like wood shavings under his knife.

"The note didn't say too much a nothin', so I took to asking around. Seems like, nobody heard hide nor hair a you coming. Brought to mind a haint, which I tend to steer clear of."

"You can see I'm no ghost, just as I'm betting you can see what folks around here can't," Larkspur began, a taste like a bitter root in her mouth. "I didn't ask for much help to get up here, because it turned out I didn't much need it."

She searched for the charm bag hidden within her skirt and brought it forward. She loosened the drawstring and reached two fingers inside.

"This," she explained, holding up a small nutmeg, "I brought up from Virginia."

She rolled the grooved nut between her fingers as she locked eyes with Silas. As a girl, she had been told by Aunt Celena that nutmeg could be used to cast a spell to ensure one's protection. While the woman had refused to teach her the spells from the old days, she *had* suggested a thing or two to drop into her charm bag or to wear around her neck.

"It reminds me of the few things I'm not trying to forget. And it helped me in my travels, protecting me along the way." She swallowed. "But it seems, I might just need something more than what I can draw from my charm bag."

She slipped the nutmeg into the velvet pouch and pulled the string tight before letting it fall against her leg. Then, in a low voice, she disclosed the information Silas would need in order to be of help.

When she finished, he remained quiet, feeling a tightening in his chest like a plank of wood squeezed between a vice. He noted this was the second time she had made him think of wood. He had reason to be cautious, as trusting the wrong person could prove catastrophic, but on the other hand, the point was to help those who needed it and that could not be accomplished without taking risks.

"Alright, I'll see what I can do," he said at last. "But mind you, no need poking your nose through this gate daily, like jack looking for the beanstalk. Don't nothin' happen until the time is right. Wait 'til you hear from me." Then he dumped the snap beans into a cloth he had used for his lunch and handed the pail back to her. "I thank you for these."

Before he pulled the door closed to catch the latch, he added, "How'd you know to come to me?"

Larkspur just shook her head, before hurrying back through the gates. She had chosen Mr. Clemons simply because there was no one else. As she made her way up the path toward the house, she looked up to see Penny standing at the at the edge of the garden. How long had she been watching her, Larkspur couldn't say.

After a moment Penny called out, "I see as I'm the only one who can be counted on to wet the tea." She looked down at the girl's feet, "Perhaps 'tis best you find yer shoes before you start a-belderin that you've caught a thorn in the toe."

Chapter 5

Zeb waited while the sound of his whistle faded. He could no longer see the dark field across the road but he knew sound had to go somewhere and hoped it would die amongst the wheat stalks, lodged by the summer winds. Part of the whistle had reached the man driving the wagon, causing the horse to be brought to a stop. Raising up from his hiding spot, the boy inched forward.

"Who's that?" the man whispered.

The boy scurried up to the wagon, holding in a crouched position. "Just me."

"Boy, what you whistlin' for? I got somewhere to be and late already." The man looked the boy over. Then with a pound of dismay in his voice, "Don't tell me you lyin' out or ...?"

The child didn't answer. He was hungry and tired and low on hope. He knew about "lying out", slaves hiding in the woods for a length of time before returning to the plantation on their own. A bit of independence and the reprieve from toil was worth paying a price, as long as the master understood the arrangement and exhibited restraint when issuing punishment.

Zeb shook his head.

"Oh, so you runnin'," Levi moaned. All he wanted was to get to his destination without any trouble, spend the night with Avery, and continue on to the marketplace by daybreak. Being a teamster, he enjoyed a relative amount of freedom traveling between the countryside and Richmond, and had assisted many runaways over the years. At the marketplace, under the noses of the white sellers and buyers, it was possible to exchange information helpful to those crossing over the Mason Dixon line, like the location of a farmhouse willing to leave out food, a steamer driven by a sympathetic captain, the Quaker Lady up the river, and numerous folks both free and bound, like him, who found ways to offer assistance when the opportunity arose. Yet, helping was always risky, and always gave him pause.

"You going somewhere directly or is you just scamperin' about any which-a-way?"

"I'm aiming to get to The City of Richmond," said the boy. He wondered if the man knew this name meant more than just a town, that it meant the name of the schooner that traveled from Richmond to Philadelphia.

Levi knew. "I see. You lookin' for Captain B. Well, you facing the right direction, but how you fixin' to get to the dock when you hidin' behind a bush? I guess that's where you supposin' I come in." Levi looked up into the night and grew silent. There were a hundred new stars that hadn't been there a moment ago.

"Suppose so," Zeb said softly.

"Don't matter what you done day before, or what you got figured for the next, the day you in just comes along to turn it all to muck." Then he jerked his thumb behind him. "Crawl up in that wagon, boy. There's room between the crates at the back. I'll cover you but don't make no noise, I got some thinkin' to do before we get too far down this here road."

Agnes had watched the summer wane, but she had not let her determination fade with it. Taking a first step to pursue the plan she had formed in her uncle's study, she decided she would seek the advice of other women who held her same aspirations. Finding a number of local names arise whenever she read anything on the topic of women and education, it both surprised and concerned her that these names, specifically Lucretia Mott and Margaretta Forten, were associated with the Philadelphia Female Anti-Slavery Society. But after a momentary pause, she concluded that just because these women might hold an opinion on the question of slavery, and most likely on a woman's right to vote, that need not complicate their commitment to education nor detract from their ability to assist her. She had set her sights on attending college and she hoped these women might advise her on how to gain entrance into an institution open to enrolling female students. Her preference was Oberlin College in Ohio, which had been accepting women since the 1830s, and from which, as she had read in the paper, Lucy Sessions had obtained her degree.

One blustery day, after securing the address to the Forten home on Lombard Street, she arrived by way of carriage. The sky above spread gray and the wind threatened to take her hat as she climbed the steps. Holding it down with one hand, she decisively turned the lever with the other, not considering that Margaretta Forten might be tending to her own business away from home. At the curb, Mr. Clemons stood near his horse pretending to not pay attention to what was transpiring behind him. When the door finally opened, a well-dressed, brown-skinned woman appeared.

"Is the lady of the house present?" Agnes asked.

"What lady would that be?" the woman replied.

"Miss Forten."

"Well, I am Mrs. Forten, but perhaps you are calling upon my daughter Margaretta. If so, she is not available to accept a visitor. She is out of the house at this hour and did not mention the arrangement of an appointment. She is normally very fastidious about her schedule. I cannot imagine her neglecting a duty. Perhaps there has been some sort of confusion."

Agnes was taken by surprise. It had not entered her mind that she could be the mother of the person whom she hoped would set her life on its proper path. She had not imagined that the members of the Philadelphia Anti-Slavery Society would be integrated, and having seen an image of Lucretia Mott, she had assumed all the women would be of her same hue.

"You must excuse me," she managed.

Her manners then slid behind a foreboding thought of what her uncle would make of her standing on the stoop asking to enter the home of a black abolitionist. And what of Bernhart? What would he think? She was struck by the realization that she did not care to guess, as she had lately resisted contemplating just what his opinion would be on difficult topics such as, say, women going off to college.

The woman raised an eyebrow, not unkindly, waiting for Agnes to gain some composure. Then offered, "It may be that I could relay a message for you?"

Agnes thought for a moment, then decided to adhere to the truth, "I came to ask her advice on the issue of education, my own to be exact. It seems an inquiry by way of post would prove more practical."

"As you like," said the older woman. "Good day to you." And closed the door.

Agnes descended the steps quickly, pausing by the coach for Silas to help her up. Her hand shook a bit as she reached for his arm, while he stood quietly masking his surprise at her decision to inquire at the Forten residence. By the time she arrived home, she had formulated in her mind the letter she would send off that afternoon. When a handful of days passed with no reply, she began to contemplate drafting a second request, but then a note arrived asking her to meet very early the next morning.

Penny was awakened by a knock upon her bedroom door. It was too early for anything but a rooster's cry or the rattling of milk bottles on a passing wagon, the sky just pink toward the east. Normally, she slept another half hour before stirring up the embers in the kitchen stove. She threw off the covers to a chill in the air and cool floorboards beneath her feet and opened the door to find Agnes standing before her in a nightgown, bright-eyed with hair ruffled. Of course she could not refuse the girl's request for assistance in getting dressed, but grumbling, she did make it clear that she would need to find a crumb or two in the cupboard before any labor could commence. By the time she reached the third floor, Agnes had washed her face, combed her hair and sat waiting.

"Never fancied the notion that the early bird gets the worm. Seems like pure blarney. No doubt a worm appreciates a decent night's rest, like the lot of us."

"Forgive me Penny, for requiring your assistance so early this morning, but I have business to attend away from home. I shall be out the door and back before breakfast is served. I will take my cup of tea at the coffeehouse to save you the bother."

"'Tis not the bother of putting a kettle on that sours my mood. 'Tis leaving a warm bed before I can see light through the window." Penny tightened the laces of the corset. "But think nothing of it, now, as I'm up. The air is cool, so you'll need your cloak. I'm afraid to ask what business calls this time o' day, just as I suppose you're afraid to answer?"

"Not afraid," Agnes piped. "Although I can't inform you just yet, it shall be good news in the end, I am convinced. Now I must be off."

Penny followed Agnes down the stairs, turning at the landings and escorting her to the front door where the young woman left out silently. Heading toward the kitchen, passing the back parlor which held the dining table, Penny glanced at the pair of windows against the wall. And there upon a chair, pulled close to the lace curtains, sat a figure silhouetted against the early light. Penny gasped, causing Larkspur to turn at the sound.

"Well, if it don't put the heart crossways to live in a house with a lass waking before dawn and another lurking about in a dreary room. What the devil are you lookin' for, if you don't mind me askin'?"

"Morning mam," Larkspur said, attempting to remove the angst upon her face before rising to her feet.

"Now I've told you about callin' me that. I can't have it. I'm far too young for any notions that I share a likeness to your own mam." She smoothed the folds of her dress that covered her hips and changed her tone. "Oh, but excuse me. I'm as grumpy as an old bear for I haven't yet laid eyes upon a cup o' something warm."

And off she went to set the kettle to boil. As she pumped the handle to draw up water, she thought about the puzzling behavior of both Agnes and Larkspur. Of late, not only had Agnes been evasive toward Bernhart, but had been buzzing around like a honey bee between her uncle's library, her writing table and the post office. She was up to something of which Penny could not guess. As for Larkspur, why had she crossed the grassy lane to converse with Mr. Clemons? It couldn't be over matters of transportation since she rarely left the house, and now here she was staring out the window, as if she had a grave matter over which to worry.

She placed the kettle on the stove and frowned. It did not seem fair that if a scandal were in the making, she not be privy to it.

༄

When Agnes arrived at the coffeehouse it was empty, save a young man sweeping the floor. She chose a table at the back, added a spoonful of sugar to her tea and began to sip in the smallest of increments, leaning her spoon facedown across the saucer. She waited. The lamps hanging along the walls offset the gloomy morning, which seemed to have failed to cross through the windowpanes. Besides the sound of the broom against the floor, the room was quiet. Suddenly the door swung open, the first of a slew of customers began to stream in and soon their voices rose like a chattering of starlings. Agnes watched discreetly, her legs shaking under the table. She added another lump of sugar to her beverage, then returned the spoon to its position on the saucer, face down as instructed. It was then that a woman approached the table.

"May I?" she asked, removing her bonnet before sitting down.

Agnes stammered, "It is just that I'm waiting for ..."

The young woman held up her palm to prevent Agnes from continuing. Agnes was expecting to meet with Margaretta Forten, who, she had learned since her unannounced visit to their home, belonged to one of the most well-reputed black families in all of Philadelphia. Her father was a successful sailmaker and community leader. The woman who sat before her, based on complexion and style of dress, could not possibly be a member of the esteemed family. Her simple Quaker attire and pale skin easily revealed this fact, but what made Agnes's mouth remain agape was that the woman before her was no other than Julianna Stone, whose family lived on Walnut Street.

"Don't worry Agnes, I was sent to meet thee by Miss Forten, a very busy woman who is in the process of establishing a school for the youth. She trusted I convey to thee her message." She leaned in and continued, "She offers encouragement and extends our assistance with thy pursuits as we believe well-educated women are essential to the nation's future. Miss Forten finds it prudent that thee meet with our group."

While Julianna spoke, she glanced about to ensure no one could hear the conversation. Her voice, she kept even and low.

"I'm sorry," Agnes began. "You have caught me off-guard, Julianna. I did not expect to see *you* this morning and now this talk of a meeting. I must be certain of the group of which you speak. I simply hoped to seek advice from those who might be in a position to offer it, not become caught up in..."

"Agnes," Julianne hummed, "I find there is a complexity to most things, yet also a road of simple truth that holds down the middle." The gentle sweep of her hair softened the cut of her cheekbones. "We have come to realize that seeking justice on one issue requires us to do so for other issues." She dropped her voice further. "We are part of the Female Anti-Slavery Society here in Philadelphia. We are not a secret organization, yet we must conduct ourselves with both courage and discretion. I have given the society members my word that we can trust thee will do the same when attending our meetings."

Agnes took a sip from her cooled tea, wincing at her indulgence with the sugar. She cleared her throat. Could she willingly associate herself with anything so controversial? And yet, the thought of being among a group of supportive women, steering her forward, was particularly tempting. Before she could speak, a couple sidled up to the table next to theirs and sat down, their parcels jarring Agnes's spoon from its precarious place on the saucer.

"Agnes," Julianna spoke more swiftly, "I can see some time is needed before a decision can be reached. Perhaps our paths shall cross at the Haverford tonight, as I have a dinner engagement at eight. Thy answer could be given then?" She smiled as she rose from her seat.

After she had gone, Anges sat staring into her murky cup.

As she contemplated the odd exchange, she began to convince herself that attending a meeting was not an endorsement of any kind, it was simply an opportunity to gain useful information under the guise of a different, albeit radical, pretext. In fact, this element, she had to admit, made it a bit tantalizing. With growing excitement, she made ready to leave, pausing at the door to button her cloak. It was then she spotted Bernhart stooped over a table outside.

The shock of him being there, infringing upon the prospect of her future with such a grounding symbol of the present, crushed every bit of her exuberance. But when she stood for a minute longer, the shock lessening, she realized that perhaps it was to be taken as a sign. Was there room for the present and the future to meld together? After all, here they both were on the same corner, on the same damp morning. She decided, fastening her top button, to interpret it as an indication of the good fortune to come. With that, she pulled up the hood of her cloak and opened the door.

ﻖ

Bernhart, too, had risen early. Amidst a morning walk through the idle streets, he had ended up seated at an outside table at the coffeehouse. Preferring the cool autumn air to the stale confines of the shop, he was nearing the bottom of his cup when the coffeehouse door rattled open and a dark figure emerged. Intrigued, he watched as a woman glided towards him with the hood of her long, wool cloak drawn about her. As she passed, her head turned so that her slender nose and her cheek caught the light, causing Bernhart to startle.

"Agnes," he called out at last, his heart minus its beat, waiting for her to turn. And to his great relief, she did.

"Bernhart," she answered, with a suggestion of tenderness laden between the even break of the two syllables.

"Why," he began, rising and moving toward her, "I am

entirely taken by surprise to find you out so early, thinking that a morning of leisure is more complimentary to your nature. Could this damp air be good for your lungs, let alone your delicate complexion?"

Anxious to return home to mull over her interesting morning, his comment squatted in her way like a bramble bush, yet she forced a smile. "Is it safe to assume that what cannot be good for me can conversely be so good for you? It seems rather unnecessary to be about at such an early hour harboring the burden of wondering how another's skin might fair."

"Agnes, you misconstrue my genuine surprise and concern for foolishness. I am merely surprised by the manner in which you swept past me and wonder what business you have at such an hour. Yet regardless, it is pleasing to see you in the gentle light of morning or the fading glimmer of evening or any angle of the sun in between."

Agnes let out a tiny puff of air. As she bit her lip to hide from his flattery, the sun broke through a cloud causing Bernhart to raise a hand above his head.

"The mist has lifted and the sun seems unbearably strong. I fear you will be overcome with heat if you do not remove your heavy cloak. And he gestured with his arms in a very helpful and innocent way just how he could assist with the cloak. "May I?"

"Don't be silly," she laughed, drawing the folds of the fabric together under her chin. "Although I do detect beads of sweat upon your brow."

From her pocket she removed a handkerchief which bore the light scent of rosewater, and brought it to his face. It was not the sun, of course, but a nervousness that had caused him to both perspire and gush with unfounded alarm. The nebulous nature of their relationship and the jolt of surprise at seeing her, had left him unnerved. Then miraculously, her eyes narrowed in that familiar way he had not been the target of in sometime.

"If you promise to be prompt I shall dine with you this evening at eight o'clock at the Haverford," she announced. "I know promptness is not your best attribute but it can easily be overlooked when it comes to the lamb chops. Did we say eight?"

"We most indeedly said eight," Bernhart beamed, feeling instantly recovered from his loss of composure. He watched her hurry off and then nearly giggled. Of late, he had been pestered by an unwelcome notion that dusting powder might be a rather banal item from which to launch his career, yet he felt certain about adding rosewater to the list of enticing scents.

ഉ

The kitchen was quiet, the late afternoon light muted and peaceful as Penny sliced the radishes and placed them upon the buttered bread.

"I hope you don't mind a light supper tonight, lass," Penny said passing a plate to Larkspur. "I can't see the use in makin' a mess when 'tis naught but the two of us."

"No, mam," Larkspur said.

Penny shot her a look. "Might it be so dreadful to try callin' me by the name bestowed upon me the day I skuttled forth into the world, no doubt screamin' at the top o' my wee lungs? I happen to think the name Penny a most wonderful thing."

Larkspur grinned. Then quietly, "I can't say you call me anything but lass. Sounds like a name for a mule."

Penny stopped chewing, then began again. When she had swallowed she replied, "I believe you to be right on that and the reason behind it ... well, call me silly but I can't say the name Larkspur fits you. It's shameless, thinkin' I know better than the parent that gave it to you, but I can't seem to get it past my tongue while I'm peerin' at that face o' yers." She slapped her knee as she chuckled. "And now you know the truth of it."

Larkspur smiled again. If only the woman knew that this was not the name her mother had given her, nor had she ever been called by it, save within the past few months. It seemed remarkable that Penny had the intuition to sense the ingenuity of the name. As the laughter died, behind it trailed a realization that panicked Larkspur. Perhaps suspicion, not intuition, had fueled Penny's comment. She glanced up to find the woman's eyes dancing before her.

The younger of the two turned away and began to gather her plate and cup to take to the sink. Penny caught her arm.

"Leave it for me, I've little else to do this night. Besides, I've got a task to put you to." She released Larkspur's arm, then patted it. "I'll be needin' you to go round to the Spiedler's place. Miss Agnes requires a coach to carry her to the Haverford tonight. See if Mr. Clemons is up for it. You do remember the fellow, eh?"

Larkspur nodded without looking up.

Penny collected the dishes. With her fork she scraped the plates clean, letting the uneaten crumbs slide into a bucket she kept near the sink. From her cutting board she added the radish tops. She would use the contents of the bucket towards tomorrow's stock. It already held a fish head, vegetable scraps and unfinished wine. She placed a chipped plate over the top to deter the flies. A second, larger bucket she kept on the floor in the corner containing items of which she could find no further purpose than to sell to the rag and bone man. It contained scraps of fabric too frayed to become dust rags or bandages, a broken milk bottle, paper not fit to write on, and bones she'd already boiled twice over. The rag and bone man traveled door to door, paying out a few pennies as he went, then sold the items to the paper mill, the glue and toothpick factory, or the fertilizer manufacturer.

Penny cleared her throat, "Take a note to leave, by chance he's not come back from his daily rounds. There's paper in the tin there and a stick o' lead."

Penny was curious to learn if the girl could read and write. She was uncertain of what this would prove or disprove but thought such information might be useful in helping her solve the mysteries swirling about the house.

Larkspur retrieved a scrap of paper and pencil, setting them before Penny at the table. Penny began to push the items back toward the girl, then caught herself as a flash of her grandfather patiently teaching her how to read came to mind, along with a flush of shame. What was the purpose of testing the girl, as if there was something to be gained by exposing her inadequacies? It was clear by the strained look on Larkspur's face that she was not about to compose a note for Mr. Clemons.

"Perhaps I should write it, eh?" Penny scribbled on the paper and handed it to Larkspur, comforted by the girl's relieved expression. "Off you go, then."

The evening started out agreeably, despite the greenish tinge to the deviled eggs and the ripping sound of Bernhart's trousers when he flicked a slug from his boot upon entering the Haverford's foyer. Thankfully the rip was well hidden behind his coat, leaving the worry to linger behind the tinkling of the cutlery, as he worked through his lamb without calamity. The spacious dining room, softly lit and humming from the sea of patrons, was warm and intoxicating. Velvet drapery softened the drumming of the rain against the windows and into the thick and slender spines of old books perched upon the wall-length bookshelf, seeped the smattering of laughter and the footsteps of waiters returning empty plates of broiled halibut and sauteed kidneys to the kitchen.

Bernhart was prattling on about ingredients for his dusting powder when Agnes brought her spoon to her mouth only to bring it back to her vanilla tapioca without taking a taste.

It seemed her eye had caught on something over his shoulder, but as he turned to look she blurted a question.

"Did you say calendula? Is that not the same as a marigold?"

Reenergized, he smiled, "Why Agnes, you impress me with your knowledge. You may also find it fascinating that in Germany we throw the petals into our stews and soups for seasoning, thus assigning the flower the name "pot marigolds." Puzzling though, why the latin would choose a word meaning little calendar."

She raised an eyebrow to demonstrate obligatory puzzlement while he continued, "But of course the name itself has nothing to do with why I contemplate adding it to the powder. Its medicinal properties are quite impressive, especially its benefits to the dermis. That is to say the skin, of course."

"Yes, I am familiar with the term?" she muttered, picking up her spoon again, stealing a glance toward the foyer. "Is that it then? Are all the ingredients set?"

With a pained look he whispered, "Not at all. There is something new that has... well, fluttered through my mind. It is merely an idea at this point, but one I shall like to explore and one on which I would like your honest opinion." He paused. "I ask you this simple question, have you not held a moth's wing between your fingertips without marveling over its sublime texture?"

"I must admit I have not found any reason to pet a moth. Bernhart, please deny that you plan to crumble moth wings into your powder?" She let out a giggle, then snuck a glance behind him before continuing in a firmer tone. "Sincerely, I must ask for an explanation before the discussion goes any further. And I do hope I shall not hurt your feelings by posing it, but you must explain to me your preoccupation with dusting powder. I admit, although you should likely not want to hear it, that I regard it merely as a talcy substance of which to keep one dry in hot weather and fair when freckled by the sun. But beyond that ..."

He dropped his eyes to the limp asparagus rod left on his plate, staggered by her disregard. Could the presence of a jar of dusting powder, perched upon her dressing table, be of no more importance than the bristles of her hairbrush or the notched frame around her hand mirror? If so, why then should he care so much? Why stand under a tree at twilight searching for the sublime? Perhaps, he realized with a sour turn in his stomach, he should have heeded the small voice within whispering the same sentiment.

The heavy silence was disturbed by a flurry of movement in the foyer behind him, commotion that seemed to propel Agnes from her seat. Looking a bit frantic, she stood up and excused herself from the tiny table, the candle flickering as she swept away.

Bernhart grasped the arms of his chair in order to turn himself to watch her go and to spot the boisterous knot of diners adjusting their hats and coats, exchanging heartfelt goodnights. She headed directly for the throng, then peeled off toward the cloak room, brushing past a more somber couple dressed in simple attire and offset from the group. He wondered if she had bumped elbows with the woman for they seemed to have turned towards each other before Agnes disappeared down a hallway.

The room settled as the company filed out. He released his hold of the chair's arms to return to the sight of the half-eaten dish of tapioca. Lamenting over her dismissive attitude toward dusting powder, he brightened when she appeared back at the table, but noticed her coat folded over her arm.

"Is everything alright, Agnes?"

"I apologize, but I must say goodnight for my stomach has begun lurching about in such an odd manner. Perhaps the deviled eggs had a dash too much paprika. Don't worry I have arranged for a coach for myself so that you may finish your dessert. I beg you forgive me Bernhart, but I really must rush off." She offered a pathetic smile and hurried away.

Bernhart sunk in his chair, deflated that the night had taken such a dismal turn.

❧

A cannon not a coach must have shot Miss Agnes from the Haverford when she heard the door bang and the glass rattle in its frame, thought Penny. And the sounds resonated for as long as it took her to remove her feet from the footstool and amble toward the front hall. There Agnes sat in a heap on the bench, slowly untying the soggy ribbons of her cap, looking miserable. Penny waited for her to catch her breath, rummaging through her pockets for a molasses drop, having learned to keep a tight lip during such moments.

At last, Agnes had the strength to say, "Oh my dear, dear Penny, my hair has come undone from this horrid rain. A facecloth at once, if you would be so kind."

"Surely a bit o' rain can't be what's twisted you into such a state." Penny's voice proved patient by the tail of the sentence if not so much at the snout.

"Yes, there is much more to it," sighed Agnes. "Nonetheless, the back of my neck feels horribly damp."

"I'll fix us a cup o' tea, then," said Penny, noting how rather unwet Agnes appeared.

She headed back where the stove in the kitchen was still warm. She poked at the fire to bring a flame back and lit the lamp on the table so they would know to pull their feet up by chance a mouse dashed across the floor. Soon she was pouring tea and after a little urging, had Miss Agnes spinning the tale of her outing, consisting of table linens, the incalculable number of tiered flounces of Mrs. Bustleton's skirt, deviled eggs and something about a slug on Mr. Hommes's coattail.

"You aim to say, not a morsel spilled from the gentleman's spoon?" Penny interrupted.

"Oh Penny, he is not so clumsy as that. Is he?" At this

Agnes stared intently at the wick of the lamp and began to worry, not over his clumsiness, but over the forlorn look on his face upon her hasty exit.

Earlier in the day it had seemed such a good idea to meet. They both enjoyed sharing together the Haverford's lamb chop, medium rare with a sprig of rosemary, but more importantly, it had been weeks since she had given him her full attention. Yet in truth, it was neither of these reasons that prompted her to suggest they dine together, but rather a selfish excuse for her to exchange information with Julianna Stone. A flush of guilt now caused her to emit a long, heavy sigh. She winced at the thought of having left Bernhart puzzled and forlorn over an abandoned dish of tapioca.

Penny, dunking a stale biscuit into her tea, wondered what Josephine would have thought of her niece coming home unaccompanied at such a late hour. At last, Agnes wound her way through the thick of her guilt and returned to the story.

Agnes drew in her breath and set her eyes upon the wooden spoon in the cook's hand. "And then Julianna Stone was leaving in her Quaker Bonnet." She looked again at Penny, and not sure where or how to begin, veered off with, "How I wish I could take her to the milliners and persuade her to add but one length of lace to her cap."

"Ah then, 'twas only a few drops o' rain that brought you such grief to arrive home in a torment?" Penny was tired from her long day. If this was all the story there was, she'd prefer to get back to her room and its bed.

Agnes sighed. "If only it were merely a few drops of rain that grieved me so." Her voice grew somber. "You see Penny, it seems the more I try to make sense of what the future holds, the more perplexed I become. How can I possibly sort it all out, as if love and calling can be kept neatly in their corners, never to run together, making a tangle in the middle? I do so think of myself as a person who speaks of the honesty lodged within her heart, yet sometimes I find it lodged so deeply no words can pry it loose."

A look of pother played upon Penny's face, caught for a moment in confusion, deepening the lines around her eyes, and leaving Agnes to wonder if she should attempt a second explanation. Suddenly, a charred log in the stove made a dull thump as it broke in two, settling Agnes's mind.

"I believe I should bid you goodnight, Penny," she said, rising from her chair.

She took the lamp with her up the stairways. When she reached the second floor, her hip jarred a small table knocking over an unlit candle.

֍

Aunt Josephine had returned from the seaside. After giving herself some time to recover from her journey, part by rail and part by coach, she felt rejuvenated. While her husband continued to attend to his affairs in the south, she threw her energies into daily volunteer work with her women's group, and sewing clothes for a local charity enticed her out of the house each morning.

On the nineteenth of September a telegram arrived announcing that Mathias Trossen could be expected to return from his travels by the end of the month. After Agnes received the telegram, she bent to pick up the paper from the stoop without glancing at the headline blazoned across the front. Tossing it upon the hallway bench, she climbed the stairs to report the telegram to her Aunt who was enjoying a monthly bath in the copper tub in her dressing room.

Minutes later, Penny found the paper splayed upon the seat of the bench.

"Compromise At Last!" cheered the headline. She began to read the article. While packed with an abundance of tedious details, it projected the Compromise would appease both those for and against the continuation of slavery. While it would restrict the western territories from becoming slave states, conversely the fugitive slave law would be strengthened throughout the nation in order to assuage the slaveholders. She skipped ahead to reach a paragraph explaining that the primary responsibility for capturing and returning fugitive slaves would now be assumed by the federal government. At this she let out a small noise, but read on. The slaveholders of the south would be relieved to know that the burden of slave catching would no longer fall upon their shoulders. Federal marshals, appointed by the government, would now be assigned this arduous duty.

Larkspur entered the hallway, carrying a stack of towels, to find a strange look upon the cook's face. "Bad news?" she asked.

"'Tis news of the Compromise. It appears the new states in the west will be free states after all, but," she sighed, "does seem more trouble for the slaves o' the south, at least the ones brave enough to run from their misery." When Larkspur did not move, Penny added, "Here are the towels. Run them up, lass, she'll be a prune if we keep at our dawdlin'." Her gaze returned to the paper.

Larkspur trudged up the stairs, her legs heavier with each step as Penny's words filled her with a foreboding dread. When she reached the third floor, she sat for a moment on a stiff chair in the hall. As the voices of the women inside the dressing room floated out to her, she rose and knocked on the door.

Bernhart, enjoying the autumn air at an outside table at the coffeehouse, motioned to the paperboy on the corner to bring him a copy of the Philadelphia Public Ledger. He gave the boy a coin and unfolded the newspaper. He forced himself to read the entire report, before he sat back in his chair. Will a compromise satisfy anyone? he wondered.

"Good morning, Mr. Hommes."

"Good morning, Mr. Spiedler," Bernhart replied, gesturing to the other chair at his table, "Would you care to join me?" The two had recently become acquainted by way of the Trossens.

"I am grateful for the offer, yet I must decline as I am on my way to the courthouse. I have a case that requires my attention." His eyes dropped to the paper splayed upon the table. "What is your opinion of today's news, Bernhart?"

"Oh sir, I must confess while I am an ardent student of a variety of subjects, politics is not one that has ever had the capacity to hold my attention in the manner it is captured by, say, a stag beetle's mating pattern or the properties of treebark. I do attempt to stay abreast of current affairs, of course, but beyond that my unrefined opinion in such matters lacks any type of authority."

Mr. Spiedler decided to sit for a moment, after all.

"Bernhart, while I support the sovereignty of each individual to follow his own path, and scientific inquiry is as lofty an inquiry as any other, I would also argue on the necessity of each citizen to maintain an informed and firm opinion on that which affects not only himself, but his fellow man. That truly is the obligation of each citizen, otherwise we run the risk of letting fools decide our fate." Bernhart nodded in deference to the older man and offered him the opportunity to continue. "For instance, the Compromise reached today may not threaten to impact upon your forays into biology, chemistry or invention, nor upon the daily lives of most of those you see around you on this fine morning. Yet, the arrangements made today will undoubtedly seep into the moral fabric of this society and add to the growing stench of its decay, for while we have curtailed the spread of slavery in the west, we have conversely strengthened its chokehold closer to home."

"Isn't compromise needed in society just as it is in nature, sir? In this case, to keep the north and the south harmonious," offered Bernhart, a bit flustered by the weighted content of the conversation, so that his elbow caught the table clumsily. Mr. Spiedler seemed not to notice.

"If good northerners like you, Bernhart," he began, "were to travel through the southern states and witness the condition in which slaves were held in captivity, I believe you would strike the word harmonious from any description to do with our nation." He stood up abruptly, tapping the iron chair leg with his walking stick. "Now, how did I come to sit when I am expected elsewhere. I must be off. I have enjoyed our conversation. There is an air about you, young man, that is most refreshing and if the words we've exchanged this morning spark in you what I truly hope they might, I have one further suggestion." The mid-morning patrons of the coffeeshop dotted the tables around them as Charles Spiedler leaned closer. "Familiarize yourself with William Lloyd Garrison's *The Liberator*. You may find the radical tone off-putting, but you will discover truths the daily paper fails to disclose."

With a pat to the younger man's shoulder, he strode off leaving Bernhart to reach the likely conclusion that Mr. Spiedler wasn't just against the expansion of slavery, but a full-blown abolitionist, advocating for the complete demise of the "peculiar institution." He sat for a while impressed by the older man's conviction.

৯

Larkspur dipped her pail into the portable bathtub, stepped carefully across the floor, and let the contents sail out the window. Returning to the tub she repeated the task countless times, listening for the muffled sound of the water to strike the ground far below.

Normally the task of emptying the large basin seemed endless, but today the young woman was not bothered by the monotony, relieved that the niece had found it sufficient to merely add warm water following her aunt's bath, rather than begin with an entirely fresh tub. She took solace in the quiet work. Her thoughts swirled back to finding Penny in the front hall that morning and the jumble of black ink marks filling the paper that she could not read. The river of her past flowed into the room.

ഉ

Larkspur had never been taught to read nor write, only schooled to speak in such a style so as to allow her mistress to go about the town accompanied by a mannerly slavegirl. It did not raise the eyebrows of the white people they encountered, as they strolled along the wooden sidewalks, ducking into the shops for new gloves or spools of thread, that the small girl was no darker than the prim and venerable woman whom she followed a few lengths behind. That her hair was thick and coarse but nearly straight when pulled tight, that the features of her face were ambiguous, was secondary to the known facts. The relationship was clear by the distance maintained and the condescending tone in which Mrs. Fenton T. Beckman, as she preferred to be addressed, spoke to the child. As well, the townspeople knew that the young thing had been acquired recently at a bargain price, suggesting the last mistress was unable to endure such an obvious reminder of a husband's indiscretion.

Too young to contemplate the identity of her father, but old enough to know that she was not white regardless of her complexion, left her little heart feeling enormously alone upon arriving at the Beckman plantation. She could not see beyond the agonizing moment in which she had been wrenched from her mother, to which it felt every fiber of her body had been attached. She moved about in a somber way and wept quietly upon her pallet on the kitchen floor for nearly a month. The overwhelming feeling of solitude did not begin to lift until the night Aunt Celena, as she was called, patted her firmly on the bottom and said, "We is your family now, child. Stop all that carryin' on and you might come to find we ain't so loathsome."

The Beckman farm, perched on the eastern edge of Powhatan County in Virginia, was a mere 300 acres in size and kept but twelve slaves to work the fields in the warm months and attend to a variety of other tasks when the ground was frozen. They were treated better than many, Aunt Celena pointed out repeatedly to Larkspur, who after a few years on the Beckman land could no longer remember much about her life on a plantation further south. Still to Larkspur, the fact that the Beckman's provided ample yarn and cloth to sew themselves woolen socks and new clothes for Christmas, and that they were allowed to keep a coin or two for the extra field work they did for the yoemen neighbors, did not compensate for the peck of cornmeal and the four pounds of fatty pork they each received per week and the occasional thrashing for any random reason. It did not negate the restriction she felt upon her body and soul as she stood, in a clean apron with head bowed, before the mistress of the house each morning to be inspected. She silently refused to accept Aunt Celena's opinion that their master and mistress were of the preferable kind.

"I tell you this, Little Del," as Larkspur was called then. "They ain't like the last ones I had before," said Celena one winter evening as they sat about weaving baskets from the broomcorn they had grown along the edge of last season's cornfield. "Them I had to fix good."

"What you sayin?" chidded one of the other women, limping across the room. "You ain't done nothin' to nobody, nohow, else you won't be sittin' here hoggin' up all the heat. Inch over some now, and give me a chance at that log."

Celena didn't move. "What you know Arlett? You ain't the onliest one to get into some tomfoolery. I done sprinkled me a little potion powder when a situation beg for it. You know when it just keeps a hollerin' and carryin' on 'til ain't nothin' to do, but oblige it."

"Just hollerin' and carryin' on," Arlett repeated as the women fell over laughing so hard that Larkspur giggled too.

"What do you mean, potion powder, Auntie?" Larkspur asked.

"Oh, she don't mean nothin', noways," Arlett waved her hand dismissively, pulling her chair up close to the fire. "Ol' Cel get twisted 'round in the head sometimes. Them Dahomey women you claim you from ain't lookin' to whisper nothin' in your ear 'bout spellcastin' and such. A dream be just a dream, I always say." She gazed at the crackling fire, then added, "Lest it got to do wit flyin' or a small opening you needin' to get through. Then you best pay some mind to it."

Celena spied the curious look on Little Del's face. Given it was a long winter's night and she knew well the art of storytelling, especially her own, she indulged the young girl, tucking a small pinch of tobacco in her mouth before she began.

Explaining how she descended from a line of women who understood how to pull down the moon and call on the rain, she winked at Arlett when she claimed they possessed the secret for keeping a man coming back. Their kind of power had to be hidden in their hair, between their fingers and in the cooking pots. The type of power not easily understood nor underestimated. They were the healers, the midwives and the sages, the old women from whom advice, herbs, tonics and potions were sought. Their magic stretched back as far as memory itself, yet as strong as it was, it had not prepared them for the arrival of the strange men on boats, carrying guns.

Celena's grandmother endured the horrifying journey across the Atlantic Ocean. Despite imagining leaping overboard into the choppy water, as it resembled home to her more than the rocking nature of the ship and the planks of putrid wood on which she was forced to lie like a small fish already dead, she had stayed aboard for the hope of finding upon the next shore something that could restore her power and grace. When she reached America she did not recognize the plants growing from the ground, nor the trees, nor the rain. Only the sky. Calling to the moon, she slowly learned to cultivate different plants to heal a wound, to ease a birth, to ward off bad luck, or to bring about a severe case of dysentery. Working alone she could not regain the strength that her former circle of women wielded, but that did not keep her from passing on her knowledge to her daughter, who in turn had a daughter named Celena.

"When we forage for them herbs in the woods on Sunday, it ain't just for the cookin' pot and the healin' jar, we pick for them that came before so they don't never be forgotten. So they endure, long as the stars in the skies." Then she began to chant a string of names that soon became a rhythm by which the little girl could work, fall asleep, or cross a grassy lane.

Shaking the memories from her mind, Larkspur finished wiping dry the copper, mopped up a few spots along the floor planks, then pushed the wheeled tub behind a partition in the corner. Before leaving the room, she returned to the window to lower it. Below, in the garden where most of the plants had been pulled or turned under and only in one corner did chard and chicory thrive in the autumn air, she spotted a charm of crows gathered in the soft dirt. Suddenly they drew still, their bodies rigid, their heads tilted awkwardly to the side. They held, and then all at once rose upward so that the flutter of their black wings and the warning of their sharp cries pierced a hole into the afternoon and caused Larkspur to stumble backward. As the birds disappeared over the rooftop, she closed the sash and hurried from the room with renewed determination, the paper's headline and now the crows sending a warning, admonishing her to make haste.

ↄ

Leaving Mercy Tubbs in the stable, despite her whining, Silas set out on foot. The trees, dappled with leaves turned the color apricot and persimmon, urged him along until he came to the outside market along High Street. Scanning the shoppers as they shuffled about, baskets looped through their arms, he searched for Erzsebet. He knew the time of morning most likely to find her purchasing food for the day's cooking, but today there was no sign of her and he had not the time to wait, for other affairs begged his attention.

"If you've no coin, be off with you," snarled a bleary-eyed seller leaning over his root vegetables.

Ignoring the man, Silas cast one last look over the crowd, suddenly catching her scarf bobbing like a small bright boat between the gray bonnets. Without looking at the root seller, he jingled a pair of coins in his coat pocket before stepping away and resuming his route up the street.

Half-way down a block on a quiet street, near the water-front, he descended a short flight of steps and nudged open the door to a crowded and noisy shop. Along with cordial greetings and firm handshakes, the mingling scents of paraffin wax and soap lather welcomed him. Attending to customers occupying a line of chairs down the center of the room, the barbers wielded their scissors and flat razor blades, while behind them perched a row of waiting customers. As Silas expected, the room was spinning with concern and speculation over what impact the change to the Fugitive Slave Law would have on the free black people of Philadelphia.

"We must consider the worst and prepare for it," stated one of the barbers.

"But how to prepare for yet a further stripping away of our rights as citizens?" asked a younger gentlemen.

The room grew silent, faces awash in the muted daylight tumbling in through the front windows, waiting for the man in the center chair to offer his respected opinion. Finally, Mr. Purvis, with his beard trimmed and his hair clipped evenly, stood up brushing his coat sleeves with his hands. He addressed the young man.

"You are too young to remember when the state snatched from us the right to vote as free black men in '38 and then burned down our abolitionist meeting hall the same year, just days after it was erected. It seemed at the time the most dismal and hopeless year, and yet looking back I see now how an enemy's tactics can, despite the opposite intention, offer a catalyst for change and even have a beneficial impact *if* we search diligently for opportunities. The mob's destruction of our meeting hall ignited public opinion in our favor and drew support for the movement to end slavery, which continues to grow thanks to our hard work. While this legislation will surely add a measure of difficulty and woe to our struggle, we must use it as motivation. For nothing shall prevent us from reaching our goal. Nothing!"

Robert Purvis, born to a free black woman from South Carolina and a white cotton broker from England, stepped toward the door, but turned before reaching it. "How to prepare, you ask? Fortify that within you which will never turn its back on our brothers and sisters still held in bondage. That within you that will insist, when our freedom is granted, on the full expression of our citizenship." He strode out into the street to carry on with his business.

As an independently wealthy man and president of the Pennsylvania Anti-Slavery Society, Purvis publicly advocated for the abolishment of slavery, and more quietly assisted in protecting and ensuring runaway slaves attain freedom. He appealed to the self-made, free blacks of Philadelphia, and as well to a small network of Quaker abolitionists, to supply funds and provide temporary shelter for runaways traveling up through the city and onward to Canada.

As Mr. Purvis moved down the street, he felt the resolve and confidence he had demonstrated within the barbershop quickly seep from him. Apprehension soon banged against his chest. The new provisions within the altered Fugitive Act allowed for the leveling of debilitating fines and jail sentences for anyone aiding runaways. He feared this would gravely hamper the collaborative effort in place, one which rested precariously on spontaneity and trust, and throw all those involved into an increased position of danger.

Reaching his residence, he closed the door behind him but knew it could not shield him from what was to come. For many years he had been a key figure in what would eventually be referred to as the Underground Railroad, and he would continue to do so for many more, but today he climbed the stairs wearily. He understood slavery as an entrenched, suffusive convention of customs and laws that challenged the moral fiber of the nation, but more so, he knew it as a singular predicament a person must endure for the entirety of a lifetime, rising each morning to face the brutality and hopelessness of it. Enduring it for the entirety of a lifetime, unless, there existed a path to freedom.

Entering his study and locking the door behind him, he was momentarily unable to appreciate how profoundly significant his work was. How it changed everything for those individuals who escaped. There would come a time when he would claim that for thirty years nearly every day he helped someone reach freedom, but on this worrisome morning his faith wavered. He lifted a plank in the floorboard behind his desk where he kept hidden his records, the descriptions of the men, women and children he had helped on their journey out of bondage. He stoked the embers in the grate until a flame, then two, shot up towards his tear-filled eyes. In his hand he held the stories of their struggle and the ingredients of their success. The words blurred together across the page as he tossed them into the flames.

෨

William Still was seated next to Silas, waiting for his turn in the barber chair. Silas murmured to his friend, "I need to see about a package by way of Virginia. Ain't got much information and the receipt is... well, too pale to make out. Comes by way of the Fenton Plantation down in Powhatan County."

Mr. Still nodded his head. "Where's this receipt kept?" The shop was noisy with conversation, so the two men had to lean their heads together to communicate. As always, they chose their words carefully.

"Young new maid at the Trossen home on Pine Street," Silas replied.

Mr. Still looked puzzled, for he knew of Mr. Trossen and his investments. "Can you meet me tomorrow night at Washington Square at seven with the receipt?"

Silas agreed, then hurried back, foregoing the haircut, only to be greeted by Mercy Tubbs snorting at him for being ignored all morning long.

After feeding the horses, he found Larkspur hanging wet towels upon the line. He opened the back gate and headed up the garden path.

"Miss Larkspur," he greeted her, lifting his hat.

"Mr. Clemons," she replied matter-of-factly, after removing a wooden clothespin from her mouth.

He looked around then whispered, "There's some business we need to tend to. Tomorrow night, 'bout quarter to seven, wait on the corner of Walnut and 8th. Me and Mercy Tubbs will come by and scoop you up. Don't be late, but don't be early just the same. Stand too long someone start to pay a mind to you."

"If I can't get away?"

"Put a kerchief in the garret window if you get in a tangle. But see, as best you can, you don't." Silas nodded at Larkspur, then added a little louder, "I shall be gettin' that dipper of water now. Thank you for it."

Filling his pail from the rain barrel and carrying it with him to the gate, he slipped out as if he had come for nothing more than a bucket of water.

Chapter 6

The rocking nature of the wagon and the measure of comfort in believing that there was someone else concerned with his well-being, lulled the boy to sleep under a burlap tarp. When they reached their night's stop, it took a firm shake to rouse him from his slumber. Levi hitched the horse to a stake and seeing no one about, motioned for Zeb to follow him toward two rows of small outbuildings. The moon had not yet risen, unwilling to alter its course for the benefit of two tardy travelers. Stepping slowly over the uneven ground, Zeb and Levi made their way by starlight.

Soon came the voices of those huddled over a large fire pit set between the two rows of dwellings. The smell from the cooking pots found the nose of the hungry boy. Before going any further, Levi motioned for Zeb to stand against the side of the first shelter, out of sight, then he knocked once before the door opened.

"Thought you be here by now," said a man's voice. "You musta come by some trouble."

"Made it, that's the truth of it," Levi replied. "Ain't no use in the how and why."

"Well, you coming in?"

Levi glanced down the lane, watched smoke curl up from

the fire, then looked back. "Ain't just me, Abram. Got a young'un with me. We'll be gone before sun-up but he's hungry and don't seem right leavin' him in the wagon all night."

Abram frowned. Levi understood why the man would say no. He knew it was dangerous. "Alright then, I best see to the horse."

"I ain't said no? Where's he at?" Levi nodded to where the boy hid in the dark against the side of the cabin. After a pause Abram said, "It'll cost you two pounds a millet instead a one. This the only time, so don't get a mind to try it twice."

Levi looked around to see if there was anyone about, then quickly pulled the boy around the corner. They both slipped by the man and into the tiny room. Once inside and with Abram glaring, Levi felt Zeb shift closer to him, brushing his elbow with a narrow shoulder. That the boy had already come to expect something from him, despite having just met, sent a tiny dart through his chest

"Some food in the pot." Abram finally said, shifting his gaze to Levi. "I'll take care a the horse." Before he left, he added, "You lucky then, no night riders out tonight."

Levi and Zeb helped themselves to a helping of beans. Watching the boy bring the bowl to his lips to catch the last drops of liquid, Levi thought the beans must be the best thing the child had ever tasted. From his pocket he took out a biscuit and handed it over, telling him to save it for tomorrow. Once the boy was asleep on a pallet on the floor, he crept outside to find Avery.

When he wrapped lightly on the brittle, unpainted door he heard her call out from the other side, "Who's that at such an hour? I done waited and waited until I'm plum through with it. All that patience just wore me out."

"Awe woman, you know you standin' right up on this door and can't but barely keep yourself from throwing it open," he teased, trying to keep his voice low. Avery rode to the market with him on market days, sold her goods from her own stall, then shared the ride back. This had been the arrangement for *nearly a year and, to Levi, was the very best arrangement he had ever known.*

Silence.

"C'mon girl, I need your help, now. It's somethin' serious."
He heard the latch slide. The cabin was dark except for the light from a single, inviting candle.

The cool weather arrived. The trees, adorned in fiery colors, waved in the shortened angle of the weakening sun. The crisp morning air, warmed so gently by midday, allowed Erzsebet a sense of tranquility she could not come by during the hot, sensual months of summer. It was not the long days of July and August that teased her with nostalgia for home, it was the nighttime, the deep, humid darkness and the slow journey of the sound of insects across her memory. It was an ache cured only by the arrival of autumn, when the beauty of things dying was only that and not a reminder of the urge to be fully alive. Autumn was the season in which she buried her desires like onions or potatoes for a far off day called winter. She had begun to imagine growing old despite her age.

Placing her basket on the bench next to her, she reached for an apple amidst her other purchases and began to shine it with the fabric of her dress. Most mornings, on her way back from the market, she paused in the square to enjoy a piece of fruit. After a few moments under the speckled bark of a london plane, she planned to return to her employers and continue the day's meal preparations, but for now she allowed the soft sunlight to touch upon the top of her head, warming her braids. She began to hum softly so that only the birds hiding in the dense bush behind her could hear. When she closed her eyes she drifted, not toward sleep but toward the past, as the apple in her hand grew heavy against her thigh.

She had just turned fifteen, in 1832, when her mother died. They had been settled into the city for a handful of years by then and St. Lucia was but a vague memory of canefields and saltwater. She had become accustomed to the noise and smell of city life, for while Philadelphia had an advanced system of aqueducts that brought fresh water to the citizens, it had not developed an efficient approach to sanitation. The pungent smell of human and animal feces from backyard privies and horse stables, along with uncollected rotting garbage encouraged swarms of insects and an abundance of rodents. To help combat the city's filth, hogs were intermittently turned out to scavenge the piles of garbage while street sprinklers, drawn by horse and wagon, came through to control the clouds of dirt and dust. These conditions, along with a void of knowledge on how illnesses were contracted and spread, made urban dwellers vulnerable to disease, especially in the overcrowded, impoverished areas. Yellow fever and cholera outbreaks were a constant threat. In 1832 cholera swept through the nation taking Erzsebet's mother and leaving the teenage girl alone in a large city to fend for herself.

Erzsebet, keeping her age to herself, was forced to utilize a number of her talents in order to survive on her own. In the early quarter of the nineteenth century, while theater and entertainment were still considered unrespectable pastimes by some, they grew in popularity in the city of Philadelphia. When avenues emerged for black performers to sing, dance and act in front of both black and white audiences, Erzsebet utilized her voice and aptitude for dancing to perform on a regular basis. At night she took to the stage, then trudged home afterward in order to gain enough sleep to attend to her domestic work by day. While she enjoyed performing and it allowed her to maintain a room above Beebe's Garment Shop, she worried that such a lifestyle would take a toll upon both her health and reputation. After she landed the cooking position at the boarding house, she decided to put an end to her work on stage.

Soon after she stopped singing, a change swept through the industry. White actors began painting their faces black and mocking the black performers style both in the theater houses and in parades on the streets, shifting the climate and closing doors for black performers. While she was glad to have ended her career before the change, it disturbed her to witness such opportunities shrink when she had always held to the optimistic assumption that the conditions of free black people would improve, albeit slowly, with the passing of time.

From her place on the bench, she began singing a song she had often performed on stage, but after a few moments the feeling as if she were being watched crept over her so that she stopped singing and opened her eyes. There was a man rushing along, as if late for a meeting, and a young couple picnicking on the grass a ways off, but none paid her any mind. When she looked down the path to her left, it was then she spotted Silas leaning against a tree. He raised a hand and came forward.

"Morning," he offered. "Begging your pardon, I couldn't help but hear you. Froze me in my tracks, reminds me of a song I mighta known some time ago."

Embarrassed, she dropped her eyes. In her hand the apple waited. He cleared his throat and came a step closer.

"A pretty song, from what I could catch. My right name is Silas. Silas Clemons if you care about the entirety of it."

"I go by Erzsebet," she offered hesitantly.

"You probably seen me and Mercy Tubbs driving the old wagon 'round for Mr. Spiedler, 'though we pick up 'bout near everyone with two legs but who don't care for walking."

She nodded, "Mercy, that's your wife?"

He laughed loudly. "Oh no now, I wouldn't put my wife in no barn. Mercy's a horse, though don't act nothin' like it. She fancies herself after the queen of England, from what I can tell." He shifted the hat in his hands from side to side then looked out across the grass. "You got a pretty voice. A real pretty voice."

She pulled on her ear, a gesture her mother had taught her in order to exhibit humility in the presence of a compliment. She recognized Silas, having noticed him at the market house and along the street driving the stagecoach.

"Some might call it peace and quiet, not having a spouse," he said lightly. "I say being alone ends up being just about the same thing as being lonely, if it goes on too long. Probably why I talk to Mercy Tubbs more than natural."

She began to rise, returning the apple to the basket and pulling her shawl around her shoulders. "I can't sit on this bench all day when work is calling. I best head on back, quick now."

"If you don't mind me keeping pace with you, I'm heading that way."

She nodded and they walked silently through the square. The soles of their feet, among the swirling leaves, vibrating above the unmarked graves of the victims of previous plagues.

৶

Bernhart stood before his work table, looking at an acorn, a maidenhair fern frond, a loblolly pinecone, damp leaves from a sweet chestnut tree, and a chunk of candle flame lichen nipped from the trunk of a red maple. Returning from a walk through the woods along the west end of the city, he excitedly peered over his new collection. From a small carrying case he removed a pair of tweezers, then opened a second, larger case and selected his magnifying glass wrapped in its velvet pouch. He hesitated, considering the best place to begin. Perhaps the leaves, for they were magnificently colored and might hold a clinging aphid or two. Or the lichen with its crevices to explore. Yet his hand, unable to resist, reached for the large acorn. Exceptionally furry and with a fringe around the edge, the cap nearly engulfed the nut beneath it, reminding him of a winter hat pulled down snug over the head of a young boy. He knew the bur oak dropped the largest acorns one could find, so he was delighted to have come across the massive-trunked tree at the time it had let go of an abundant crop.

While he held the acorn in his hand, having yet neither drawn his magnifying glass to it nor plucked at any part of it with his tweezers, he sat down upon his stool. Something about its appearance pried open what he had tried to keep shut since the night of the outing at the Haverford. Despite a handful of pleasant occasions spent with Agnes since then, she continued to seem distant. In response, he had ardently rallied his attention toward his work, telling himself she merely needed some space and that he would benefit from focusing on his own endeavors. But the acorn, with its fuzzy cap, seemingly unable to survive without it, convinced him to alter his approach.

"Very well," he conceded to the object in his hand, "I shall see to it," for in that moment, Agnes seemed the very thing he should not attempt to survive without. He would arrange to see her that evening.

The bur acorn slipped from his fingers, knocked against a wooden dish, and bounced to the floor. It took a moment before he found it, dusty and resting against the baseboard. Brushing it off, he chose to tuck it into his vest pocket as a reminder of his task. When it didn't fit comfortably, jutting out in one direction and into his flesh in the other, he slipped it into the pocket of his sack coat which he still wore from his outing. Satisfied with its location, he removed the daily paper from another pocket, lowered himself onto the stool, unfolded it, and began to read.

Scanning the day's stories, his eye caught on an article regarding Bartram's Garden. The botanical garden was to be sold. "Oh no," he cried out to no one but the battalion of wounded soldiers that had suddenly formed a line across his heart.

The Bartram family had founded the garden over one

hundred years earlier and now after three generations of establishing and maintaining the elaborate grounds, even shipping plants and seeds across the Atlantic, it was now to be sold to a man named Andrew M. Eastwick. Tossing the paper aside, he felt compelled to share the tragic news with Agnes immediately. He rushed off, troubled over the idea of losing his favorite place on earth.

৩

Bernhart sat on the bench in the hall while Penny went to announce his arrival to Agnes. She did not mention that the young woman was preparing to go out. When she knocked upon the bedroom door, she found Larkspur fastening Agnes's hair into a low bun.

"Beggin' your pardon," she began, "but yer Mr. Hommes has come to call. I had not the heart to tell him of yer plans elsewhere, believin' that would come easier from a prettier face than mine."

Agnes closed her eyes and then stood up, burdened by the thought of having to receive Bernhart. "Has the courtesy of requesting a reception prior to arriving fallen entirely by the wayside? It is as if all social norms have crumbled in this new age."

"Seems," whispered Penny as she retreated to the hallway, "not a thing you would mind if the corset went with it, eh?" At this all three women smiled and headed down the stairs.

Agnes and Bernhart sat in the front parlor for as long as it took Penny to rummage up a plate of cardamom wafers and a warm pot of tea from the kitchen. She sent Larkspur in, knowing Agnes would not appreciate a tray of refreshments prone to lengthen the visit, yet she could not be so rude as to fail to offer a bit of something.

Agnes was saying, "I'm sure it will all work out. Perhaps the new owner plans to preserve the garden just as it is." She turned her head as Larkspur placed the tray on the table, "Oh Larkspur, thank you but that won't be necessary. Bernhart, at the risk of appearing impertinent, and while I assure you I have found our time together most pleasant, I must excuse myself for I have an engagement that calls me away from home this afternoon. I cannot linger another moment or I shall be terribly late. Larkspur, could you bring me my cloak and gloves?"

"Oh," was all Penny could hear him say from where she stood pretending to wind the large clock in the hallway. Such a sad sound drew her into the room. She made her way toward the tray of tea and wafers. The young couple remained seated, a wall of disappointment building between them, while the acorn lie forgotten deep within its dark pocket. When Penny stole a glance at Bernhart's face, she thought to change his name to Burned Heart, he looked so close to tears. She could not bear it.

"Seems a cryin' shame to waste a perfectly good pot o' tea. If the lady has errands that have been put off twice over so they can't be put off again, I don't see as how that means Mr. Hommes can't stay for one o' me famous wafers." She lifted the tray and continued, "Did I bother to tell you that for a time I was known as Plum Penny, for I could make a plum puddin' like no other in Croagmuckros nor the hamlet one over. Oh, there's the lass now with yer things, Miss Agnes. Be off then, I shall see to Mr. Hommes so that his spirits return."

After the heavy door had closed behind Agnes, Penny motioned for Bernhart to follow her back to the kitchen where it was less drafty than the front of the house. While Larkspur went out to check the cellar for root vegetables, the other two sipped their tea.

"You may join us lass," Penny said to the young maid when she returned, "'Tis not a crime to break for tea. The Trossens pay no heed to how we go about gettin' the work done, just so we do in the end."

Larkspur was unaccustomed to sitting idle in the middle of the day, especially in such company, so she continued scrubbing the vegetables at the sink.

"Chamomile makes a lovely tea, doesn't it?" Bernhart said, deciding that a kitchen might prove his favorite room in any house. The warm cup of tea and the busy room began to lighten his mood.

"Good for the skin," murmured Larkspur, turning from the sink with her clean vegetables ready for chopping.

"Yes?" he perked up.

"Helps with healing a wound." She hoped that would end the conversation.

"Ah, you've seen it administered?"

Wiping clean a knife upon her apron, she replied, "Done so myself. After you clean out the wound, you need to see that it doesn't turn ugly. For a scratch chamomile or sweet marjoram will do, but for a deep cut, or if a poor fool steps on a nail, then best to get some jimsonweed."

"Jimsonweed?" His eyes widened.

Despite her hesitancy to reveal too much of anything, she could not resist indulging in the topic. "Crush the jimsonweed in a spoonful of lard and then rub it into the foot. Put a dab on the nail too, if the person was keen enough to save it. Then bury it so as to send the poison into the ground with it."

Bernhart was amazed. Considering himself somewhat well-read on the medicinal properties of plants, he was startled to find a mere maid with such knowledge and, as well, amused over her advice on how to apply the liniment.

"Fascinating. And from whom would you purchase your collection of herbs and roots?"

"Purchase? No sir, we found what we needed foraging through the woods or, when we could, we grew it right in our own garden."

"But how had you learned of the plant's healing qualities and how could you be certain of how to apply them? For Jimsonweed, I've read, can prove quite poisonous when taken in excess."

She shrugged, "I learned from the old women, although I

only know half as much as they did," Larkspur, with a growing unease over being asked so many questions, could not deny enjoying it.

"And how did *they* come to know so much on the topic?" he persisted.

"Passed along from one to the next." She was surprised that he wouldn't know how healers learned their trade.

"So it was not information accumulated from books?"

"No sir, we never did any reading," she replied.

Filling Bernhart's cup and then pouring one for the girl, Penny noticed the flush in Larkspur's cheeks as she sat at the table chopping. She sipped her own tea and reached for another wafer.

"If I may ask, where is it that you were raised?" he continued with an inquisitive look upon his face.

Larkspur, removing a few sprouting eyes from a potato, flashed it at Penny. "I thought you lacked a fondness for these?"

"Prefer to never see one again, but 'tis the Trossens I cook for so I do as I'm told. Most o' the time, that is," Penny laughed, then turned to Bernhart. "Mr. Hommes you can't rightly tell me there was no healer back in yer wee german village. One who could come to see about you when you were ailin'?"

"Why of course, we sent for the physician a few towns over when necessary."

"Course you did. But supposin' you only had aches and pains or took to your bed for somethin' you didn't need botherin' the doctor over? Or for the birthin' of babies or for the mendin' of a wounded heart? For that only a wise woman could be trusted. Back home our bean feasa was Moll McCourt. 'Tis she who brought me in the world and helped me through it. Dipped me in the holy well many o' times."

He cleared his throat. It was rather difficult to hear such talk given his full confidence and commitment to the wonders of scientific progress. For he was certain, even if others were not, that a theory would soon emerge to explain just how disease was spread, and an end to epidemics would follow. He trusted that the reputation of physicians would soar, as would the trust in their medicines. Yet, he found himself happily falling backwards toward his childhood.

"Why Penny, I believe you have dislodged a very early memory of mine for I have not thought of Frau Kniefle in a very long time. I do recall that she would amble up the stone path to visit with my mother, smelling as though she had slept on a bed of pine needles. Not an unpleasant smell at all. On the contrary, rather lovely. So many questions she would ask before scribbling a recipe upon a very small piece of paper. In return, my mother would send her off with a loaf of bread or a sweet cake.

"In my young eyes, she appeared as old as the hills and as strange and dark as the heart of the forest. I do remember my father teasing that the Hexenmeister would one day chase off all the cunning folk for trying to steal his magic. Yet, my mother drew the recipes from the pot on top of the mantle when she needed to bring down my fevers or ease the pain of a bee sting. I rather forgot all about it, until just now."

"'Tis true then, Mr. Hommes, that a book is not the only place from which a thing can be learned," said Penny smiling.

He nodded his head, smiling as well. "Larkspur, do you know much about calendula or marigolds as they are commonly called?"

Larkspur explained how they had wrapped a poor man's protruding veins in a warm compress so he could sleep at night and had once tried to improve a little girl's vision by placing three petals from three different flowers on each eyelid.

"Why three?" Bernhart found his interest in calendula returning.

The girl looked at him, not answering for a moment. "Everybody knows three and nine are the numbers to rid poison from the body. When you fix the tonic or prepare the poultice or brew the tea you have to tap into the mind's power to heal. We gave that tiny gal a chant to say when she took it, something rhyming with the number three." She added, "I don't remember that one working so good."

"Intriguing, although I cannot understand the purpose of incantations," he commented.

Shrugging, Larkspur slid the vegetable tops into a pot, then stood to fill it from the spout at the sink so she could begin the soup broth. Turning her back to the others, she did not find it necessary to explain how the rituals that went along with the remedies helped convince the healer and the one to be healed that they both possessed a power. A miraculous, some might say magical, power. Believing it would work was half the cure. The rhymes helped the person remember how to take it properly, which was essential, for Mr. Hommes was right, too much of certain things could prove deadly.

༄

While Bernhart was having his tea, enjoying himself more than he had in quite sometime, Agnes sat stiffly on a wooden chair in the corner of a crowded parlor. She did not know whose home she had entered, as she had accompanied Julianna Stone without asking any questions, and had slipped in just as the meeting was called to order. An hour later, when it had ended and the women began to stir, exchanging further opinions or inquiring over each other's well being, Julianna turned to Agnes with a smile.

Rising from her chair, Agnes asked, "Do the meetings always progress in such a way?"

"What is thy meaning?"

"Simply that there was so much dialogue, such an impassioned exchange of ideas. Is it common to feel such a charge in the air?" Agnes's cheeks were flushed, her heart beat against the fabric of her dress.

"Why indeed, the meetings tend to be quite spirited," Julianna laughed. Then with concern, "Is it too much for thee?"

Agnes did not at first answer. She clasped her hands together and looked out through the window. The day was dying, the promise of night eased across the sky, one star waving hopefully above the rooftops. Bringing her glance back into the room, the din of conversation in her ear, she fixed upon the painting above the fireplace mantle. Her eye stuck to the myriad range of hues and colors without seeing how they came together to result in a unified landscape. Surprisingly, each part held a beauty separate from the whole that she had previously failed to appreciate. At last she turned to her new friend and replied, "It is not too much, Julianna. Not too much at all."

With an empty wicker basket looped through her arm, Larkspur pushed open the back door to encounter an unexpected assault of cold air. Retreating back into the kitchen, she wrapped a scarf around her ears. She had begun running occasional errands for Penny, as the passing of time had made her less cautious, and today she had arranged to meet Mr. Clemons to exchange any news. She tried the door again and charged forward into the weather.

Upon reaching the market house, she found the area abandoned by the sellers who had been ill-prepared for such a biting wind in the middle of October. They were likely to reappear tomorrow, for they still had produce to sell before the winter fully set in, but for today Larkspur would need to make her purchases at Cullinans, the storefront grocers. About to set off, her eye caught on a stationary figure in the shelter of a lonely stall, an old woman settled upon a crate, hunched over a few small baskets. A pervading stillness suggested that the woman, wrapped in a wool blanket and face shielded by a scarf, had fallen asleep. Curiously, Larkspur moved closer, continuing until she could peek into the baskets, finding all were empty save one, which held a bunch of bound beets.

"I been waitin' on you," came a husky voice that made Larkspur stumble against the baskets.

"Pardon?" She righted the baskets.

"Is you the gal meant to meet Silas?" She had somehow, without using her hands, parted her scarf so she looked out with one eye. "Yep, you is. You ain't yet fancy the notion you one a them, has you?"

"You know Mr. Clemons?"

The woman ignored her attempt to steer the conversation. "No matter who you fool, can't fool you ownself. Sell the soul tryin' and never do. No never do. Can't, cuz ain't no truth to it! You is what you is, in the night time and again come daylight. Don't matter how you talk neither, that ain't nothin' but a fashion. Only what you *know*, that be all that counts." She drew a deep inhale. "Thing I say is, take a hold and be glad for who you is, lest you lose your mind wonderin' who gonna love you. Us might. Onliest ones."

Larkspur could now see her face, skin weathered like smooth, dark leather, and she understood that the old woman was warning her against passing as white. "Yes mam," she said, hoping to get back to the topic of Mr. Clemons.

"Well, you want them beetroots or not? Catch me some chilblains out here waiting half the day to sell some little old bunch a beets. No doubt, sweetest ones you done ever gonna taste, but chilblains all the same."

Larkspur couldn't help but smile, "Yes, then. How much?" Picking the bunch from the basket, she held it up in the gleam of the overcast day. The green tops with their crimson-veined stems stood vibrantly above the bulbous roots. The sight and weight of them nudged something deep within her that she wanted to recognize.

"Ahhh," murmured the woman, watching Larkspur, "Ain't

that color for nothin'. Beetroots make you ache for that some-body. Yes sir. You best find you a man quick, if you ain't git you one yesterday. But maybe you ain't tryin' to fool wit none a that. Then stick to the tops, them just keep the blood from goin' watery. Both though," she grinned, "get you to the biffy reglar." Her laughter fell without a sound as she rocked back and forth, mouth open and eyes closed.

As Larkspur reached to retrieve a coin, the woman cried, "I don't need no money." But changed her mind. "Then again, I best take it since it pro'lly belong to that no count Trossen mister." She winked at the girl. "Think I don't know you. I been seein' you come by. And I got ears, too. Askin' Silas for help. Umph, you lookin' at help right now and can't see it. Si and them might could help wit a thing or two, but I be the one to hook you a man, if'n you want one that is. Ain't just beets that do the trick."

Larkspur laughed so that when the tears sprung to her eyes she might succeed in hiding her feelings, strong as crimson and heavy as the beets in her hand, from the old woman.

It was to no avail. "Seems like you done left somebody back on the road you done come up? Waitin' on him, too, huh?" She started collecting her baskets before adding, "Gal, Silas be headin' back wit Mercy Tubbs to his stable. Go round and see 'bout him right soon." She stood up, swaying a bit. Come back 'n see me when you ready to find the kingdom to go wit that key."

She inched away, leaving Larkspur to stand all alone in the market, hand searching for the shape of the key through her clothing, while the old woman's feet echoed against the emptiness.

The cold finally forced her to move. She put her head down and set out to collect the things she needed, a hand-ful of carrots, two onions and a cut of beef shank wrapped in newspaper for the evening's stew. When she reached the narrow alleyway, she hoped to find Mr. Clemons still tending to his horse. Rapping on the gate, she heard the horse bray just as the latch lifted and Silas, broom in hand, motioned her to follow him.

Once inside the stable, where it was considerably warmer, Silas continued his task of sweeping the trampled hay into a corner pile. While Larkspur stood waiting, he began spreading a fresh bale about the floor with his hay fork.

"Spoke with Mr. Still. He said nobody heard nothin' by way a the grapevine telegraph. No one that match who you looking for. Now, he said, that don't mean your friend ain't making his way, just mean ..." Silas tipped his head to one side, "just mean no word on it. He suggests sending off a letter as that might work better than waiting on word a mouth. He's real good with the pen, so he'll help write it up. You got someone trustworthy still in Virginia?"

Last month Larkspur had rode with Silas to meet Mr. Still in Washington Square. She had worn her bonnet low and kept her umbrella open despite the suspension of the rain as the three stood at dusk along a quiet path. Silas had explained that if anyone could help it would be Mr. Still, given he was the clerk of the Anti-Slavery Society. William Still with his penetrating eyes and kind smile, asked Larkspur a number of questions until he had gained enough information to tip his hat and stride off leaving Larkspur feeling relieved and confident.

But now as she stood in front of Silas and his hay fork, considering the suggestion of sending off of a letter, addressed and sealed with wax, requesting information about the whereabouts of a runaway slave she was flushed with irritation and disappointment.

"No, there's no one. The farm was about to be sold and with it, all of us." Her voice changed when she added, "Not together but separately, in every direction."

She thought of Aunt Celena, nearly given away due to her

age to a man heading toward the Carolinas. It seemed the others were all doomed to be traded further south as well. All except for herself, who was purchased by a newly married couple hoping to improve their social status in Baltimore with their very own slave.

It all happened too quickly. Larkspur hadn't time to gather her belongings, leaving behind her medicinal pouch of dried herbs, and the tiny vials of tinctures and tonics. All she could keep was the amulet about her neck, the charm bag buried within the folds of her skirt and the memory of her hurried good-bye. She had grasped Aunt Celena's hands for they had only a few minutes alone together, a few dire moments before their parting. And while she would sorely miss the woman who had treated her like a daughter, she also needed to discuss another matter. An urgent matter.

"If you see him, tell him…" She had trouble getting the words out. "Tell him the first chance that comes along, I'm gonna take it." The old woman knew about the young man on the neighboring farm. "And if he can, if he can see to a way, meet me before the cold arrives. Just like we planned."

She clung to Aunt Celena, despite her name being called from outside. The older woman wanted to advise her to put aside her foolish notions, to bank nothing on the folly of romance and the ache of love. Wherever you land, build yourself a life with what you find, she wanted to explain, but only whispered, before pushing her young friend toward the harsh voices. "Be what you can, Little Del. Ain't no shame in that."

Silas's voice pulled her from the memory of that awful day. "There might be somebody who knows when he left and how, otherwise ain't much Mr. Still and them can do. Think on it. Think real hard on who might could know."

She hurried across the lane, over the hard ground of the backyard and through the Trossen's kitchen door, shook to the bone from both the cold and Mr. Clemon's improbable assignment.

Moving through the next few days disheartened and detached from her work, Larkspur banged about in her tasks until Penny warned her that Mrs. Trossen might take notice, despite the woman's despondency, if the ash pot was knocked against the floor any harder. Apologizing, she tried to remind herself of the importance of maintaining her position of employment, one for which months ago she had been extremely relieved to acquire. Such relief was now tarnished by a growing feeling of despair, for no matter how hard she thought, there was no one to whom she could send a letter asking for information. Instinctively, she reached for the amulet around her neck, pulling the string out from where it hid behind her dress. She squeezed the worn key tightly, and continued solemnly with her work, her thoughts narrowed on the young man she once met at the fencepost on Sundays.

ॐ

Penny couldn't help but notice the change in Larkspur, and, after dinner when she retired to her own room, she found her spirits dimmed as well. She told herself it must be the shortened days, the sky now dark before the meal was finished, but she knew it was something about the girl that stretched out the shadows the lamp cast upon the wall. Her somberness seemed to be rubbing away Penny's own amiable disposition, and she now sat on her bed feeling heavy.

A soft, slow tune came to mind, one of her mother's favorites. She thought of the country in which she was born. While the famine continued to devastate Ireland, she no longer allowed herself to dwell on the ongoing tragedy of it. When the potato blight first began to spread in 1845, it ravaged the Irish Lumper that the poor grew exclusively in their meager plots. She had fretted over her family's well-being, despite a letter from her mother insisting that she was not to worry. Then a year passed and a second letter arrived addressed in an unfamiliar hand. With dread, Penny broke the seal, and read the awful news sent by a neighbor. First her poor grandparents and then her sweet mother, taken during the winter by pneumonia. The money she had been saving, enough for one ship's passage but not three, was still hidden in a box in her room.

Reaching for a book amidst a stack on her table, she drew out a worn slip of paper pressed within the pages. Having discarded the neighbor's letter, she had saved an attached note from her mother. It contained just one line: *Farewell my bright lucky Penny.* For the past four years she had pledged to have each word ring true, to not dwell on Ireland's ongoing misery nor on the despair of being left alone in the world, but to be bright, to seize luck and to do her best to fare well. And she harbored pride and satisfaction in having done just that, although, and too often, behind the genuine optimism and her habit of gratitude, sorrow often lingered. Tonight it rolled down one cheek and then the other until her shoulders shook.

Larkspur, padding through the kitchen for a spool of thread from the sewing box, halted upon hearing the sobs. Thinking to tiptoe away, to retreat to her room in the garret and mind her own business, she froze with indecision. After a moment, the crying quieted and was replaced by hushed singing. Struck by the mournful notes, the younger woman found herself drawn toward the sound. Spellbound, she crept into the pantry. It was there, in the small dark room, Larkspur understood that it was not only the beauty of the voice that intrigued her but the novel idea that Penny had endured a past, just as she had, and just as likely clung to the idea of shaping her own future.

Larkspur nearly called out the cook's name, nearly knocked upon the door that stood ajar to answer the invitation of the beckoning light stretching toward her toes. But trust was an idea in which she did not yet believe. Her retreating steps were like a feather against the wood until a floorboard moaned. The singing ceased, yet she continued through the room, along the hallway and climbed the stairs toward her own solitude.

Chapter 7

This time the boy curled up inside a crate. A blanket was draped over him and lima beans poured on top. By the time they reached the market, just before sunrise, he had developed a strong dislike for the smell of the legumes. When the wagon stopped and while the morning still hung gray and opaque, Levi and Avery quickly pulled Zeb from the crate and brushed him off, immediately placing a basket in his hands. They set up their stand as if all three had been sent to sell the produce, figuring blending in was often the best form of disguise. The morning sped along and the boy proved rather adept at procuring a good price for the goods. According to plan, when it was time to break for the mid day meal, Levi drew the boy to him.

"You go with Miss Avery now, hear?" he whispered. "She'll see you to the docks, but you gonna have to go some of it alone." The boy nodded, anxiety rising in his face. The man continued, "You got this far, ain't no point in worrying now. They gonna want money for the ride so figure a way to sneak on like the other stowaways be doin'." The boy nodded again, but patted his cap where some money was sewn into the underside of it.

Levi smiled. "I see. Then you tell the men collecting

*tickets, Mr. Dart sent you to help the captain clean the deck.
Don't give no money to no one but Captain B. You be needin'
bout ten dollars to get all the way to Philadelphia. You ain't
got that much, tell him to drop you in Salem. That's New
Jersey, where the Quaker Lady been known to help."*

The boy swallowed hard, "Who's Mr. Dart?"

*Levi laughed. "Nobody I ain't never met. But sounds im-
portant, don't he? Alright then." He put his arm over the boy's
shoulder. "What name you go by, boy?"*

"Zeb."

*Avery cleared her throat to signal they were wasting too
much time. She nudged the boy by the elbow.*

*"Alright then, Zeb," Levi murmured looking the boy in
the eye. "Alright."*

First the sharp, November wind began to blow across the river
and up through the streets, whipping around buildings, tugging at coattails and chafing bare cheeks. Then the unwaver-
ing cold settled down on the city like an unwanted guest
arriving early. The hands of those unloading shipments at the
docks, or saddling their horses or carrying the chamber pots
to the backyard privy quickly turned raw and stiff. Philadelphia citizens moaned with indignation that winter should
come so soon, forgetting how they leveled similar complaints
each year prior.

For Larkspur, having survived her winters huddled inside
thinly boarded slave quarters, she found her trips to the market and her tasks in the backyard entirely bearable given the
amazing welcome of a warm, steamy kitchen upon her return.
Penny, as well, was undaunted by the weather for she too had
known a cold in her youth from which a change of season was
the only escape. Agnes, on the contrary, found the cold nearly
debilitating. From where she spent most of the day in the upstairs drawing room, her hands and feet seemed perpetually

frozen. Despite having pulled her chair closer to the fireplace and having insisted Larkspur feed the fire regularly, she required a shawl around her shoulders and a blanket about her legs as she sat for long hours reading.

"Perhaps another log?" she suggested to Larkspur.

"I don't believe another will fit just yet, miss."

"Well what good is a fireplace if it can't properly heat a room? Is it not horribly frigid in here or do I just imagine it so?"

"Hard for me to say, as I've been up and down the stairs so often. Moving about keeps me plenty warm and then with the cookstove in the kitchen…"

Throwing off the wool blanket around her legs, Agnes stood up. "While you may suggest that physical exertion would lessen this penetrating chill, as you see I have much to do here without taking on another activity, be it pillow fluffing or silver polishing." Pointing to a stack of books that began at the floor and climbed to the seat of her chair, she added, "I can not emphasize the necessity of remaining on schedule with my preparations, for I am still struggling with my review of Latin and have yet to attempt Greek since I find it altogether impossible to maintain concentration when my feet and fingers feel so numb."

Larkspur recognized that Agnes was working herself into a panic, her words spurting out upon her short, shallow breaths. Forgetting her role as a maid, Larkspur reached out and took both of Agnes's hands, squeezing them gently between her fingers. "Are you wearing that contraption around your waist again, Miss Agnes?"

Stunned by the calming effect of having her hands held, it took Agnes a moment before she shook her head.

"Good, then breath back here." Larkspur moved a hand to where Agnes's ribs wrapped around her back. She focused on slowing her own breath until Anges unknowingly began to match the rhythm.

"Miss Agnes, your hands don't feel so cold to me. It might be that they've grown a little numb, for your breathing seems stormy."

Larkspur closed her eyes in order to encourage the other woman to do the same, but also so she herself could digest the idea that she was standing there holding the hands of a white woman without it evoking within her any malevolence. After a few moments, Larkspur released Agnes's hands, noticing a new softness about her face.

"It's not good to sit in any one spot for too long, no matter what needs accomplishing," she said gently. "Come down now to the kitchen and get you some tea. Maybe you can tell us about the things you read in those books."

Smiling to himself as he dismounted from the carriage, Silas was thinking about his time at the market with Erzsebet. She had inspected each item with scrutiny, turning them over in her palm, while he strolled alongside inquiring as to how she would put her purchases to use. With the onset of cold weather, the sellers had diminished but there were still those peddling wheels of cheese, bottles of milk, root vegetables, grains, legumes, salted meats, tallow candles and bars of soda ash soap. Erzsebet teased that her skin deserved castille soaps from Italy, and Silas assured her that when Mercy Tubbs found a way to transport him across the Atlantic, he would return with a variety of european bars wrapped in fancy tissue paper. He now chuckled to himself as he wound the horse's reins through the loop of an iron post on Second Street outside of O. Conrad's Watchmaker and Jewelry Shop. He needed to pick up Mr. Spiedler's repaired watch.

A hard shove wrenched him from his thoughts, his head snapping back in alarm. Before him stood a burly man with a yellowed mustache, his coat unbuttoned, hands ungloved, head bare, as if impervious to the climate. A worry as hard as steel pressed against Silas's chest. When the man's voice slid out sideways from under the mustache, a rotting smell seemed to accompany each syllable that dropped toward the stones underfoot.

"You got papers?" He raised a hand to his coat, parting it to reveal a flash of a badge, before letting his arm and his lapel fall back into place. "And whose horse is this?"

While Silas had been a free man for over ten years, he had no papers in his pocket as proof nor had he ever been concerned over producing them, especially to a stranger on demand. Yet he knew the man, most likely a bounty hunter hired by the federal government, would not accept the explanation that somewhere in his rented room was a document verifying his free status, nor would the man care to know just how Silas had gained his freedom. As early as 1780 Pennsylvania had declared bondage illegal and passed a law allowing any slave brought to the state and kept there for longer than six months to be granted freedom. Most visiting slave owners, from businessmen to politicians, were savvy enough to shift their slaves before six months elapsed, but the man who had brought Silas to Philadelphia fell ill and was unable to mind his affairs accurately. The Anti-Slavery Society, the same men he now assisted, had helped Silas secure his freedom.

"This horse is owned by Mr. Spiedler," he finally responded, surprised that at such a moment it would bother him not to argue that Mercy Tubbs belonged, at least in spirit, to him alone. "I been working for him going on ten years." Silas's voice shook the tiniest bit and the horse snorted as if she noticed.

Laws had been set in place to protect the black population in the state, even one passed just three years prior prohibiting Pennsylvania sheriffs and constables from aiding in the pursuit of catching fugitives, yet there were many dynamics, such as the revoking of voting rights, mob violence and lack of employment opportunity, that threatened full citizenship. Now with the change to the Fugitive Slave Law, the fear of conditions worsening hung in the air like spoiled meat. Talk intensified within the walls of the barber shops, the church halls and in the Anti-Slavery office. Agreed upon, was the necessity to raise more money to help with legal fees and to accommodate the physical needs of the fugitives in order to move them more swiftly and carefully through the state. Silas thought of the dedicated men and women with whom he had worked alongside for years. Those who had sewn clothes, cobbled shoes, drafted letters, prepared meals, fabricated papers, and opened their homes to strangers. Together, their strength and defiance against slavery had both inspired and grounded him. He looked to it now in this challenging moment, leaning against the resolve and power that comes from acting on clear and unarguable principles. He nearly smiled, knowing such righteousness could not be reduced by the words or actions of any man, badge or no badge. Not even the foul-smelling one looming before him, swaying now as if he were a clock about to chime.

"We'll see about that." The deputy spat on the ground, just missing his own boot. He then rubbed his jaw and moaned so that Silas guessed he needed a tooth pulled, which would likely rid him of both pain and stench.

"Mr. Spiedler lives just 'round the corner. He can tell you himself, if you ain't tend to believe me."

The man's eyes narrowed. "I'm not going around no corner to check on the words of a liar and, no doubt, a thief. I'm bettin' you stole this horse, just like your stealing your master's property by running north. Thinking you can run off and cheat him out of his investment like it's not a crime. Ain't no going around a corner gonna help you now. We'll leave all that up to the judge." And he moved to grab hold of Silas's arm, when a voice called out.

"Mr. Clemons." It was Bernhart advancing quickly. "Just

my luck to find you, as I was hoping for a lift to the apothecary. I've a few items to…" He broke off when he reached an angle at which he could see the face of the man in front of Silas.

"Is everything alright here?" he added, as an odd feeling crept over him.

"Not to worry, Mr. Hommes," said Silas, untying the reigns from the hook. "I shall be happy to take you where you need to go."

"Not so fast," demanded the deputy, turning to Bernhart. "Not so fast. Do you got any idea what can happen to a foolhardy person trying to get between the capturing of a runaway? I'll tell you, it can get you six months in jail. Mind you to find another way to get where it is you're going and leave me to my business." Revealing his badge with one hand, the other hand moved again to his jaw.

Confused, Bernhart took a step back. Not until he looked over at Silas did he begin to discern the situation. The newspaper articles and his conversation with Mr. Spiedler came back to him so that he realized this man must be a federal deputy commissioned to recapture slaves. The ridiculousness of mistaking Mr. Clemons for a runaway would have caused Bernhart to laugh if not for the grim and ominous weight of the accusation. He adjusted his hat and took another step, this time toward Silas.

"Preposterous, as I rely solely on Mr. Clemons for my transportation and no one else. Furthermore, my good friend Mr. Spiedler would vouch for his long-standing employment. In fact, this man's services are a benefit to the entire neighborhood. Ask anyone you like. If he were to be suddenly apprehended for any length of time a ruckus would ensue as we could not get along without him."

He patted Silas on the back and added, "Now did you say you were searching for a runaway horse? Have not seen one. Sometimes the hogs, set loose to scavenge the garbage left about the streets do take an unfortunate, wrong turn. You might consider one of them a runaway, although I would wager a corpulent hog wouldn't get further than a hungry neighbor's dinner table." At this Bernhart chuckled, totally amazed at his own performance. "Shall we then, Mr. Clemons? I've to look for a remedy for a toothache."

The two men mounted, Mr. Hommes joining Mr. Clemons on the bench rather than inside the carriage. Without a glance at the silent deputy, their victory sounded loudly as Mercy Tubb's hooves knocked against the uneven cobbles. Upon turning the first corner, the men doubled over with laughter, marveling over the ham dinner remark and the diagnosis of a rotten tooth. Yet after a little ways, Silas let forth a long whistle that seemed to put an end to any sense of relief, leaving in its wake thoughts of how narrowly disaster had been avoided, in addition to the uncertainties of what the future might hold. For the remainder of the ride to the apothecary, the blue shadows cast by the failing sun seemed to follow the riders with each turn.

The sewing box stood on its long legs in front of the sofa where Agnes and Aunt Josephine sat darning socks, with both flaps turned up to reveal trays filled with spools, thimbles, pins and needles. When Mathias entered the front parlor, he paused as if surprised by the task of the two women. He moved across the room to the fireplace and splayed his hands in front of it.

"What on earth are you doing?" he said. "Is that one of my socks?" The two women stared at him, then looked at each other.

"What do you imagine becomes of your socks when they sprout a hole?" replied Josephine.

"I suppose I've not given ample consideration to the matter. Seems a drab task. Surely, dear wife, you spend enough time with the Ladies Needlepoint Club that you could let the maids tend to the mending of socks."

Josephine smiled at her husband, "The maids have plenty to see to with the upkeep of the house. I can't bother them with our stockings." If only he knew that her club had recently been sewing socks and scarves for one of Julianna Stone's charity groups. The nice Quaker girl always knew what poor souls needed a handout to get them through the winter. The women felt both useful and generous knowing their needlework was assisting a family who had come by a bit of bad luck or a young fellow just arriving from a far-off land.

Josephine plucked a needle with a large eye from the pincushion and began to thread it. "And of course there is the sewing of their own dresses and aprons and what have you. It is fortunate we are able to rely on the haberdashery for your garments and dressmaker for ours. If not, we would need to sit the new girl down to sew the day long."

Agnes removed one stocking from around the darning gourd and replaced it with another. "Have you heard, people have begun purchasing sewing machines for their homes? Can you imagine a machine within one's own household that zips along the fabric in the wink of an eye? Wouldn't Penny love it?"

Mathias frowned. "And then what would Penny do throughout the day if we bought a machine to replace each of her tasks?"

Agnes thought of how Penny seemed always busy. Even while she sipped her tea there was a boiling pot to keep an eye on or beans that needed to be sorted through for pebbles. She was rarely seen sewing at all. Agnes had to conclude she did most of it in the evening when her other work was finished.

"I wonder would she spend her time in the drawing room behind a book?" Mathias said, as he moved away from the warmth of the fire and began buttoning his overcoat.

Agnes dipped her head towards her work. So he had noticed, despite being out of the house most of each day since his return from his travels. She remained silent, hoping he would leave the matter alone.

"I must be off now for there is much to do," Mathias announced, striding out of the room. Then just within the archway leading to the front hallway he turned and added, "Josephine, I shall be leaving for New York early next week. Please ask Penny to see to the preparations."

"North, not south this time?" she asked.

Mathias reached out a hand to touch the woodwork that framed the arch, running a finger along the carved grooves. Having spoken little about the trip to Louisiana since his return nearly a month ago, he did not care to discuss it now. In fact, he closed his eyes, hoping to thwart the memory of an incident in New Orleans that had left its mark. Up until that day he had been able to dismiss the striking discrepancy between the warm hospitality southerners displayed towards their fellow citizens and the merciless behavior they exhibited towards their slaves. And up until that day he had continued to tell himself that slaves, despite his surprise over their utterly wretched and bleak living conditions, did not possess the intellectual nor emotional sophistication of the white race. He had convinced himself of this notion up until the hour he was strolling through the French Quarter, having just finished lunch, and heard a din as he passed the main entrance to the St. Louis Hotel.

He could see through the entryway and glimpse the domed ceiling of the rotunda, and curiosity led him inside. A chandelier hung overhead and the walls, painted a pale blue, were adorned by paintings with wide, golden frames. A wonderful shaft of afternoon light stretched from the high windows onto the heads of the people gathered below. It was then Mathias noticed the presence of a stone auction block against one side of the room. The competing voices of the auctioneer and the audience suddenly rose as a woman and child were prodded up onto the obtrusive platform. They held to each other for a brief time before being pulled apart by a strong arm.

Mathias found it an incongruous sight, two cowering figures dressed in rags, now separated from each other by the ocean of a few feet, amidst the elegance of the room. Despite having witnessed a number of outdoor slave markets, a strange feeling spread over him as he stood in a room used for concerts, masquerade balls, and dinner ceremonies to honor prominent political figures. The beautiful rotunda, designed to accommodate elaborate social gatherings in the evening, functioned as a human trading den between noon and three on afternoons.

He removed his hat, mopping the perspiration from his brow, and made to leave just as the small girl, no older than six, began thrashing and crying, even kicking at the man separating her from her mother. Those standing about laughed while the girl was briskly subdued. When the spattering of laughter died, a new sound rose which caused a hush to fall upon the room. The sound came from the open mouth of the mother, emitted as if from the darkest cave of the human heart, from the deepest pit a soul could plummet, left to rot and be forgotten. A sound that Mathias had never heard before nor would again, piercing him in the chest, straight through to the shoulder blade. For the deep, low wail, bleeding down the blue walls, was the mother's last sign of love for a daughter she knew she would never see again.

The clanging bells of a nearby church broke the spell and suddenly the shifting of feet, the waving of arms, the murmuring and bickering took up again like a rush of children in a school yard. Yet during the brief moment, for Mathias, the notion of a slave possessing an underdeveloped set of emotions was proven undeniably false, for what he witnessed was the epitome of suffering, the essence of pain and love. Now sinking to her knees, the mother's gaze locked on her child being carried away, and the sound, which no longer came from her mouth, continued to reverberate like a blacksmith's hammer against the flat, metal center of Mathias's conscience. He spun and fled.

It was not until he was back in the city of Philadelphia, that he could begin to discard the cloying sentiments of that day. Still, the memory would not entirely dissolve, persuading him to relinquish the business of slave trading and stick to the moving and selling of cotton, which he found more palatable.

"Are you feeling unwell, Mathias?" His wife's voice brought him back to the present.

He smiled at the two women with their darning gourds and turned to excuse himself just as the doorbell rang. Bernhart rushed in along with a swirl of cold air.

Entering the room, where the two women remained perched on the sofa, he was met with a warm grin from Mrs. Trossen and a small smile from Agnes. "Forgive me. I'll leave you to visit. I must be off." With that Mathias hurried out the door.

After a round of exchanged pleasantries, Bernhart leapt into an account of yesterday's incident between Mr. Clemons and the federal marshal. As he relayed the details, his voice effusive, Agnes was struck by how impassioned he appeared and Mrs. Trossen shook her head a number of times before stating, "How unfortunate for Mr. Spiedler that his driver has to be harassed in such a way when he has provided such trustworthy service to all of us."

Chapter 8

"Ticket?" the ticket collector had asked each of the travelers in front of Zeb, but when it was Zeb's turn, the man only growled low, "Git," like he was speaking to a dog. The boy had no time to mention needing to see the captain before another arm grabbed him and pulled him to the side.

"I'll take care a this one," the new man promised, dragging him by the collar over to an area crowded with trunks, barrels and crates. Zeb, cowering under the man's strong arm, feared looking up.

When the man whispered, "You think you can just get on like that, boy? You must not have any sense." Zeb raised his eyes to find a brown-skinned man guiding him through the scattered objects, before pulling him behind a large crate. "Sit. Now, you got some money?"

"I need to see the captain."

The man laughed, "How you plan to see the captain without a coin to your name? S'pose I gotta take you on back to the ticket man. You already know, he's meaner than a snake."

Zeb felt his heart race. Trying to get up, his legs wobbled, and he dropped back down. Levi's face popped to mind and he remembered.

"I must see the captain. Mr. Dart will be real angry if I

ain't help like he told me to. Expects me to mop the deck and all."

"Mr. Dart? I don't know any Mr. Dart."

"That's the man who saved Captain B the time he fell overboard and almost drowned." Zeb watched a puzzled look wash over the sailor's face, which quickly turned to a frown, before he stomped off. Later, when he snuck the boy on board, he brought him to the captain's quarters muttering, "This is a crafty one, boss."

Despite her heavy quilt, Larkspur woke early from the chill in the air. On this early December morning the window of her room was icy, and the sky behind it a dull gray. Her narrow room in the garret had no fireplace, but it drew heat from the floor below if she left her door open. Wrapping a shawl about her shoulders, she trudged over to look out the window. A light snow had fallen during the night, dusting the city. While she had seen snow a number of times, the beauty of the street's transformation into a clean sea of white made her sigh. It was early and not a soul had ventured out to disturb any of it. She shivered and remembered why she had gotten out of bed in the first place.

Penny was always the earliest to rise. She'd poke at the embers in the stove until the kindling caught, then move upstairs to light the tinder bundles Larkspur had prepared the night before in the bedrooms and dressing rooms. Larkspur would come along later to add the heavy logs, as well as tend to the fireplaces in whatever rooms the Trossens would utilize throughout the day. With Mr. Trossen away, his study was left cold now that they had convinced Agnes to lug her books into the drawing room or even down to the kitchen where it was always warm. Penny's second order of business required returning to the kitchen to fill the kettle, so that when Larkspur arrived they could begin the breakfast preparations as the coffee brewed.

As Larkspur entered the kitchen on this day, she found it cold and silent. The cookstove appeared abandoned and the lamp left dark upon the table. Spinning around, she slipped through the pantry to knock lightly on Penny's bedroom door. When met with silence, she pushed in and crept toward the bed to find Penny moaning softly in her sleep, shivering despite flushed cheeks. Touching her forehead, Larkspur felt the fever that had descended, like the snowfall outside, during the night. She turned, hurrying back to the kitchen. The house was soon blazing, with fires in the hearths, the tea kettle steaming, pots bubbling. As she loosened the lids to the tiny jars of her strange powders, the dirge of familiar names fell methodically from the young woman's lips.

∾

Agnes was surprised to find her room so filled with light, and the flames leaping behind the firescreen. Had she slept the morning away? Padding over to the window in her wool stockings, she soon realized it was the bright snow that added light to the room. How lovely. She quickly splashed her face with cold water from the washstand, tied up her hair and slipped into a simple daydress, then headed downstairs.

Agnes paused at the kitchen doorway. "Are we celebrating the winter solstice so soon? There seems such a flurry of activity and do I smell pine cones or is it rosemary?"

"No celebration. Penny's sick."

"Oh dear, what ails her?"

"Fever. Been sleeping all morning." Larkspur stirred the batter to the biscuits with a wooden spoon and grew quiet. Having crushed fresh ginger, dried yarrow and bee balm with her pestle, she planned to steep the mixture in hot water as soon as Penny awoke. The herbs would open her pores, sweating would control the fever and release the toxins.

Lifting her gaze, she added, "There's one thing I'm needing,

Miss Agnes. Can I bother you to find a length of ribbon? Red ribbon."

"Ribbon? Seems an odd request," mumbled Agnes. "Red, you say?"

"The color of strength." Larkspur nodded, causing Agnes to shrug her shoulders as she set off to search the house, pleased to have a task.

By mid afternoon Penny remained in her bed, having stirred only once so that Larkspur could give her a few sips of the warm elixir, before falling back into her fitful sleep. Larkspur sat on a barrel in the pantry, one eye on Penny and one on the simmering pots upon the stove, aware of the unease that grew within her as the sun traveled away from the day. She understood that fever was a good thing; a sign of the body fighting off that which means it harm. Having felt Penny's forehead countless times to know that the fever had not shot too high, concern still gnawed at her as did frustration for neglecting to gather a better array of ingredients to protect against whatever ailment was bringing about Penny's fever. Understandably, her attention had been elsewhere since arriving in Philadelphia, but at the moment she could not dislodge the sense of ineptitude that moored her to the barrel. The herbal tea, with a crushed mustard seed added, and the stringing of an amulet of protection from the bedpost - a red ribbon adorned with green pine needles and sprigs of dried heather - was as much as she could think to do.

Suddenly, she had an idea. She stood up, admonishing herself for not coming to it sooner and headed up the stairs to the first landing.

Knocking on the door to the drawing room, she called, "Miss Agnes?"

"Come in," came a sleepy voice. "I seemed to have dozed off again. Mathematics will do that. How is Penny? Up and about, yet?"

"Afraid not."

"Oh, I was certain a day of rest would have her back on her feet. I can't remember a time when she's been too ill to get out of bed. Has she eaten much?"

"No, miss. She's still asleep."

Agnes let out a little puff of air and wished her Aunt had not left yesterday to visit friends in New Hope when presently they could use her advice.

"Do you think calling upon the doctor is in order?"

Larkspur looked at Agnes for a moment, "Rather, I think it best to call for Mr. Hommes."

"Bernhart? Whatever for? While he may know a great deal about many subjects, including the name for everything green and scratchy, he is no physician. And I dare say, he is a bit too clumsy to be trusted to carry a hot bowl of soup."

"Just the same. Perhaps Mr. Clemons could fetch him."

"Well, I suppose, if you think it necessary. Would you like me to stay near Penny while you send word to Mr. Clemons?"

"I was hoping you could run out, as I don't prefer to leave Penny." Larkspur was quite amazed that she was placing demands on Miss Agnes and yet she no longer felt like the maid, let alone a fugitive. In the role as healer, she felt in charge.

"Is it that serious?" Agnes grew afraid for the first time.

"Most likely not," Larkspur replied, yet something inside her was not convinced and it was not just the part that earlier in the day had recognized the existence of a fondness for the feverish woman downstairs. She had long ago learned to heed her instincts, and she was not to deny them now. "And tell Mr. Clemons we're gonna need him too."

By the time Bernhart and Silas arrived in the kitchen the sun was nearing the horizon. Penny's condition had not varied. Larkspur quickly closed the door leading to the pantry as the men stomped in through the back. Hushing them and pointing to chairs, she placed bowls of stew on the table without bothering to ask if they were hungry. The copious provisions in the Trossen house had not ceased to amaze her and having served Penny very little nourishment all day, she compensated by the heaping bowls she set down. When Agnes entered the room, she set a bowl in front of her as well. The three ate silently, the tense air in the room creating an abeyance to the typical social norms. Then Larkspur explained what she needed.

"Yes of course, I know just where a beautiful stand of dogwoods grow. The west end of the city, just before the river," Bernhart offered.

"And you're sure they're Flowering Dogwood, not Jamaican?" asked Larkspur, "The two can't be confused. We called it a hound tree but it can go by a number of names."

Bernhart put up his hand. "I am most familiar with it. Cornus Florida is the latin name. It can be distinguished from the other dogwoods by the flat-topped crown."

The two looked at each other, each impressed by the knowledge of the other. A filament stretched between them in the silence of the warm room.

"It likes to grow under red maples or hickories," Larkspur added.

"Oaks as well. And what is it you need from the tree?"

"I need the bark to boil for tea. Bring two handfuls and if possible the very end of a few narrow branches about as long as your arm, just to chew on." Then she peered out the window at the darkening sky. "Can you and Mr. Clemons set out first thing come morning? The fever might break before then, but if not, the sooner the better."

Bernhart followed Larkspur's gaze. He knew the wooded area well, but had never ventured through it at night. Standing up abruptly, he strode to the window. Unable to see the moon through the pane, he knew it was up there for the sheen it cast upon the thin layer of snow.

Turning back he asked, "How does Mercy Tubbs take to traveling at night?"

Silas had already imagined them setting off through the streets, reaching the edge of the neighborhoods, and then weaving their way through the woods toward the Schuylkill River. "She moves just fine, but accustomed to a path with street lamps," Silas said.

"Oh Bernhart," Agnes jumped in, "do you think it wise to attempt such a thing after dark and with the snow? What if you were to lose your way?"

"It is only a short stretch of woods and travelers have been know to travel at night for all sorts of reasons, this being no more harrowing than any other," Bernhart assured her. He remembered the Black Forest back home and the occasional man who showed up in their village after venturing through it for weeks or even months. They seemed to have acquired a certain stillness that he envied.

Silas looked less certain of the plan, but when he again glimpsed the determination on Larkspur's face, he figured it was a deed that needed doing. The men, given blankets and extra lanterns, set out at once. Agnes went to sit with a book before the fireplace in the front parlor. Larkspur found herself alone in the kitchen with Bernhart's statement about traveling at night lingering in the corners of the room. An array of tumultuous thoughts arrived, for night always follows day, like the day she escaped.

ॐ

By the time they arrived in Baltimore, Larkspur knew. A dank, moldering feeling settled in her stomach as she lugged the trunks through the small house she was to occupy with her new master and mistress. Like a blanket, his gaze lay too long upon her, and worse, the smug curl of his top lip suggested his determination to get what he desired. Unable to bear the thought of it, she began to imagine a route to freedom. At first it was as thin as gauze and no more than a daydream, but then a solid shape of a plan began to formulate in her head. One she would not have guessed, had the man's brutal nature not emerged, herself capable of carrying out.

Before long, the day arrived. Larkspur quietly informed the mistress of what was to take place, then left the house while the other woman's mouth hung agape. With her charm bag, her key pressed against her heart, and a small amount of money that she and Aunt Celena had saved from selling brooms sewn into Mistress Pixie's old dress, she headed toward the harbor. Keeping her eye upon the shadows cast by the morning sun, the shadows of dandelions and sparrows, of parked wagons and long lampposts, she avoided the faces of those around her.

At the corner of Pratt and Howard she stopped. There rose a bare brick wall, and hiding behind it sat a treeless yard where slave traders detained the poor souls, some fugitives but others not, destined to be sold down river to the cotton plantations. Pretending to fasten a button on the stained gloves she wore, another item she had openly pilfered from her mistress, she waited. When she determined no one on the street would notice, she slipped between the wall and an adjacent building where an alley led to a brick she had previously discovered was loose. She wiggled it free from the others, then called inside. One eye, which she had come to know, appeared.

"Hello John," she whispered.

"Hello Delphinium," the eye whispered back. "Ain't na worry, girl, dint nobody go by Ignatius come through."

"Alright then." She placed three ripe blackberries, which she had plucked from a bush along the way, in the space between them. It was all she had this time, but she thought it might be her best offering. Good-bye John, she thought as she wedged the brick back in the wall after the berries and the eye had disappeared.

A few years after Little Del had grown tall enough to be called by her full name Delphinium, a young man had arrived on the neighboring plantation. His name was Ignatius. The first time Delphinium saw him, during a Sunday worship in the woods halfway between the two farms, he stood against a tree with his head tilted to one side, as if, she thought, he was listening for the sound of something far away. When their eyes met, she felt a drop of honey land upon her tongue. The following week, they both lingered near the fence post after the preaching was over and the others had dispersed. Neither knew how little time there was before the Beckman Farm would be sold and she with it.

She slipped out of the alley and back onto the street. Irrational as it was, for there were other places a runaway could be retained, and there was no clear reason to assume Ignatius's travels had brought him through Baltimore, she now felt she could leave the city. Her recurring nightmare that he would be captured by traders, taken to the Pratt Street slave pen, then walked in chains to Fells Point to be shipped back south, had never come true.

Now she hurried toward the harbor docks, suddenly panicked at the thought of not boarding the boat in time. She was able to purchase a ticket for a steamer leaving within the hour. She squeezed her charm bag thankfully. While she stood in a line waiting to board, she drew not a look, nor a raised eyebrow, nor a comment from the white folks around her, giving her a strange new understanding of the advantage of her outward appearance, while inward she was dumbfounded, as she remembered John and the others in the yard, by the utter folly and disgrace of the world in which she now moved about.

෨

The wheels of the coach made barely a sound in the soft snow. Silas brought Mercy Tubbs to a stop when the path was no longer cleared well enough for them to continue with the carriage.

"This be 'bout it then," Silas said.

"The dogwoods are still ahead, say one hundred yards, and off to the left," Bernhart stated, jumping down from the wagon. "I can go alone by foot, if you prefer to wait with the horse."

Silas did not prefer to wait with the horse, nor did he prefer to leave her and tromp through the woods with Mr. Hommes. While they were in a desolate area and it was unlikely anyone would come along the path at such an hour, it was just the kind of remote place he had strictly avoided since his encounter with the deputy.

Bernhart sensed Silas's apprehension, so he offered, "Shall we unhitch the horse and bring her along? It truly is not much further."

Since the incident last month, Bernhart had found himself thinking of it often, as well as wondering about Silas in a way he had not done before.

"We gone leave her here, but best we be quick about it."

Silas descended to the ground, reaching back for a lantern, which he handed to Bernhart, and then sought another for himself. The two men set off, following a footpath deeper into the woods. They did not go far before reaching the trees. While Bernhart cut away at the bark, it began to snow. Silas saw the first flakes swirl in the glow of the lantern he held up and then soon the snow made a line along Bernhart's coat, from one shoulder to the other. When Bernhart's hands grew too cold, Silas offered to cut the thin branches requested by Larkspur. They exchanged lantern for pocketknife, and as one man took off his gloves and the other fumbled to pull his on, they heard the noise. Immediately, Silas turned to start them both running in the direction from which they had come, the lanterns swinging, the bark stuffed in Bernhart's pocket, and Silas surging ahead eager to discover what had made his horse cry out.

When they reached the spot where they had left the horse and carriage, they found neither. For a moment they watched the snow fill the tracks left by Mercy Tubb's hooves, then they took off again, sprinting along the grooves left by the wheels of the missing wagon. Bernhart struggled to keep pace with Silas, his chest burning in the cold, but when Silas turned back and drew a hand to his ear, Bernhart detected the rattle of the coach bouncing over the ground up ahead. The next turn brought the horse, carriage and a lone figure into view.

Silas darted to the side of the road to find a rock, then sprinting until he had gained ground, threw the rock so that it struck a tree just ahead and to the side of Mercy Tubbs. The horse was brought to a stop by the person holding the reins, while Silas and Bernhart continued approaching. Silas let out just one low whistle into the quiet night, so that when the leather straps snapped to make the horse move again, she would not budge.

"You there," Bernhart shouted as they neared the rear of the carriage. Silas had picked up a heavy stick that Bernhart assumed he would use against the man, but instead he wedged the stick between the spokes of a wheel, while Bernhart advanced around to the side of the coach. The figure, which appeared hunched over and rather small, had yet to turn toward them, filling Bernhart with trepidation. Then, as he reached the point at which he could see the profile of the driver's face, his trepidation was replaced by relief. The figure on the bench was a boy with raw, red cheeks and no cap over his stringy hair. His hands were bare and his breeches did not cover the holes in his stockings.

"Young man, this horse does not belong to you," Bernhart began, ordering the boy to dismount. The boy dropped to the ground, and stood with his arms wrapped around himself, partly in defiance but more so to stay warm, while he was lectured on the perils of thievery, compromised integrity and frostbite.

Finally Bernhart concluded, "Despite your error in judgement, we do have room on the bench for three if you are traveling in our direction. Of course, first you must apologize to Mr. Clemons for absconding with his horse."

The boy's face, which had begun to brighten at believing he had found the type of fellow who might give him a coin at the end of the ride, suddenly turned stormy. He looked back and forth between the older men, wondering if he was sincerely being asked to offer an apology to a negro.

"I see that you enjoy walking in the cold at night," Bernhart said as he hoisted himself up next to Silas, who held the reins ready in his hands.

It was not long before the boy caught up to the carriage. After he mumbled an apology, he was allowed to climb up and slip under a wool blanket between the men. As they headed back toward the city, Bernhart looked off into the dark woods and wondered how was it that neither age, hunger, nor torn clothing proved as defining as the color of one's skin. At the other end of the seat, Silas kept his eyes on the ground. With the sway of the lantern, the light that cast upon the new snow rocked back and forth, stretched and retreated just beyond the horse's precarious footsteps, reminding Silas of both the need and the futility of being careful.

ৡ

At the onset of the day's ride, the steamboat plowed smoothly through the Chesapeake Bay. Delphinium stood in one spot on the deck and watched the water against the side of the boat, feeling a sense of relief she had never enjoyed before. Had she known that the railroad would have taken half the time for the same cost, she would have still chosen the river route, as the sight of the water moving in one direction and she in the other seemed like the perfect image of freedom. For the first few miles she did not lift her eyes as tears slipped from her cheeks into the swirling current.

After passing through the series of locks connecting the bay to the river, the day passed as they headed steadily up the Delaware. By evening, the trees along the banks darkened and the sky grew quiet. She was tired and hungry, and had found a spot on deck near a family with three young children. While the father cut his eyes away from her and the mother pretended she was not there, one of the children smiled, and after a nod from his mother slipped her a crust of bread when the father's back was turned.

She must have slept, for when she awoke it was very dark without a star visible in the night sky. The boat was no longer moving. Anxious voices swirled about and then a man with a lantern hurried past without offering any explanation. Alarmed, her first instinct was to recoil behind an object, but then she heard footsteps and the voice of the husband explaining to his wife that a snag lay up ahead.

"A snag?" the wife asked worriedly.

"It's nothing more than a fallen tree blocking the way."

"As wide as this river is, how can a tree stop us?"

"They say we've just passed Tomkin's Isle, and there seems to be a stretch of sand bars making it difficult to pass when the water's low," he pointed beyond the boat into darkness, "and now with the tree down." His feet shuffled off and he could be heard grunting softly as he bumped into something.

Word traveled from passenger to passenger that there was no way to maneuver around the snag in the dark and that it would require daylight to clear the tree and continue the last leg of the journey. When a handful of travelers, including the husband and wife, insisted they be allowed to disembark so that they might spend the night on the river bank rather than on the cramped boat, Delphinium decided to do the same rather than risk staying alone throughout the night upon the stopped vessel.

Following the others onto the New Jersey side of the river, she stood apart, unnoticed in the dark. Voices argued over the distance to Billingsport, some deciding to set out immediately so that by morning they could finish their travels by coach rather than wait the uncertain length of time it might take to clear the toppled tree.

Delphinium, with very little money left in the hem of her skirt, decided to remain close to the boat. Searching for a spot in which to settle for the night, she crept across a small clearing, followed what seemed a path lined with brush on both sides and lowered against the first tree trunk she could find as it was too dark to go any further. Off to the left she could hear the trickling of a creek running inland. After awhile the clouds must have thinned for a spattering of stars appeared overhead. She began silently reciting Aunt Celena's list of names, matching each name to a star. She was not frightened by the night itself, its rustlings, its biting insects, the occasional animal noises, it was the people within it that worried her. Come morning, she would slip back onto the steamer.

৽

When Bernhart, Silas, and the would-be thief arrived back at the Trossens, the boy was fed, provided an old sweater and cap, and after one last chiding, sent on his way. Bernhart and Agnes settled into conversation, their chairs dragged near the stove for warmth. When Silas stood to leave, buttoning his coat at the door, Larkspur quietly incurred his help. She handed him the tray containing the pot of tree bark tea and motioned him to follow into Penny's room. Once inside, she pressed the door closed until it clicked behind them, and pointed for him to set the tray on the bedside table. Under a heap of blankets, Penny appeared fast asleep.

Before she could speak, he whispered, "I been thinking with all that's going on, it ain't safe for you to bide your time here much longer. It's best you head on up to Canada. You might be getting by for now, but somebody's bound to come snooping 'round sooner or later. Seems just a matter a time before ..."

Frowning, she replied in a voice just as hushed as his, "Seems safe enough." She sat on the edge of the bed, holding the back of her hand against Penny's forehead. "It will have to do."

"Not with them new laws. Barely safe even if you been free all your life."

Silas looked at Penny, to make sure she was still asleep, then back at Larkspur. He wanted to tell her that most runaways didn't make it. That most were caught and sent back to endure unspeakable punishment and the same dire conditions from which they'd fled. He wanted her to realize how fortunate she had been to get this far and that she shouldn't squander her chance waiting on someone else. And yet, instead of speaking, he dropped his head and chuckled at himself. Didn't he place himself in jeopardy everyday by helping Still and Purvis? Didn't those men and the others risk everything for complete strangers? And actually, when he thought about it, wasn't that the only way to stay sane in a country that allowed and encouraged and justified the owning and selling of human bodies? To struggle against the degradation and abuse, to defy it was the one power they had. He knew men and women who had made it to the north only to turn back around to retrieve their loved ones. How could he convince Larkspur to be less than any of them? And why should he?

She stood waiting. With optimism, he offered, "Your man is young and healthy, right? And coming from as close as Virginia. Those the ones that tend to make it."

Her eyes smiled. "I told him I'd be waiting, Mr. Clemons. Gave my word."

"Your word, I always say, is about the only thing you can hold onto." He paused, then added, "Mr. Still say he sent off a letter to try to find something out."

Larkspur had been unable to offer Mr. Still the name of anyone in Virginia, despite his request, so Mr. Still had sent a letter off to someone he communicated with regularly about travelers moving north.

Her voice shot with excitement. "To who?"

"Ain't sure exactly but there's people along the way that know about such things. You said he woulda tried to come by boat so probably he asked somebody along the river instead of in the railroad towns." He scratched his chin and wiggled his toes, which were still cold from the outing. "It tends to take a bit of time for letters to go back and forth."

Penny stirred and Larkspur took the opportunity to rouse her from sleep. Motioning to Silas with her eyes that their conversation had ended, she propped Penny up on the pillow to offer her the tea, while Silas slipped out of the room and then the house.

Larkspur watched Penny settle back into sleep, having succeeded in getting her to drink nearly half the cup of tea. It would take some time for the elixir to begin to reduce the fever, yet she thought Penny appeared more peaceful already. She sighed and then finally forced herself to rise, leaving the door ajar so she could hear if Penny called out. She passed through the pantry, and found Agnes and Bernhart alone in the kitchen nibbling on roasted chestnuts at the table. With expectant faces, they looked up.

"It shouldn't be too long before she starts feeling better." Her words, husky and sluggish, were laced with exhaustion. She had singularly handled all of the day's chores, and yet the worrying and searching for a remedy for Penny, had proved most draining.

Suddenly she wondered aloud, "Did I serve the evening meal? It feels like midnight, but I couldn't guess what time it might be."

"We have eaten plenty," Agnes assured her. "You fed us before we sent the men on their adventure in the woods." She turned to Bernhart, "Tell me, were you at any point frightened traveling through the snowy forest or was it all as comical as it turned out?"

He smiled at her, running his hand over his beard to brush away the crumbs. "The urchin *was* a rather comical sight propped up upon the board, I give you that. Yet, until we discovered the source of the theft, the possibility of Mr. Clemons losing his horse was rather alarming." He paused here, tracing the handle of his tea cup with his finger. "It is not just that, Agnes. There is another element of fear and worry for him, that the three of us know nothing about. Imagine moving through one's life knowing there is a chance one's freedom, one's ability to come and go as he pleases, is tenuous. That it can be snatched away either through mistake, or false pretext, or even by a sanctioned law." He exhaled through pursed lips and added, "I can't say I understood the weight of it until last month, when Mr. Clemons was apprehended by that foul man with the badge who threatened to force him into permanent bondage."

"Oh, it would not have ended as such," Agnes interjected. "Surely Mr. Spiedler would have arrived in time to sort it all out."

"Mr. Spiedler is the very one who asserted how easily it could have turned out as such, disastrously such. How swiftly Mr. Clemons could have been dragged south into slavery and never heard from again."

"Mr. Spiedler seems to hold a firm stance on the issue of slavery, for I've heard him speak of it many times at my uncle's gatherings. Surprisingly, he seems to take a personal interest in it."

Agnes was not actually as surprised by Mr. Spiedler's interest in the topic, as much as she was surprised by her own growing association with it. By now she had been to a handful of the Female Anti-Slavery meetings and heard the moral argument against the continuation of slavery, as well as reasons why those in the north should help see to its demise. She could not object that slavery was completely wrong and needed to come to an end one day, yet she had done her best to resist feeling obligated to take a stand against it, as the other women had chosen to do. She wished to keep her focus on her goal, rather than be distracted by an issue with such complicated and widespread ramifications.

"He does seem rather personally invested," Bernhart agreed, then yawned for it had been a long day for him as well.

"I reckon Mr. Spiedler considers the poor slaves to be actual *persons* who think and feel and get tired by day's end." The tone of Larkspur's hoarse, weary voice turned their heads. Standing at the end of the table, she spoke with her eyes fixed to the flame flickering about in the lamp. "People who love their children and prefer their backs not get lashed, or their ankles shackled, or their mama's wrenched away never to be seen again. Seems like the only way to view it, *is* as a personal matter." She paused, then added, "Except for someone fooling themselves into thinking slaves can't be real, living persons." Overcome by a strange emptiness, as if she had nothing left either to give or to keep, restraint and caution had settled at the very bottom of her hallowed thoughts, a dangerous place for someone hiding a secret.

Agnes and Bernhart did not respond. They merely watched Larkspur's face, which drooped for a moment from the stabbing ache, which attacked her at various times, of never having the chance to see her mother again. Of never feeling the soft skin of her mother's face or watch her long fingers braiding hair. Even after Larkspur turned, climbing the back staircase to prepare the hearths on the upper floors, the remaining two were unable to break the sadness of the room with common words. When Bernhart bid Agnes goodnight and departed, they were both left with the impression that the night had split in two. Upon reflection, they would recall how the evening's beginning was marked by the strange, magical feel of adventure, but the end would be cloaked by a dark, somber truth that neither the candle on Agnes's bedstand nor the sheen of the street lamp upon the snow at Bernhart's boot, could penetrate.

୨

The night of the river, after edging away from the other travelers and crossing the clearing, Delphinium awoke a few hours later to the sound of men approaching. From their slurred speech she knew they had been drinking and that there were two, maybe three different voices. Having not expected anyone else to venture so far from the boat, she had settled against a tree with her feet stretched out across the faint path. Now the men were snaking their way along it and nearly upon her. Rising to a crouched position she darted up the path, staying low to keep her cover. Then she wedged between an opening in the thicket along the stream's bank. The thorny branches clutched at her clothes and her skirt caught for a moment, until she yanked it free and pushed through. The soft dirt of the riverbank gave way, and losing her footing she landed on her knees near the water's edge.

"What the devil?" one man cried.

"Draw your gun, soldier! Sounds like a tiger," another quipped, yet it grew quiet and she knew they were waiting on another noise. She stayed on all fours, her hands in the dirt waiting to spring into action. She matched the men's silence but readied herself to flee along the shore if they advanced. The water was low, given the dry season, so there seemed to be space to run, but she couldn't be certain what lay ahead in either direction.

"Tiger my arse. Opossum more like it." A pair of footsteps drew closer then stopped just on the other side of the line of bushes from where she crouched.

"And what if it's a fair maiden that needs to be rescued?"

"Rescued from a drunkard like yourself?"

"Now you're catching my meaning." The man's words were thick and seemed to snag in the tiny branches that separated him from Delphinium. Her heart beat so loud she worried he would hear it.

A deeper voice announced, "I've enough of all this. My flask is dry and the captain'll be looking for us. The bastard."

Another man laughed in agreement and after a long moment, she could hear the rustling of the cattails as they turned around, one bumping into another which gave them a reason to argue as they retreated from where she knelt. Still she waited, unable to convince herself that it was safe. Finally, she crawled a few feet up the bank and tucked herself underneath the overhang of tree roots. She forced her thoughts to turn to Ignatius, of his hands on her skin and the current of heat that radiated from his touch. She imagined him holding her face in his palms and with this she began to calm herself. Much later she dozed off and when the day dawned, she decided against returning to the boat and its sailors.

Brushing the sand and dirt from her dress, she then set out in the direction pointed to by the group of the night before. By midmorning she reached Billingsport, bought herself some fruit from the grocer and sat on a bench in the town center until a brown-skinned woman came by.

"Pardon me," she said softly. "How much farther 'til Philadelphia?"

The woman dropped her eyes and said, "Not sure, mam. I just know it's across the river and up some." She looked up quick and then back down again.

Delphinium realized the woman thought she was white. "You mean I'm not even in Pennsylvania, yet?"

"No mam, you on the Jersey side of the river." There was a pause while Delphinium wallowed in her dismay. The other woman began to ease away.

Delphinium reached for her sleeve. "Please, you don't understand. I'm trying to get up north. I *need* to."

The woman raised her chin and stared, "Oh. I see." Fear shot through her whisper. "I can't help you. I got children at home who need me."

She hurried off, but before she got too far away she turned back and then nodded at a man across the square selling flowers on the corner.

There were no customers in front of the seller's buckets, so she approached. Explaining what she needed without mincing words, she inquired if they were anywhere near Salem, where she had heard shelter could be found with the Quaker Lady.

Showing her a handful of lilacs, he motioned for her to smell them. Then in a hushed tone he explained that it was better to head up to Free Haven than to go down to Salem.

"But call it Snow Hill when you tell the driver where you want to go. Not everybody knows, or needs to know, we took to calling it Free Haven since some Quakers bought up the land and thought to sell it to black folk. It's not but fifteen miles." He bent down to arrange a bundle of wild daisies, but kept talking. "You got fare for a stagecoach? From there they can steer you on to Camden. That's just across from the city." Then he lifted his voice, took back the flowers and said a little louder, "I understand, mam, if you don't favor lilacs."

During the bumpy ride to Free Haven, Delphinium decided she would need to choose a new name by which to call herself, as much as it saddened her to abandon the one given her by her mother. Suddenly, she remembered the other word by which the purple flower was sometimes referred and whispered it a few times to herself. So when she arrived in the small town, and was directed toward a particular house that opened the door to her, she introduced herself as Larkspur. After a simple meal, she was shown to a room where she could sleep and informed that she was to travel with Mr. Mott to Camden in the morning. Without ample time to tidy herself nor even clean the dirt from beneath her nails, she was awoken at dawn and hurried on her way.

꙳

Silas, stomping his cold feet, pounded against the icy door leading to where Erzsebet stayed. A dim light shone behind her curtained window situated above the garment shop, but it was taking so long he wondered whether she had been struck with a fever as well. He hesitated to knock again, worrying he might disturb the shop owner who sold coarse fabrics, made-over garments and used men's clothing, and lived with his family in the back on the first floor. Finally, the door unfastened and Erzsebet motioned him in.

"Took you so long to answer, I got scared you caught the fever the cook come down with at the Trossens," he whispered as they ascended the stairwell, which curved harrowingly at the top. "That's why I'm so late. Took me on a wild goose chase looking for tree bark out near the Schuylkill. Seen as the girl said she knew how to boil it right so as to bring down a fever, I agreed to get Mr. Hommes through the woods. You okay, Erzsebet?"

She turned and smiled, comforted to hear him speak her name. It was not the first time she had worried over him and she guessed it wouldn't be the last. When they reached the top of the stairs, she helped him out of his coat and they settled near the fire, each in a rocking chair. A pot of warm soup hung from the hook that swung out over the embers. As she dished out two bowls, Silas returned to the topic of Penny's health.

Erzsebet interrupted, "Don't know why you worry so over them. You know they don't give a thought to what ails us."

"Most likely not, but guess I can't stop myself from being human. We meant to care, ain't we?" In response, she tilted her head to one side. He continued, "Anyways, the Trossen cook ain't like most."

"How so?"

"She don't act no better than us, and come to think of it,

don't act no worse than those she works for. She won't let the Trossen women get nothing over on her. Runs the house, if you ask me, without them knowing a course." He laughed. "Most of all, she be who she is, don't matter who's around."

"Well that's the difference, then. We can't afford such luxury. The new gal surely can't. She's pretending from the moment the sun comes up 'til it drops at night. You talk to her yet?"

Silas raised his eyebrows. "I tried, sure did, but she aint ready to listen. She set on waiting for whoever he is she thinks she waiting on."

Erzsebet smiled, her face more relaxed now. "Just like there's no chance in me talking you out of helping runaways when they come through?"

"Naw, ain't no chance. I wouldn't be here if no one helped me. So since I got a coach and Mercy Tubbs, I help when I can. Delivering food, clothes, maybe shoes here and there. Then sometimes, it's the people themselves need to switch from one place to another 'til they move on up. It helps that Mr. Spiedler don't ask no questions. Probably knows more than he lets on. All the same, ain't like he offered his assistance." He rubbed his hands together, then continued, "Now with the change and them deputies roaming around, we gotta worry about all us already free not getting kidnapped. Ain't that something?"

The room grew quiet. They had not touched their food. She nodded at his bowl and they began to eat, but after a few bites he put his spoon down and said, "Each one a us knows the risk, but we also tasted the power in saying we doing it anyway. After that, ain't no going back."

That was precisely what Erzsebet was worried about, for last week she had offered Silas a few jars of stewed tomatoes and a sack of barley that she didn't think would be missed from the boarding house. How was she supposed to say no the next time there was a need for help? She looked down at her soup.

Quietly finishing their meal, the rustling fire and the whistling wind against the panes filled the silence. And because they were still new to each other, also within their silence hung an expectancy for what was to come. The slow unfolding of their relationship hovered delicately between them. When the log in the fireplace sputtered and popped, Erzsebet shifted in her chair, then rose to gather their bowls. Their hands brushed in the exchange, making her hurry away to the table.

Silas thought about Bernhart. After tonight, he felt a growing affinity towards him that had sprouted from the episode with the bounty hunter. Now, sitting before the fire in the tranquil room, rocking ever so slightly in his chair, he made a decision that brought to mind a bolt sliding open in its socket. To conclude that Mr. Hommes could be confided in and turned to for assistance, engendered Silas with a boost of confidence. He hoped the need would not arise, but if it did it was invaluable to know where to turn.

"Well, I best be gettin' on home for it gets too late."

"Stay just one minute more," she said softly from her chair, pulling a shawl around her.

"You cold? I'll put another log on."

"Best not, I've enough to get through the night only if I space it right," she called.

"I'll fetch you some from the wood yard first thing in the morning," he promised. "I'm warm enough now, anyways."

❦

Larkspur had made up a pallet on the floor next to Penny's bed. There was barely space for her to roll out her quilt, but she knew she would be unable to rest on a barrel in the pantry or on a stiff chair in the kitchen. While the floor was hard and cold under her, exhaustion allowed her to fall asleep immediately, without time to think about the past, including those she had left behind. She slept soundly.

When morning dawned, face damp with perspiration, Penny propped herself up on one elbow and said, "Are you tryin' to turn my heart cross-ways? Lying down there, I thought you were a mutt come to bite my toes off. Goodness gracious lass, what are you doin' there?" Then she collapsed onto her pillow. "Seems my fever has broke."

Larkspur struggled out from under her warm cover, rising off her pallet to take a look at the cook. The sparkle had returned to her eyes.

Chapter 9

*Z*eb gave the captain all the money he had, which did not amount to the ten dollars needed to travel the entire route to Philadelphia, and was then sent below deck where he was told to wait in the hold for the duration of the two-day journey. Climbing down the ladder, his feet landed on the solid boards of the floor of the ship but his eyes proved useless in the encompassing darkness. He heard a shuffling off to his right, but he dared not move until his pupils widened.

The hold was damp and sour smelling, as if it had trapped, over the years, every odor that had dared to seep down into the boat's belly. Underneath the pungent stench was the suggestion of rotting fish and below that, human fear. Zeb's eye caught on a thin line of light stretched across what seemed a stack of trunks. The light came from above as the hatch had been left ajar.

"Here," called a weak, pained voice. Dropping to his hands and knees, Zeb crept forward to reach a figure leaning against the ballast. The shadow of his head slumped to one side as if it were too heavy for his neck. Nothing more was said, so Zeb waited, listening as the man's breathing slowed and rattled. An occasional scrape or cough rose up from around the inky space, suggesting there were others waiting for the schooner to set off on its northern coarse.

The letter Mr. Still had sent off to his contact in Salem, New Jersey remained unopened until just after the new year. On its slow journey, first across the river on a ferry and then bumping along on the mail wagon, it hid inconspicuously in the bottom of a burlap sack, before arriving at its destination, under the door of a humble little house of a woman known as the Quaker Lady.

A young child picked up the letter, knowing to fold it within the pages of her grandmother's special book above the fireplace. After a few days Grandma Goodwin came upon the letter. With a finger she broke the seal, knowing where the letter originated despite the seal having no defining mark, to avoid disclosing specific information. When she read that a parcel belonging to a young man named Ignatius (sometimes called Nate) had not arrived as expected, her eyes widened, for the feverish boy who had appeared months earlier had repeatedly uttered just that name during his days of delirium. She would need to drive out to the farm where the boy, still recuperating from his prolonged illness, was being harbored. She read the letter once again, then tossed it into the crackling fire.

ൟ

Agnes stood before the mirror in her bedroom, waiting for the sound of the doorbell below. The aroma of the food prepared by Penny and Larkspur drifted up the stairs, and although she hadn't eaten much earlier in the day, the smell only agitated her empty stomach. Due to arrive any minute, Bernhart was to dine with her and her aunt and uncle, and yet she felt that she would prefer to spend the rest of the night standing before the mirror rather than tromp down the stairs, dragging her news, like the weight of her skirts, behind her.

Bernhart was running late. The usual mishaps had slowed him down, the cuff that required replacing after plunging into the washbasin, the return up the flight of stairs to retrieve forgotten gloves, the icy sidewalks. His tardiness was accentuated by the indirect route he traveled to reach the Trossen door, circling the block twice in order to sort out a few nagging thoughts. While it was not unusual to be invited to dinner, he sensed Agnes had a distinct purpose behind tonight's invitation. Having alluded to nothing, yet harboring that pensive look on her face, he anticipated that she would reveal the source that had been, for the past few months, deflecting her attention away from him. The frightening possibility of her choosing to devote herself to someone else filled him with apprehension, and yet his yearning to discover the truth compelled him to stop procrastinating and make an arrival.

Penny, whose strength and wit had returned full fold since her fever, had outdone herself with the meal. The peppery roast pork was tender, the parsnips and carrots savory, and the thinly sliced and browned onions melted into the salted broth. She served the bread warmed with butter and offered a dish of pickled vegetables before she sent Larkspur out with the roast. Unfortunately, no one took any satisfaction in the meal except Mathias, who mopped his broth with his bread and called for another helping. The others at the table were too preoccupied with their thoughts.

It wasn't until the dessert plates had been cleared and they had moved to the front parlor for tea, that Agnes felt it was time to speak. Aunt Josephine sat on the edge of her chair, the tension in the air suggesting the evening would contain an announcement. Assuming it would have to do with Bernhart's intentions for her niece, she tapped the heels of her shoes against the floor in nervous excitement. Clasping her hands together in her lap she looked back and forth between the young couple as her tea grew cold and the fire in the hearth crackled. Agnes cleared her throat, opened her mouth, and then cleared her throat again. The pained expression upon Bernhart's face, as he waited for Agnes, contrasted to the relaxed and oblivious air Mathias exuded sitting upon his stuffed armchair, patting his belly.

Agnes tried again. Not only was she faced with the difficulty of the subject matter, but she was suddenly paralyzed by the realization that it would have been more suitable to discuss the matter with Bernhart privately rather than in the presence of her aunt and uncle. But it was too late for that.

"Dear?" Aunt Josephine finally said when Agnes had cleared her throat a third time, parted her lips, but not yet spoken. The question seemed to draw forth Agnes's voice.

"Aunt Josephine, Uncle Mathias," she said slowly, looking at each as she said their names. Then turning, "And Bernhart. My dear Bernhart, you must forgive me for what I am about to tell you." She drew in a deep breath and forged ahead. "I do it with a heavy heart for I suspect it will not be easy for any of you to understand and yet my heart, conversely, is lighter than it has been since I was a young child. For there is a certain joy in choosing one's own path that can not be matched by anything else I know. Not even, I suppose, love."

Mathias's voice sprang forth like an animal crashing noisily through the woods, "What are you rummaging about for, Niece? Get to the point." Agnes cast her glance toward the flames of the fire so her uncle would not catch her irritation. That he thought she was prattling on, that he wished to rush her to some point as if the expression of her feelings was not prudent enough for him to bother considering, sent a red bolt through her. Yet, it took only a moment to push the anger aside, for when she glanced up she met Bernhart's eyes.

"What is it, Agnes? What is it that you need to tell us?" There was tenderness in his question that she thought was tinged with a sense of dejection but also a bit of relief. On his face was that look of curiosity of which she was so fond. Her eyes welled up but she willed the tears not to fall.

Josephine chimed in, "Really dear, what is it? I absolutely can't imagine."

Agnes found that if she kept her eyes on the rug, following its patterns and avoiding the faces of those in the room, she was able to announce her desire and plan to move to Oberlin, Ohio to pursue a college education. Without pause she explained how Oberlin College welcomed the attendance of females and that she had not only sent off a letter requesting admissions but that she had recently received a reply from the administration. Here she stopped and finally raised her chin to find her uncle harboring a condescending smile and her aunt looking utterly shocked. She did not dare glance, just yet, at Bernhart.

Mathias launched into a verbose soliloquy on the fancy notions of young ladies, to which no one else in the room listened as they were all absorbing what Agnes had just declared. When the rampage began to lose steam and Mathias needed to stop to catch his breath, Bernhart interjected in a near whisper, "And what of the reply?"

Her face transformed so suddenly, that both Bernhart and her aunt gasped, for they had never seen happiness flood over her in such a way. Immediately Mathias began again, in the same vein but with a bit more vehemence, until finally his wife issued a firm, "Mathias!" In the silence she locked eyes on her niece and felt that prick of desire inside her that she had spent a lifetime ignoring.

In a decisive tone, she said, "Well, I happen to think it's a scandalous idea. A rather scandalously, wonderful idea."

Agnes rose suddenly, moving to her aunt with tears spilling over as she hugged the older woman. From his chair, Bernhart smiled. Out of all the words Agnes had uttered, *not even love*, tumbled through his mind like a young child rolling down a hill. So she does love me, he thought, so she does.

و

Despite Josephine and Mathias bickering about it for weeks, when the letter from Amsterdam arrived, offering permission for their daughter to attend Oberlin, the matter was settled. Josephine saw no need to inform her husband that she had worded an initial letter to Agnes's parents very carefully, so that they may have concluded that all parties in Philadelphia were in firm support of the endeavor and that young women going off to college was a new and acceptable trend in America. Mathias threw his hands in the air, feeling outnumbered. He had other business to put his attention toward, so if his brother wished to fund Agnes's educational pursuits, he decided to leave the matter alone.

Preparations ensued at once, for Agnes was expected at Oberlin by the beginning of spring semester. This was the part that didn't sit well with Josephine. She did not understand the rush. Why not wait until the following fall, when school years are meant to begin? Agnes explained that an opening had presented itself, and, now that the decision was made, she was anxious to begin.

Neither Penny nor Larkspur begrudged Agnes for the extra work involved in preparing for her departure. They were both impressed by the young woman's ambition and warmed by the happiness she exuded. It was only when the trunks were packed and then unpacked and then packed again, that Penny let out a few huffs.

"Miss Agnes, must I remind you, the stamp on yer ticket says the train's not pullin' out for two days? I can't see the sense in packin' it all up knowin' we'll be draggin' the whole of it back out each time the clock strikes the top o' the hour. Supposin' you explain that to me, eh?"

"But Penny, I must determine what will fit, and what I will need, and what I'm forgetting." She plopped down on the chase. "How does one surmise what to take on a journey so far from home?"

"I should think you'll be doing little else than stickin' yer nose in a book, just as you do now. All you'll be needin' is perhaps a pair o' spectacles when the eyes give way."

Agnes smiled, wishing it was that easy. "I shall need two quilts, I presume. You know how I am. And extra wool stockings. Despite it being called spring semester, winter is bound to rage on for another ..."

A pounding on the front door, followed by the bell being pressed repeatedly, startled both women. They were in Agnes's bedroom on the third floor, and stood wondering if Larkspur would see to the caller. When the pounding and trilling returned a moment later, they moved immediately down the stairs, turning at the landing on the second floor. They hurried their steps, for whoever was at the door urgently wished to have it opened. A blast of cold air swept in as Penny yanked at the door knob. Agnes waited near the base of the stairs, as something kept her from peeking her head around to see who it was. She watched Penny's posture, hoping for a clue.

"I want to see the master of the house."

It was not the man's attire that gave Penny a frown, although his ragged trousers and coat looked to be slop clothing, roughly made and not well cared for. It was not even the scowl upon his face that matched his gruff voice. It was something about his eyes that jabbed a thorn into her and made her think immediately of home, of the bay on which she boarded the boat to begin her voyage across the Atlantic. She shuddered, then realized the man was waiting for an answer.

"What's that yer askin'?" she said.

"The master of the house, is he in?" The man's tooth had been pulled so there was a gap on the left side of his smile, on the occasions he chose to smile. This was one of those occasions because as he stood on the cold stoop waiting for Penny to respond, he concluded that the distracted, simple-looking maid might be of great use to him.

Dropping her shoulders a notch, she was relieved that the man was without a celtic accent, as he reminded her of a lecherous character who had given her some trouble aboard the ship. She had put the man off but only after her heel had slid along his shinbone accompanied by a slew of her father's curse words.

"Mr. Trossen's not in. Was he expectin' a hammer to throw itself against the door? If you don't mind me sayin'." She was not impressed with the sudden grin he had acquired.

"Are you not going to invite me in? I have business to discuss and I don't appreciate being kept in the cold."

Penny squinted her eyes a bit and replied, "Many a ragged colt made a noble horse, so I ain't leavin' you on the step for that pitiful jacket yer wearin'. I'm leavin' you there cause if you ain't thought to offer me yer name, most likely you ain't got an ounce o' pride left in it. A name is a powerful thing, a friend o' mine likes to say. 'Tis a truthful statement, I've come to think. Now, unless you can offer an explanation that'll turn you into St. Patrick, we best say our good-byes."

Off to the side, Agnes could not contain herself, and let out a tiny gasp of dismay. Then quickly covered her mouth.

"I see," the man said. "If a name is all you need, you can call me Federal Marshal Diggs." He unbuttoned his coat to reveal his badge, and pulled it back still further to show the gun strapped to his holster. "I come to discuss a matter with Mr. Trossen but since he's not available, seems like I'm forced to come in and take a look around."

He pushed past Penny to find Agnes standing in his path in the hallway.

"Wait one moment," Agnes's voice rose. "You have not the right to barge in. My uncle will look most unfavorably at your attempt to enter our home without an invitation. He is a powerful businessman and surely will not appreciate such a gesture."

"Your uncle may be powerful, but if he's harboring a fugitive than he's guilty of a crime." The man revealed his imperfect smile again.

"I've never heard of such a ridiculous accusation. We are not harboring anyone in this house." Agnes could feel her hands shaking and a prickly flush of emotion moving up her neck into her cheeks, yet she made herself tall and looked the man in the eye.

Reaching into his coat pocket, he pulled out a piece of paper and unfolded it to reveal a sketch of a woman's face and the words WANTED printed below it. To Agnes, apart from the wide spacing of the eyes, it was a rather nondescript face, poorly drawn and the mouth distorted by the well worn creases. Penny pulled the paper from the man's fingers and looked at it, then dropped her hand to her side.

"What makes you think we take to the notion of hidin' criminals? We keep our vegetables in the cellar, not vagrants and such. Check for yerself if you please, we've nothin' to hide." She threw one palm up to signal he could do as he liked, quickly tucking the sketch in a pocket, then added, "Take your chances as to whether Mr. Trossen'll take kindly to the intrusion."

The man did not move, looking between the two women. "Word has it, you've recently taken on a new maid."

Penny had kept her ear cocked for noises from the kitchen since the slave catcher stepped inside the house, and now she forced herself to appear unmoved by his question. Agnes just furrowed her brow, confused as to why the man would find their new maid of any interest.

Before Agnes could speak, Penny began, "If yer speakin' of my young cousin who I twisted the arm of Mrs. Trossen to convince to let stay as to relieve me of a bit o' the enormous heap o' work around here, than you can promptly remove her from yer mind. Just because you may be a fellow new to town, and luck has it the girl happens to be a young unattached lass, she's not available for any kind o' courtin'. Unless it's Prince Charmin' himself who comes to call, any lad must wait until I'm dead and gone before he comes forward with such a blarney idea." Penny set her hands upon her hips and huffed, "Now, it would serve me nicely to get back to my tasks before the day's end and I'm sent back on the boat for failin' to get a single chore finished."

Agnes did not say a word, despite her confusion. Whatever the reason Penny chose to lie about Larkspur, she decided it was not the time to find out.

The man looked at Penny for a long moment, then asked, "So she's your kin, huh? Come from Ireland as well?"

"Not a t'all. She's born here in America. Daughter of my dead husband's uncle. Rest their souls as they have both gone on to muck about with the saints." She made the sign of the cross. "Although, I can't say a good thing about her mother, besides havin' the name Brigid. But that's neither here nor there," she huffed, "as I can still hear the clock tickin' away as if it's the very sound o' me chores piling up in the hallway right here with us. Now will that be all?"

"Is the girl home?" he asked, ignoring Penny's movement toward the door to see him out. This time he issued the question toward Agnes.

"Well," Agnes replied, "I believe she is gone upon an errand. Isn't that so Penny?"

"Yes, she has gone to get some trimmins, ribbon and an arm's length o' lace. We shall be sewin' tonight, if you care to know. I can list the other chores needin' to be tackled before we can get to our needles and thread. I know our tasks pale compared to the excitin' business of yer work Mr. Sir Deputy, but nonetheless they are tasks still the same."

He weighed the information he had been offered, then turned. "Make sure to tell Mr. Trossen I called." He tromped out to the landing, down the steps and disappeared into the street.

It was only when the door was closed, that the two women began to shake, eyes wide, for the temperature in the house had dipped from the door being left open for so long. Moreover, the whole exchange had ruined their nerves. Without speaking, they hurried towards the kitchen.

❧

Before the pounding upon the door, and while Penny and Agnes were still staring into the trunks contemplating what else could be stuffed inside, Larkspur's scrubbing of the planks around the cookstove was interrupted by a tapping against the kitchen window. Silas motioned her to put on her coat and come to the door. Ushering her by the elbow in a way that told her not to question why they were crossing the frozen yard, they slipped through one gate and then another, and into the stable where Mercy Tubbs looked up as they entered.

"I beg your pardon at rushing you out," he began, his face tense, "but the slave-catching man is headed for the Trossens. Same man tried to pick me up the other time."

"How do you know?"

"A friend come by to tell me."

"Is the man looking for me?" Larkspur said, incredulously.

"Not sure. Maybe some other runaway, maybe not. Asking around if anyone showed up lately in the neighborhood. And Mrs. Blair said nobody 'cept the new maid at the Trossens, but she ain't black." Silas raised his eyebrows. "Man said he was going to check things out either way. So I came straight away to get you out from that kitchen."

"And you think it might be me, who he's looking for?"

"He asking a whole lot a questions and now people being told the law says they have to help or the marshall take to charging them with a crime." Mercy Tubbs moved about in the stall behind them, thwapping her tail against the wall.

Silas continued, "Ain't no way a knowing, right yet, if he's looking for you or somebody else. But if he getting paid to do it, then he'll stay at it. How rich you say your master is? How much could he pay for a reward?"

Larkspur paused for a rather long moment. "Not much at all."

"Hmmm. Either way, he probably wants back what he

sees as his, so he'd be willing to pay otherwise he'd be out the money he spent to get you." Silas was just thinking out loud, not even looking over at her. He continued, "We gotta get you away from here. You gotta go. You gotta keep moving. This ain't no place to stay if you ain't all the way free."

Silas now looked at her, feeling the cold begin to bite through his clothes. She began to shake her head slowly but firmly so that Silas took off his hat and scratched his head.

"Figured you might say that. Just figured you might." He put his hat back on. "Then for now, until we find out more, you need to crawl behind those hay bales in the back. Put some loose hay over you to stay warm. I'll try to get an extra blanket from the house."

Larkspur did not move. Finally she took a step toward the hay bales.

"Mercy Tubbs will keep you company 'til I'm back." He stroked the horse's nose, then eased out into the cold afternoon, wondering what to do next. After a moment he headed into the Spiedlers for a blanket, deciding there was no way to intercept or intervene in what was about to happen at the Trossens.

৯

It had come to Penny the night of her fever. Perhaps it was the conversation between Larkspur and Silas she must have overheard despite her semi-lucid state, that convinced her she could know of something without understanding it. When she woke the next morning and looked at Larkspur, the secret that had sat between them like a mist of rain, splashed over her. Why o' course, she said to herself, looking at the girl's full features, her thick hair pulled back and wound tightly in a knot, usually kept under a bonnet or scarf. Watching her hands as they nursed her back to health, the darker skin above the nail bed and at the knuckles, she remembered when the girl had first arrived, with no belongings and looking like she had crawled out of a thicket or been climbing a rough-hewn cliff. So, she'd been running. But Penny chose not to say a thing, for it mattered profoundly and then, conversely, not at all, merely depending on how one had to look at it.

Now she rushed into the kitchen, with a perplexed Agnes at her heel. They found the room empty, in a gray, still light that was filled with little of anything. It was the thieving hour of day, the dead of afternoon, when Penny had to be careful not to let it overtake her, especially on gloomy, winter days. The hour that could suck up the present and replace it with the somber moments of the past or even the ones yet to come. It could drain away her optimism and her strength if she did not sing her way through it, or chase it out with conversation or the aroma of sweet and yeasty things. But today, she found the room not only empty of Larkspur, but empty of sound and smell and something else. Gone was the way things had been. It would be different now. The thieving hour had won. She felt a weight pull her slowly down into a chair, ignoring Agnes's inquiry into what had transpired in the front hall and why anyone would think it a good time to sit down to contemplate life, as Penny seemed to be doing.

Another memory came back to Penny as she stared at the swirls in the wood of the floor planks, the abandoned pail, and the rag hastily dropped beside it. At a young age, when she realized her father would never return from being lost at sea, she had crawled onto her grandfather's lap and cried upon his shoulder. He patted her back.

"Here, here wee one, while yer eyes are waterin' I shall tell ye a secret. One ye might not understand right off but seein' as I can't recall but one wise sayin', it'll have to do." He paused for a moment, lowering his chin towards Penny's head. He whispered, "I once heard it said that when the temple bell stops, the sound keeps right on comin' from out o' the flower."

He reached over and nipped a stem of chickweed from where it grew close to the ground against the stone wall.

She lifted her head. "From out o' the flower?"

"Indeed."

"From what part o' the flower can sound get out?"

He chuckled, "Oh the very middle, I suppose. The very center o' the middle."

He pointed to the stamen set between the five small white petals. Taking the tiny flower from his hand, she looked up at him as if somewhere inside the petals and inside his words, the thing she needed was hidden, then she went back to his shoulder and continued to weep.

Now sitting in the kitchen, the thing she needed was there before her. Her father, and then her mother and grandparents, were not gone even though they had stopped ringing, for they were still coming out of her. She was not all that alone, she realized, and she had known it all along, even if it took until this moment to understand it.

She stood up and patted Miss Agnes's arm. "We can't leave Larkspur on her own."

Agnes did not understand Penny's meaning, for she had no inclination that Larkspur was anyone but who she seemed to be. When she shrugged her shoulders in confusion, Penny decided that perhaps it was better to leave it that way.

"What do you mean, Penny?"

"I only mean," she sighed, "the lass can't be expected to prepare the entire evening meal after runnin' the errands and scrubbin' the floorboards. I shall come up and help with yer packin' after I've got dinner goin', if you don't mind."

"But Penny, do you have any idea why that man would come to our door? Would suspect us of harboring slaves? Does he suppose we are involved with the Anti-Slavery Society? What would give him such an impression?"

Agnes knew she had done nothing but attend several meetings and spend a few hours in her room upstairs mulling over the moral obligations of free citizens. Surely this couldn't provide a federal marshall a reason to pound upon their door?

"I don't see the point in lettin' one unpleasant visit take us under. I'm bettin' Mr. Trossen will know just how to handle it, if it's even worth mentionin' to him. Now off you go, with all that there is to do, you best be at it with no further delay."

She directed Agnes out of the kitchen before Agnes could let her thoughts move beyond her own possible connection to the man's interest in their household and to the other puzzling issue that she wouldn't think of again until later, like why had Penny alleged that Larkspur was her cousin?

Once Penny was alone, she threw on her coat and headed to find Mr. Clemons, the sketch still stuffed within her apron pocket.

৯

Folding the letter and pressing an H into the warm wax, Bernhart stared at the seal while it dried. Perhaps his father would be disappointed, but he had come to understand how the dreams of one generation, so optimistically placed upon the next, could come to feel like small lead weights sewn into the seam of one's own plans. His father had wanted Bernhart to follow in his footsteps, either as an inventor or by assuming responsibility of the family's pillow factory. Tomorrow the letter would be postmarked and on its way by stagecoach for Sullivan County, Pennsylvania. While it might take a few weeks to arrive, there was no changing the content of the message once he dropped it at the post office in the morning. He had to trust that his parents would adapt to the notion of their son foregoing the acclaim and excitement of invention for the less glamorous role of a gardener.

He dabbed at the wax, which was now firm under his fingertip and tried to imagine what lay ahead. Immediately following Agnes's announcement, he had been filled with a sense of consternation, as if a wave had knocked against him and the undercurrent swept out his feet. For although he had not yet determined just when to ask for Anges's hand in marriage, he had expected that one day they would be wed. Now he could not be sure of anything. A few nights after the dinner party, when they were able to share a moment alone, he revealed his troublous mood. She tried to assure him that her pursuit of an education did not suggest there was no hope for their future together.

"Perhaps that is true, Agnes," he had sighed, unconvinced by her words. "Or perhaps you shall find the most pleasing accommodations to persuade you to stay in Ohio and never return."

"Pleasing accommodations? I am going off to gain an education, not book a stay in the Girard Hotel. On the contrary, I've secured modest lodging within the household of a family near campus. I'm told they have young children, so I imagine their noisy scampering will force me to hole up in my meager room."

He smiled at her before replying, "It's not your living arrangements I'm concerned with, but the classroom itself that would captivate your attention. That is what I worry losing you to, Agnes, given your inquisitive mind."

She clasped his hand. "Inquisitive just like yours, Bernhart. It is only that I have been discouraged from exploring my curiosity, while you have not." Then her face lit up. "You should come with me! Yes! That would solve everything."

He let go of her hand. "No, I don't think it would. I have had my nose in one book or another for many years and only recently have I begun to ask myself why. I've come to realize that I've been searching for an *idea* to latch onto. And while I've acquired an abundance of fascinating information, what I have not found is the *idea*. Something tells me neither would I find it at your Oberlin."

"Then where shall you look?" She posed the question with such a practical tone that he imagined turning over a sofa cushion to find an idea, shaped like a glass marble or a lost thimble. Had he been proceeding in such a silly way all this time, under the assumption that to come up with an invention was just a matter of finding where it lay hidden? He felt exhausted by the futility of his approach.

He dropped the burden onto the floor beside him. Imagining the heavy thing striking the soft carpet, he shifted a foot out of the way. When he looked up into Agnes's eyes, he remembered their walk through Bartram's Garden last summer, the strand of hair he had brushed from her cheek. On that day, amongst the green splendor of sprouting life, he had been filled with profound contentment. He realized, only here did he enjoy a sense of harmony that he had not found elsewhere. Suddenly his face brightened. Surprisingly and amazingly, he did have an idea.

After he left Agnes that day, he rushed home to compose a letter. This one to Mr. Andrew M. Eastwick, inquiring into the owner's need for assistance with the upkeep of the grounds of his newly acquired garden. By listing his extensive knowledge of native plants and conveying his exuberance for getting his hands in the particular soil belonging to Bartram's Garden, Bernhart hoped to secure a position with Mr. Eastwick for the upcoming spring.

Now rising from his desk, he went to place the letter for his father in his coat pocket so that he would not forget it come morning. As he reached inside, his fingertips brushed the scratchy cap of the bur oak acorn still buried in the bottom of his deep pocket. Taking it out and turning it in his hand, he remembered the day he put it in. How had the hard object managed to hide in his coat all this time, he wondered, without the lucky thing slipping out through the tear in the pocket lining?

～

Two floors below Bernhart, Erzsebet swept up the crumbs from the day's cooking. The evening meal, for the four tenants who stayed in the boarding house, was finished and waiting in the warming oven. They could help themselves, depending on when each arrived home, or in Bernhart's case, grew hungry. While she swept, she planned out the meals to prepare for the next day. When she finished, she looked out through the lone, basement window to see that the sky had grown dark, then climbed the steps to the main level of the house to retrieve her coat from where it hung in a narrow back hallway that led outside. At the foot of the door, a slip of paper lay upon the floor. Hesitantly she picked it up, unfolded it and saw Silas's scrawled penmanship. H was all he had written, but she knew what that meant. He was seeking her help.

Knowing she kept little food at her own home, as she most often ate her meals where she worked and had nothing but a fireplace to cook over, she headed back down to the kitchen. Gathering a few biscuits and two baked potatoes from the warming oven, she wrapped the food in a cloth and tucked it in her basket. Lowering the wick on the lamp, she turned to leave the room, only to be startled by the presence of a man standing across the room watching her. His name was Borbola, a tenant who had recently arrived from Hungary. While he spoke little english, the rigid way in which he continued to stare at her in silence, seemed laden with opinion.

She did not know if she should attempt an explanation. Since it was acceptable and expected of her to take her meals at the boarding house, there was really no reason why she couldn't carry her dinner home with her, yet the fact that she was placing the food in the basket for someone besides herself, left a measure of guilt hanging between them.

Just then, Bernhart clanged his way down the stairs and into the kitchen. "It is rather dark in here. Are we running low on lamp oil? Oh, hello Barbola, I almost missed you in the gloom." Erzsebet turned up the wick so that light spread toward each wall. "Good evening, Erzsebet. And you in your coat when this room is the warmest of the house."

"I'm on my way." She was relieved to see Bernhart and

added, patting the handle of her basket, "I packed up a little something for later. My stomach's acting funny tonight."

He nodded as if that was the most reasonable thing he'd ever heard. She felt better and didn't bother to glance at Barbola as she brushed past the two men, up the stairs and out the back door. The cold air against her face was welcoming as she hurried through the dark streets toward home. She did not wonder for whom Silas needed the food, not expecting it to be someone she knew.

৽

Penny nearly lost her footing as she hurried through the yard, then picked her way across the lane, stepping over the frozen ridges and muddy ruts, to reach the Spiedler's back gate. When she tugged at it, the latch seemed frozen. She jiggled it and pulled harder, but it did not give. Pounding her fist against the wood of the gate, barely a noise reverberated in the frigid air, so she tugged again. Frozen? Perhaps Larkspur had not come this way. She stood there imagining where the girl could have run off to, but no other place came to mind. Finally, she surrendered to the cold and turned back for the Trossens.

Silas, having wound a rope through the latch to keep it fastened, stood in the yard clutching a blanket, listening for her retreat. When she did, he slipped into the stable and found Larkspur standing next to Mercy Tubbs, stomping her cold feet and looking restless. He admonished her for leaving the hiding spot and explained he had just heard someone trying the gate.

"I believe it was only the cook, but no sense taking chances. 'Til we know what happened over there, we gonna keep still."

"No surprise Penny would come looking, she's bound to wonder where I am. It's gone dark already."

"Yeah they may wonder, but that ain't what I'm worried 'bout right yet. We gonna get you to Erzsebet's for the night.

She stays above the garment shop. We'll figure out the rest as we go."

"Maybe we could go to Penny for help."

"Why you think that?"

"I gotta feeling about her and I tend to trust when I get a feeling about someone."

"You might be right." He remembered his conversation with Erzsebet on this topic, and yet thought it necessary to proceed with caution. "But *tend to* ain't good enough, right yet. Got plenty of black folks around here to help us, once we get to figuring what help it is we need, exactly. Figuring *that* out, Penny might help us with. But the keeping you safe part? We'll start with the good people we know already. Now I just gotta see to Mercy Tubbs and then it be about time to go. Erzsebet should be home soon."

As he brushed the horse's coat, he explained to the animal that, as always, she'd be alright on her own. "Don't I always come back come morning, ol' girl?" Then he led Larkspur into the night, with her shawl wrapped around her head for warmth and to shield her face. Guiding her elbow, they sought the empty, narrow streets over a direct route until they reached their destination, knocking only once before being ushered inside.

ص

That night, while Larkspur slept next to Erzsebet, who woke in the night to add a log from the box Silas had filled, Penny tossed about on her lumpy mattress. When the first rays of light woke her, she popped out of bed to take on the cold house by herself. As soon as she could break from the morning chores, she returned to the Spiedler's back gate. This time the latch lifted and she eased into the yard. Mr. Clemons was drawing the horse and carriage out of the stable as she approached.

"Mr. Clemons," she called out, her breath a puff of steam against the cold air. He waited for her to reach him, his face stoic. "I've been worried sick for not knowin' where the lass has slipped off to. Surely, you might know."

"The lass?" He maintained a passive look.

"There's no time for shenanigans, Mr. Clemons." She lowered her voice. "I've caught on to Larkspur's secret and I don't rightly care to be left out from helpin' her. No frozen gate shall keep me from it. She nursed me back from the fever and has come to feel like a friend o' mine. But if that is not reason enough then moreso, she's a fine girl and deserves to be considered as such. Now I'm assumin' it was you who found a safe place for her to stay the night, eh?"

Silas could not help but smile as he stepped back into the shadow of the stable and motioned for her to do the same. "Why Miss Penny, you ain't shy to cut right to it. Larkspur said we could trust you, and I guess you gonna twist my arm until I'm forced to agree."

"So she's safe, then?"

"For now. But I need to know what the slave-catchin' man said. Who is he looking for?"

Penny pulled the folded sketch from her pocket and showed it to Silas. "Claims to be searchin' for this woman."

"Well that don't look a thing like Larkspur, now does it?"

"Not a bit. That's what I come to tell you. She's safe to come back as the deputy's lookin' for someone entirely different." Her face held enough trepidation that Silas knew she didn't really expect him to readily concur.

"'Unless it's a trap. Unless this one," he tapped the drawing, "he caught already and returned last week. Now he's on to searching for a runaway light enough to pass for white." There was a pause while they both stood in the cold morning oblivious to the temperature. "Can I keep this paper?"

Penny nodded. "The man asked to speak with Mr. Trossen. That was before I told a wee lie that Larkspur was a cousin o' mine. I can't bet one way nor the other if he took it for the trickery it was. But what happens if he comes back and she's not in the house where she's supposed to be?"

"And what happens if she is? You'll have to put him off again. I aim to figure out what he's up to just as soon as I can. Give me the day to ask around."

Penny nodded again. "But Mr. Clemons," she said slowly, "might you have to send her off so that I'll never lay eyes upon her again?"

She did not wait for an answer, for she knew she was being selfish, putting her own feelings before Larkpsur's safety. She closed the gate behind her, her heart catching on the icy, metal latch.

ᦞ

Mathias, who had business to arrange in Northern Liberties, left the house after breakfast. Josephine and Agnes had plans to head to Chestnut Street for last-minute items Agnes needed for her journey the following day. On the way they would drop off a bundle to Julianna Stone for her charities. While Josephine gathered the knitted shawls and scarves, Agnes slipped into the pantry to find Penny searching for a jar of stewed tomatoes.

"Good morning, Penny. The rooms upstairs are especially drafty today. It seems Larkspur has forgotten to tend to the dying embers. But no matter, my aunt and I are preparing to go out for the next few hours."

Penny realized she had not returned upstairs to keep the rooms warm, a task belonging to Larkspur. Nor had she emptied the chamber pots, nor wound the clock, nor rinsed the dishes from breakfast, nor swept the front rooms which Larkspur did on Tuesdays.

Penny nodded and squeezed past Agnes to stand over the stove. Agnes joined her, extending her hands toward the warmth. "Where is Larkspur?"

"I sent her out as I'm low on butter. Nearly had to churn my own this mornin'. Shame if I'd have to take on that task again, now that butter can be had for a small price from the market house. And soap cakes. A loathsome task, makin' those. I'd prefer a hole in my stockin' or to eat cold eggs than to stir lard and lye together." She laughed, hoping Agnes would move onto another topic. "'Tis cold out there today. Shall I expect you back for lunch?"

"I don't think we shall return in time, but I have agreed to an afternoon walk with Bernhart. Do you think you could have a pot of tea ready for us afterward and perhaps a small meal. It shall be our last together for quite some time." Agnes's chin quivered for just a moment. Then she gained her composure, leaned closer and whispered, "I'm curious why you kept from us that Larkspur is your family? Did you think my aunt and uncle would somehow mind? And then to willingly divulge such information to that awful man yesterday, I find it odd."

Penny stared at Agnes, unsure of how the younger woman could readily absorb the complex information from her books and yet seem to lack the ability to put two and two together. "'Tis a complicated thing, family matters."

Rubbing her hands together, Agnes waited for more and finally said, "Well, do you think that man will return? I don't suppose you told my uncle about him before he left this morning."

"Seems not a thing to bother him over. I wager that deputy is more like a wolf who fancies huffin' and puffin' rather than the blowin' of a thing over." She reached across the stove for a lid and placed it on the simmering pot.

Agnes sensed Penny knew something she wasn't revealing. She hovered in a moment of uncertainty, wondering if she wanted to press to find out. Before she could decide, her aunt called from the front of the house needing a basket for the knitted items.

Penny rushed to collect one from the corner, then handed it to Agnes. "Off you go. With so much to do today, Miss

Agnes, don't let any o' this nonsense get in the way o' preparing for yer upcoming journey." The look that the younger woman gave, before rushing out of the kitchen, left Penny doubting that Agnes was the impervious rock she had likened her to a few moments earlier. She lifted the empty jar from the table and set it, with a tiny clink, in the crowded sink.

She worked hard through the morning and into the afternoon, never appreciating Larkspur more as she emptied the chamber pots and wound the clocks, and worrying about her to the same degree as she hauled firewood up the stairs. Finally, she paused for a cup of tea and a slice of buttered bread. Normally, there was little that could distract her from savoring her afternoon tea, but today her mind was scattered so that she was surprised when she reached the bottom of the cup. Suddenly, a banging on the front door reverberated the length of the hallway, through the back parlor and into the kitchen where she had just begun to rise from the table. Startled, the chair toppled behind her, clattering to the floor.

Bernhart had deposited the letter for his father at the post office and now angled toward Pine street. Without a snowfall in over a week, a griminess adhered to the slick sidewalks, but Bernhart did not notice as his step felt lighter than it had in a very long time. As he passed the open door of a bakery, and the smell of cardamom and cloves wafted out, a yearning seduced him to step inside. Loaves of fresh bread and little lumps of soft buns lined the shelves, but upon the counter lay a tray of sweets; rows of butter cookies, thin wafers, lemony crisps and lady fingers. Yet it was the almond-scented, crescent vanillekipferl that made him smile. Cookies his mother had made so often.

"Ah, you should've come in Dezember. I had for you all the weihnachtsplaetzchen to choose. Now just these." A small, stooped woman behind the counter pointed with irreverence at the tray of sweets. "Hemma can make you gingerbread same like home, but only Dezember time. Too late, now." She waved her hand in disappointment at his tardiness.

"If only I had walked by your shop before today. Accept my apologies Frau Hemma. Perhaps you will fill a small box for me? One of each kind so that I can determine which one reminds me most of my lost days of youth."

The woman's face lit up so quickly that he knew how happy she was to have tricked him into making a purchase. She perched up on tiptoe to reach the tray of cookies, then filled the box. "Come back tomorrow, tell me which taste just like lost youth."

Bernhart paid the woman and rushed out, eager to get to Agnes. After their walk, he would present the box for them to share. A small, last celebration. Although they would be separated, he could not deny feeling optimistic that they were both about to take a promising turn. Pausing for a horse to pass and two men pushing a cartload of bricks, he then hurried toward the Trossen's home.

ও

The chair remained overturned back in the kitchen, while Penny opened the front door slowly, dreading who she might find. The day was cold and mostly overcast but at the moment the sun shot between a part in the clouds so that a glare glanced off the houses across the street. Her eye caught here first, on their grey stones and opaque windows, before dropping down to the boy standing in front of her. With the light behind him, she could not make out his features, but then remembered the young urchin who had tried to steal Mr. Clemons's coach and horse.

"Well, you don't say," she murmured, amazed the boy would have the nerve to show up again. Hunger and cold will do that, she thought, steal your pride. He seemed to have grown a foot. "C'mon then, before you freeze yer britches." She gestured him in, wondering why he didn't have the good sense to use the back door like most beggars did. As she tugged at his threadbare jacket, she felt him resist, leaning away. With the shift, the light fell upon his face differently and Penny realized it was not the carriage thief after all, but a negro boy with a cap pulled low over his head.

"And who are you?" she demanded. Hesitancy washed over the boy's face and it looked to Penny like he might turn and run, so she whispered urgently, "Hear me now, I won't hurt you." Pulling him in, she quickly guided him down the hall, all the way to the kitchen before he could respond.

"Lad, next time the back door, so as to be safe. Instead o' comin' through the front for all the world to take note."

The boy, whose eyes pulled toward the fire in the cook-stove, said, "I know to use the back, mam, but all these houses stuck together."

Penny nodded, "There's an alley, but I don't suppose 'tis the easiest thing to find if you don't know to look for it. Now, who are you and how'd you end up on the front stoop?"

Before the boy could answer, again came a noise from the front of the house. This time it was the trill of the door-bell and it pierced both the boy and the woman like a dart. Penny immediately thought of the deputy and given the frightened look on the boy's face, put a finger to her lips and whispered, "Come."

Leading him through the pantry and into her small room, she opened the wardrobe, parted the clothes, and issued him inside. "Remember, not a sound. But you know that o' course. When I get back, you shall tell me your proper name." Then she carefully pressed closed the doors of the wardrobe until they made a tiny click, paused and then turned toward the insistent bell.

୨

Larkspur awoke when she heard Erzsebet stirring. Sharing a weak pot of coffee and a buckwheat cake, they sat at a small table while the sun rose slowly over the city. As light seeped through the front windows, with it came a feeling of ease that Larkspur had not yet experienced since arriving in Philadelphia. This morning there was no requisite for her to affect to be someone she was not. She no longer needed to closet the truth, to hide a memory in the strings of her apron, conceal a penchant in the braid of her hair, stuff her pockets with her opinions. For working in the Trossen kitchen had required a denial of her past, of the layers of sound and smell and impression that had shaped her own, particular world. She would have thought it a world, as exacting as it was, worth dismissing, but she had found such a denial only another diminution of her personhood.

"So you thinking to go?" Erzsebet's voice broke through the placid silence of the room. "North, I mean."

She didn't answer, running her hand along her skirt. Tucked within the folds, the velvet of her charm bag hopped into her fingers like a kitten into a child's lap. Placing the small bag upon the table, she worked the drawstring open and then left the bag sitting there with its contents waiting at the bottom. The purple had faded, except for where the bag had been drawn closed and a few thin, dark streaks had been spared from the effects of sunlight. Larkspur liked the deep, purple lines for they reminded her of long ago when Aunt Celena had suggested what talismans she might place in the bag: the key for opportunity that she now wore around her neck, a nutmeg for protection, an acorn for luck, a smooth stone for peace, grains of salt to ward off impurities, mustard seeds for health, a sprinkle of dried sage for more protection. There was the memory of one rose petal that had crumbled into dust, for love. She had chosen purple fabric from which to sew the bag because it was the color of wisdom and mystery. So too, the color of her name. The D she had stitched in a silvery thread.

She now traced the D with her finger as she spoke. "Aunt Celena was the first to show me. She said to peer real close to spot the four true petals of my flower. Tiny things, the same color as the sepals on the outside. She said the true petals were "inconspicuous." Said it knowing I didn't know what such a big word meant, and she wasn't quick to tell. Said everybody should come to their own understanding of what things mean." She sighed, then added, "Aunt Celena could throw around fancy words. They just stuck in her head, even without knowing how to spell 'em."

Erzsebet sensed that the young woman across from her was working her way through the past, despite the future looming so harrowingly in front of her. She asked tenderly, "Which one you call your flower?"

Her voice caught in the middle of her name, "Delphinium. That's the name my mama gave me."

"She named you after a flower?"

She closed her eyes so no tears would escape, "Purple and poisonous. But they say you can use it for ink, the juice of the petals is so dark."

"Maybe your mama wanted you to learn to read and write your letters," Erzsebet offered.

"Or poison somebody."

Erzsebet began to laugh, but stopped when she saw how serious and grim Larkspur appeared. A silence descended until Larkspur began in a dry, low voice.

"I don't believe I can go north. I told him I'd wait here, in case he can make it. There ain't no good reason to think he's coming, but all the same, I can't start imagining he's not. So I've got a mind to wait, just like I said I would."

"Well, you found you a good spot, but no telling what those people gonna act like if they find out you ain't white? Or maybe you hoping to go on passing?" Erzsebet tried to keep a neutrality to her voice, not let on how this seemed a betrayal to those who did not have such a choice.

Larkspur lifted the charm bag and placed it in her palm. The past months had been strange. For the first time in her life she no longer had to remind herself to expect to be treated as a slave, to guard her every movement and spoken word. For the first time she had not the constant worry that each day her body could be met with some form of violence. How much of her new freedom could she attribute to her escape from bondage and how much from being mistaken as white, she couldn't decipher. Either way, she had never anticipated that the arrangement at the Trossens would go on indefinitely, especially if Ignatius succeeded.

"I expect the truth is bound to come out. But for now, I don't believe that bounty hunter is looking for me in particular," Larkspur stated. She withdrew the smooth nutmeg from the bag and held it tightly in her palm.

"How you so sure?" Erzsebet asked, eyeing the nutmeg with interest for she rarely could find a nutmeg to grate into her coffee or add to her cakes.

"I saw to it." The words came out like wooden blocks knocking against the table between them. Larkspur reached out and placed the nutmeg in front of Erzsebet.

"This nutmeg helped me on my way north. Offered me protection and some luck. But you letting me in your home is putting you in harm's way, so now I want you to have it so nothing bad comes your way." She smiled as she set it in front of Erzsebet, then her face grew somber again. "I figured the best way to leave Baltimore, was with no one trying to come after me."

༄

Penny felt suddenly alone as she stood in the front hall. Her earlier relief over Agnes and Mrs. Trossen being out of the house was now replaced, especially with the child hiding in the back, with vulnerability. She felt ill-prepared to face the federal marshall on the other side of the door. Her confident attitude of yesterday had scampered like a mouse along the baseboards of the empty house looming behind her, and disappeared into some dark crevice.

A hand pounded against the door making her jump. She reached out and yanked the knob, knowing she could delay no longer. Throwing her shoulders back, she felt a small surge of yesterday's defiance return as she swung the door open.

"Bejapers!" Penny cried, for it was not Diggs at the door but Mr. Hommes standing with his hat crooked on his head and a small box in his hand. Behind him the clouds hung low but had not yet begun to drop snow.

"If ever before I was pleased to have you come by unannounced, that day pales to how mighty thrilled I am to lay eyes upon you now."

She put her hand on his arm, leaned out behind him and looked up and down the street, then sweeping him into the house as she had the boy a few minutes earlier, she added, "Ah, Mr. Hommes. Our own, dear Mr. Hommes. I shall be needin' yer assistance. Follow me."

Knowing they were pressed for time, yet with much to explain, she sat Bernhart down at the kitchen table.

"I've no time to wet the tea or bring down a biscuit from the press, for there is a development to tell you of. You won't believe it, but you must, for 'tis true. There is a child hidin' in the wardrobe. I'd wager he's a runaway, but I hadn't the time to ask for all the trilling of the bell and shufflin' up and down the hall. On top o' that, there's the chance, the awful chance, the rotten fellow with the badge might come back."

Penny spoke quickly so as to prevent Bernhart from asking questions. When he opened his mouth to speak, she quickly continued, "Yes a fellow with a badge, claimin' to be a federal marshal or some such title, came by yesterday pokin' his nose around and wantin' to speak with Mr. Trossen. But I shall get to that later for I remind you of the youngster crouched in the closet. Now, what I'm needin' from you sir, is to help me figure out what we might do to get dog-wide of the deputy."

Bernhart raised his eyebrow, uncertain of her meaning. She added, "To keep clear o' the likes of him."

"I see," he mumbled. "Yes, what to do. What to do? I don't suppose you're in favor of following the law and handing the boy over to the marshal. You should know the penalty of harboring a runaway is now a heavy fine, or worse, prison. There is much to lose, I'm afraid, by aiding a slave."

His words grounded Penny in the seriousness of their decision. Then she thought of Larkspur over whom she might need to make the same decision. Knowing that she would risk such penalties for Larkspur, how then could she not for a child?

"Mr. Hommes, 'tis true we put ourselves in a heap o' danger, but certainly it can't compare to the danger this child has risked stealin' away, nor what he would face if we gave him over. I'm supposin' I would feel like a no good coward, in the presence of the young lad's courage, to not offer a hand."

He tried to imagine if Penny had taken the opposite stand, elected to turn over the fugitive. Would he have nodded and concurred in the same way he was now nodding his chin? He could not be sure.

Despite the rapid pace of his heartbeats he kept his voice calm. "I believe we might look to Mr. Spiedler for assistance."

"I'd have to disagree with you, sir. I'd wager 'tis Mr. Clemons who could be of most help."

"On the contrary, I know Mr. Spiedler takes a firm stance against slavery. Surely he would know what to do. And, I would not want to jeopardize Mr. Clemons by dragging him into this."

"There would be no draggin' involved," she muttered.

"How's that?"

"Well, I've only told you the half of it. Besides the boy in the closet, we've a second, what am I callin' 'em? Oh yes, developments. The deputy fellow of yesterday wasn't here to pay a friendly visit. No, he came askin' after our own, dear Larkspur. Well, if I didn't nearly stab him in the toe with the fire poker. Now Mr. Hommes, I'm sure yer askin' yerself, what the devil does a bounty hunter want with Larkspur. Well, the truth of it is, despite her appearance..."

Bernhart held up his hand, for suddenly the truth jumped forward and he only needed a quiet moment to make sense of it. He pictured a furtive Larkspur gathering her herbs in the garden and remembered how reticent she was to speak of her past. Why of course, he thought to himself, but in the next moment was struck by the idiosyncrasy of it.

"What a strange thing," he found himself saying out loud, "that someone's identity can be governed by nearly indiscernible factors. Such a convoluted predicament which Americans have entangled themselves. I suppose I must say *ourselves*."

Penny nodded. "Yes but what I'm sayin' then, Mr. Hommes, is that Mr. Clemons has taken Larkspur off somewhere safe until we can be sure the marshal means her no harm. So there's that to sort out and now the boy..."

Just then Josephine and Agnes swept into the house with boxes and parcels, calling from the front hall that they were home. Penny groaned and Bernhart glanced nervously at the pantry door leading into the back bedroom. He reminded himself that he had been invited to spend the afternoon with Agnes before tomorrow's departure.

"I shall try to find Mr. Clemons. Keep the boy here until then," Bernhart whispered to Penny before the aunt and niece called again.

Penny nodded, then bellowed, "Back already, eh? Mr. Hommes has just arrived. I've not even the chance to offer him a tea biscuit."

As the two marched noisily toward the front of the house, the boy shifted his position, his foot bumping against the side of the wardrobe.

❧

As Silas and Mercy Tubbs wound slowly through the streets, the clouds lowered like a wool cap over the city. Large, wet snowflakes began to drop upon the slick, brown coat of the horse, and upon Silas's sleeves. When he ushered Mr. Spiedler out of the coach, the men's boots left marks in the snow.

"Silas, it may be that the snow will force you to put the carriage away. If so, I shall make it home by foot."

The gray-haired man turned up his collar and sloshed off while Silas sat for a moment debating whether to take Mercy Tubbs to her shed. He decided to abandon such caution and head directly for the barber shop so that he might procure the information he sought regarding Diggs. The slippery cobblestones slowed the journey through the hushed and rather empty streets. When he arrived, tied the horse to a post and placed a blanket over her coat, he was startled to spot Erzsebet pacing in front of the shop. As he moved to greet her, the wet snow reached for the hem of his trousers.

"I've been waiting on you," she began, clasping his forearm. "Little while ago, I stopped by home, just to check. Larkspur was gone." He raised his eyebrows in alarm while she continued. "My guess is she went right on back to the Trossens. This morning she said something about fixing things so there wasn't no reason to worry that somebody was coming for her."

"Fixed things how?"

Erzsebet just shrugged. "Didn't say exactly but she didn't seem no way worried over that bounty man." She squeezed his arm. "I have to go. Be careful, Silas."

Silas ducked into the barber shop. It was quiet, with only a few customers. He quickly found out there was no real information on Diggs, but there was news of a young boy, just arriving in town, who seemed to be in search of a woman fitting the description of the maid over at the Trossens.

Despite his urgency to get Mercy Tubbs into her stable

and locate Larkspur, it was a slow tromp through the snowy streets and then as he passed the shops on Chestnut Street, Mrs. and Miss Trossen spotted him, hailing him for a ride back home.

လ

In Baltimore, she endured a number of anxious months of his persistent gaze and snarled lip, before he reached for her as she passed through a dark room, tearing the sleeve of her dress when she pulled away and fled down the stairs. It was then Larkspur began to imagine more seriously how she could ward off his advances.

She was thankful the house was small and the mistress never out of earshot. So far, she had never been left alone in the house with him. Yet often, she lay on her pallet on the kitchen floor worrying that he might come down for her. Then one night the commotion from above began. The first time it sounded as if a table had been overturned, followed by a small cry and then silence. The next morning, Mistress Pixie had a mark across her cheekbone. Progressively the clamor from upstairs grew louder and occurred more regularly, so that some mornings dawned with the mistress unable to leave the house due to the bruises to her skin or the aching of her body. She often took to her bed once her husband left for the day, leaving Larkspur to wonder over the woman's condition. She was rebuffed the first time she offered to prepare a liniment, but when a cup of a bitter smelling brew was set before the mistress to ease the pain to her ribcage, she conceded to its warmth.

Larkspur could not understand why the man chose to beat his wife and not her. Had he been a plantation owner he would have known that beatings were, if not considered a necessary measure of control, at least a customary benefit to the free labor the enslaved provided. But since he did not descend from landowners, could barely make enough money to afford to dwell in a mediocre neighborhood in Baltimore, and had been convinced by his wife to purchase Larkspur despite arguing they couldn't afford it, perhaps he harbored a particular set of frustrations only wife-beating could alleviate.

The abuse went on throughout the spring season. While Larkspur continued to nurse Pixie and avoid the master, she sought out a woman selling herbs at the market. The shiny black berries of belladonna, she was told, which Larkspur knew by the name of banewort, could be mistaken for blueberries if hidden in a pie. "But you'll have trouble finding it growing around here." The woman's eyes grew hard. "I only got the root. Deadliest part of deadly nightshade. Be sure you mean it, hear?"

Larkspur paid the woman for a small vial of the dried root, and took it back to the sad, dank house. She crushed it with a stone against the floor and added it to the pot of vegetables stewing over the fire. She told Pixie to serve it to her husband but to be certain not to ingest it herself. When Pixie's face flashed, first with indignation and then doubt, Larkspur responded.

"Looks to me like that man is intending to keep on beating you, I expect, for the rest of your life. Or his. Your life, I come to argue, is as important as his. So I'm proposing a way to stop him." She held up her hand so the woman would remain quiet. "First, his eyes will grow big, his head will ache. Get him in the bed before he falls. Make him think you're taking good care of him. Later, he'll have trouble speaking, take to thrashing. Eventually, he'll grow real quiet. The next morning, put on your black dress and call for the undertaker. Say one of his seizures finally took him in the middle of the night. Only thing you can't mention to anybody in this new town, is that you once tried to own someone who was never meant to belong to you."

Then she turned and marched out the door, banking her life on the other woman's desire to stay alive.

લ્ર

"Ah, Bernhart," Agnes beamed. Her affection and attention for him had returned, even swelled, in the last few weeks since her plans no longer weighed secretly and heavily against her conscience. "Is it so late that it is time for our outing?"

"Hello Bernhart. If you'd be so kind." Josephine handed him a few paper sacks and plopped onto the bench to remove her damp hat. "Mr. Clemons has a few more to bring up. It has begun to snow, I thought surely the wheels of the coach would get stuck in the sloppy mess. I recommend you two exchange your outdoor plans for a sit before the fire."

Agnes sighed in what sounded like concurrence.

"As Agnes wishes," he responded, "I shall see if Mr. Clemons needs a hand."

He ducked around the women, rattling the umbrella stand before edging through the door. Spotting Silas beside the carriage, he hurried toward him to offer help.

Then under his breath, "Mr. Clemons, we have a very pressing matter on our hands. I am taking the liberty of seeking your help, for Penny suggests you are our best bet."

Silas interrupted, hearing the duress in the other man's voice, "Is it the girl?"

"No. On the contrary, Penny says it's a young boy." Bernhart reached for a package from the seat of the carriage, as a pedestrian passed by.

Puzzled, Silas asked, "Have you come from the house, Mr. Hommes?"

"Yes."

"Is Larkspur inside?"

Bernhart drew his head back. "No, I understood Larkspur to be in your care."

Silas nodded ever so slightly, snow had collected across the bill of his cap.

"It's just Penny and the boy," Bernhart added.

"A boy?"

"That is what I've come to tell you. Penny says that she has hidden a small boy."

"Hidden? Hidden where?"

Bernhart lowered his voice. "Inside the house. She believes him to be a runaway." He shivered, standing without a coat in the falling snow. "And she's anxious to find him refuge. Only now that Mrs. Trossen has returned it seems the situation has grown even more urgent."

Silas held up a hand. He needed a moment to think, to sort things out. He handed the younger man the remaining parcels.

"I'll come 'round back, soon as I can. Tell Penny to expect my knock."

Larkspur left the nutmeg on Erzsebet's table and picked her way down the steep, turning staircase. Once outside, she felt the premonition of snow even before she turned her face upward. Intending to return to the Trossen's house, she found herself drawn in the opposite direction, toward Front Street, and as she approached the waterfront the sound of a barge's horn bumped against a sky that had grown heavy and gray.

Wrapping her shawl more tightly around her neck, she remembered the bright morning she had rode the ferry into Philadelphia. Fear had sat like an unripe pear on her sternum, but she had ventured forth with nothing more than the charms in her velvet bag and the key around her neck. Aunt Celena, who had explained that a key was a sign of power, said finding one whose corresponding lock was unknown was a hopeful sign of what lay ahead. One day she would discover just the thing it opened.

With the sharp river wind against her face, she wondered if she had already done that. Could it have been as deadly as banewort? Could one's future turn on a crushed root dropped into a bubbling stew? And how could such a pivotal moment arrive so convincingly, despite its wickedness, that it appear more like fate than a deliberate, murderous decision.

It seemed, as she looked across the river, the past was waving accusingly at her from the far shore. Was she to assume blame, even though her mistress had served her husband his dinner? Had the situation demanded her to take the action she did or had there been another way? Her culpability in the matter now washed over her as if she had stepped into the water and come out drenched to the bone. She bent over with dread, her legs buckling so that she dropped down on one knee to the frozen ground. First a sob escaped and then her stomach turned, as she struggled not to vomit.

"You catch yo death out here, gal. And get me dem chilblains goin' agin. Saw you movin' like de grim reaper hisself through dem streets. I come to follow so you ain't to sling yoself in dat dere river. What you thinkin' child?" Larkspur looked up to see the old woman from the market who had sold her the beets. "Getty up hey and gimme yo hands."

When Larkspur was on her feet, the old woman took her hands, closed her eyes and grew completely still. Larkspur could feel a current pass between them.

"You set dat down, now. A hard life turn a man cruel aginst a good thing. Dat man better off now, ain't no more hurtin' goin' on. You leave dat 'lone." She opened her eyelids and pierced Larkspur with a crow-like gaze, causing Larkspur to gasp, first with surprise at the woman's words, and then at the seed of relief taking hold somewhere within.

"No need to have your mind twined up in dat no more. You set dat down, hear?" the woman repeated before dropping her eyelids again. There was a long pause in which Larkspur's relief began to dissolve, for she sensed the woman had more to say.

"Now, second matter. You still waitin' on somebody." Again a pause, then a hoarse whisper, "I ain't thinkin' he gone make it."

Larkspur pulled her hands away. "Don't say that. Don't…"

Her voice trailed off as she felt the ground below her seem to shift. A blackbird landed in the tree above and let out a wretched cry.

"Who? Who do you mean?" Larkspur's voice jumped out. "Ignatius? How do you know he's not coming?"

She did not doubt the woman's ability to sense that which was closed off to most people, for she believed there were those who walked between worlds. She merely wished to hear a different tale.

"I know 'cause he say, *howdy, howdy, howdy.* He right here, same like your mama. They both wantin' you to know dey done gone over." She let out a little chortle before adding, "Each time you thinkin' on 'em dey take to grinnin'."

Larkspur moaned at the mention of her mother. She began to weep, while the black bird peered silently from above.

Suddenly the woman opened her eyes, her voice changing as she mumbled, "We done 'bout to catch our death standin' on de water like fools. Come." She reached for Larkspur as she turned her back to the river. The far-off barge sounded its lonely horn.

"Is that all? Is that all they have to say?"

The woman shuffled along for a few steps before muttering, "Well, dey both say, ain't just one lock to open." She tugged Larkspur's arm. "Now come along and take me home."

Gazing at their feet, as they moved away from the waterfront, they did not notice the first snowflakes sifting through the afternoon air. The bird twitched its head and watched them go.

୬

Agnes untied the string around the box of sweets so as to enjoy their kaffe and kuchen, as Bernhart tended to call it, and grew increasingly upset over Bernhart's despondency. He glanced impulsively toward the hallway and shifted toward the edge of his chair each time Penny entered the parlor. Finally, when Josephine excused herself so that the two could be alone on their last afternoon together, but before Agnes could admonish him on his behavior, Bernhart lurched forward, his coffee sloshing over the rim of his cup as he thumped it against the table.

"We must go speak with Penny in the kitchen."

"Whatever for? I would much rather…" she did not finish for she felt a sob welling in her throat. She managed to blurt out, "Why are you acting so strange?"

Leaning toward her, he took her hands in his. "Oh Agnes, I've upset you. But you do not yet understand."

Then in a hushed voice he divulged the fact of the child hiding in the back of the house, and the pressing need for them to act swiftly and carefully to ensure the boy's safety. In the same way Penny had assumed, that in a dire moment, noble qualities would emerge in Bernhart, so too had Bernhart made such an assumption of Agnes, granting no room for a conversation to the contrary.

Penny crept back into her room and motioned for the boy to come out of the wardrobe. "Sit on the bed now so yer legs can stretch a bit. I've brought you some fancy thing called a pfeffernusse. Now, tell me yer name, lad."

He took the powdery cookie as if it was not something to be trusted and told his name.

"And tell my how you came to choose stoppin' here, Zeb, at this particular house? Certainly not just a lucky guess that we'd be servin' sweets?"

"I'm looking for someone named Delphinium."

Penny's brow furrowed. "Then I think you may be mistaken for there's no one here by such an odd name."

Before either could say another word, a soft knocking

sound seeped through the pantry to let Penny know that Mr. Clemons had arrived. She told Zeb to wait on the bed and hurried to the rear door.

Issuing Silas in, she said, "So Mr. Hommes has told you of the predicament, then?" When he nodded, she added, "Can you find a place for the boy?"

Silas kept his voice very low. "Well the truth is, the boy came through yesterday and been shown a safe place. Suppose to move on tomorrow or the day following. Only thing is, seems he got something to take care of first. That's why he risked coming over here."

The back door popped open and in with the cold came Larkspur wrapped in her dark scarf spotted with snowflakes. She had only a moment to look surprised at the two staring at her before she was met with Penny's embrace.

Penny, stepping back, wiped her eyes with her apron. "When you get used to losin' those you love, 'tis a joyous thing when one comes back." Then she helped Larkspur out of her overclothes and steered her toward the stove where the fire inside blazed.

"Glad you're safe, Miss Larkspur," said Silas.

"All the same, I'm not entirely certain 'tis safe for you here?" added Penny.

As if her body had suddenly grown as solid as a tree trunk and the bottom of her feet had taken root, Larkspur felt grounded by the earnest concern in the faces of the two standing before her. For the first time in her life she felt at home. It took a moment for her to find her voice.

"You're gonna just have to take my word for it. It's safe, safe as can be. Besides, if someone comes looking, you can just say you've been fooled by my appearance." She cleared her throat, "But the truth is, I'm not planning to worry no more over what might happen next. I've had my fill and then some of worrying. Seems just another way of being shackled to one place. I'm done with that now."

She then walked over to the table and pulled out a chair. Feeling strong but weary, she closed her eyes and thought of Ignatius. Could it be true, as the old woman said, that he would not be coming?

Just then, Bernhart and Agnes tumbled into the kitchen like noisy boxcars, and Bernhart began to inquire over the whereabouts of the boy.

"Ah," said Penny, "common sense would say the less involved the better, but I see we shall all walk the plank together, if things go awry. I've left the boy with a few of yer sweets, supposin' you don't mind."

"What boy?" asked Larkspur.

"I suggest we keep our voices down," said Agnes, surprisingly calm and forthright. "I hesitate to involve my aunt in all of this and surely my uncle should not catch wind of it." She swallowed and continued, "Now, I believe I know who we can contact for help."

The others in the room stood dumbfounded until Larkspur asked again, "What boy?"

After Penny explained the presence of the boy and shared Silas's knowledge that a secure location had already been arranged for him, she went and retrieved the boy. She steered him to a chair at the table, introduced him by name and then suggested Agnes listen for her aunt's footsteps by chance she descend the stairs.

Silas asked the first question. "Son, we ain't got much time for chit chat. We need to get you back to a safe spot. Why you risk coming out in broad daylight and what you come to say?"

Zeb locked eyes on Larkspur. "Is your name Delphinium?"

Larkspur was still seated, so they sat across from each other with the table stretched between them. To the surprise of many in the room, she nodded.

Silas asked, "How you know that, as you just got to town?"

"The Quaker Lady in Salem, that's where I hid all through the harvest season, being too weak from the fever to get out a the bed. Quaker Lady come one day with a letter from Philadelphia. Had two names in it I heard before. Nate and Delphinium. So when I was strong enough, I made my way north 'til I reached this city. I asked around to find out where you stay at." He kept his gaze on Larkspur.

The room held silent despite the number of people crowded into it. Penny considered lighting the lamp on the table but then the boy started again.

"I come to tell you something you probably ain't gonna wanna hear, but I been asked to do it, so here I am."

Larkspur grew as still as the herbs drying in bundles above her head. Her voice rasped, "I already know he's not coming. I guess it's best to know why."

"Who's that? Who's not comin'?" asked Penny, striking a matchstick and lighting the lamp. The room brightened. Bernhart and Agnes exchanged glances.

The boy began. "First I met him, we was on the schooner coming north. He was already in bad shape but he called me over to sit by him down in the hold where we was hiding. Had a wound in his side but he never mentioned how he come by it." Zeb brought his hand to his side for a moment. "It was real dark down in that hold but he called me over, maybe 'cause he knew I was scared or maybe 'cause he was. Either way, ain't no one trying to be in the bottom of a boat alone."

Zeb swallowed. Silas shifted his weight from one foot to the other, while Penny blinked to fight back the gloom spreading between the four walls, despite the lamplight. For everyone, hope seemed to catch on a barbed fence while they waited for him to continue.

"Go on, son," Silas urged.

"Told me to call him Nate. He was thirsty. Finally they lowered down a pail of water and we got him a cup full. He seemed better after that. Started talking. Said he had a story and he wanted me to hear it, 'bout a girl named Delphinium and his plans to find her. By the time it ended, all his strength seemed to had run back out."

Although the boy had not taken his eyes away from Larkspurs, he felt the presence of the others in the room lean inward toward the story, as if they were dandelions tilting their heads toward the sun. Moving to stand behind Larkspur, Penny thought to place a hand upon her shoulder but the sorrowful tale anchored her arm to her side.

The boy continued, "That's why I come. He hoped I might get to tell you. Said he wanted you to know something important, something that meant something to him. He said, 'tell her, make sure you tell her, that I didn't die as no slave. I died free.' So that's what I came to tell you. Your Nate died free."

Larkspur sat motionless, a tear falling from her chin landed upon her dress. Beneath the soft fabric the dull key lay quiet.

"What else?" she whispered.

He remembered the sky that night, so he told her of that.

Chapter 10

Hours into the slow journey, the man began to stir and then let out a low moan. Zeb inched closer. "You alright?"

He did not immediately answer but after awhile, the boy felt a hand reach for his arm. "I caught a blow to my side. Bit more rest and I'll be good as new. Bleeding done stopped. Thirsty though," he coughed, "you got any water?" The boy had nothing to offer but the biscuit, which the man refused before sinking back into a fitful sleep.

By the next day, Zeb had been able to give the man water from a pail that was lowered down. The hold had suddenly brightened when the hatch was opened and the handful of men, that Zeb now realized were strewn between the cargo, passed around the ladle and then brought it to Zeb before the hatch was closed and all went dark again.

Hours later, the man began to whisper to the boy. "It's time I go on up now." Zeb didn't respond, hoping for the man's words to make more sense. "I'd like to see the sky. A dark hole ain't no place to die. Can you take me up?"

"It ain't safe. They might catch you," the boy warned.

The man let out a tiny laugh. "But I ain't running no more. They can't do much to you when you ready to die. And

*not a thing once you're dead. Seems a pity, but as long as I die
free under the sky, I don't mind. Naw, I don't mind."*

*So Zeb, with the help of another man, ushered him up
the latter. When Zeb opened the latch, they found the bril-
liance of the night sky, a slivered moon and an abundance of
glittering stars, beckoning them into the light.*

*There seemed no one moving about so they crawled in
the direction of the stern and finally leaned against a small
cockboat, the man exhausted from the effort. Then after he
caught his breath, he looked up and smiled.*

*Above, the sky stretched endlessly, black as ink. Within it
a million tiny points, each one barley a glimmer but together
a radiant band. A luminous dance of shimmering light willing to share its glory indiscriminately, willing to flirt with the
hearts of two young travelers searching to find a way through
the dark.*

*"Ahh, Delphinium always did say the sky was full a noth-
in' but magic. If you get to see her, tell her I seen it to be true.
Tell her, Nate done seen it to be true."*

*After a while, after the man told the boy about the warm
glow of Delphinium which brightened his short life, he closed
his eyes for the last time. Zeb remained at his side awhile
longer, then he crept back to the hatch and down the ladder
into the hold, leaving Ignatius under the full watch of the
star-strewn night.*

Agnes loosened the top button of her coat, finding the day
surprisingly mild, and hurried along toward the post office.
She was sending her weekly letter off to Bernhart before her
morning classes. It had been a long few months of bitter
weather, so the gentle touch of spring against her cheeks lifted
her spirits. She stepped carefully along the wooden sidewalk,
pausing to turn sideways when meeting another pedestrian so
as not to step off the slats into the soft mud. The Ohio winter had offered a deluge of snow and now the spring seemed

intent on lodging mud between the laces of her boots and clinging to the hem of her skirts.

Slipping the letter into the postbox, she rushed toward campus, preferring to arrive early to her classes. While she found the small town of Oberlin to be lonely and mundane, with odd wooden houses detached along unpaved streets, she had no complaints regarding the campus. Academia agreed with her. The leather book covers, the rambling professors, the rise and fall of voices in debate, the angled walkways between lecture halls. Even the drafty windows didn't bother her. It reminded her that she was indeed a genuine student. If only in place of her well-worn journal, she had Bernhart, Penny and Larkspur to sit down with to discuss the day's lessons. She hoped to convince Bernhart to come for a visit over the summer months.

The first to arrive in the classroom, she hung her coat in the cloak closet, settled into a seat and arranged her books about her. A moment later, a woman bounded in, her feet clicking against the scuffed floorboards, and took a seat next to Agnes.

"Hello there. I've just joined the class. Do you think I'm foolish for beginning at such a late date?" She gave a little laugh. "You see I was taking classes in the Female Department when I was made aware there was such a thing as a Teacher's Department. Just in name alone, it is a department much more suitable for someone who knows perfectly well how to be female already."

She smiled brightly then clasped Agnes's hand. "My name is Lucy, just like Lucy Stone I'm proud to say. You know, Lucy Stone the magnificent orator on the woman question? She graduated from Oberlin just a few short years ago."

Agnes, at first confusing Lucy Stone with Lucy Sessions, the first black woman to graduate, merely nodded.

"Did you hear what she's up to now? She's joined the Anti-Slavery Society. She's both a suffragist and an abolitionist!"

Lucy clutched Agnes's arm. "Perhaps I should lower my voice, I do get so excited about it all."

Agnes finally spoke. "There seems to be an abundance of Lucys graduating from Oberlin."

"Yes? Well this one plans to join them. Now, tell me your name and everything else there is to tell?" Agnes delightedly obliged.

ཙ

Brushing the dirt from the knees of his trousers, Bernhart then straightened, relieving the stiffness in his back. He had spent the afternoon tending to dormant flower beds, working the stiff dirt back to life. While he could have assigned the men under his supervision to such a task, he couldn't resist doing it himself. He now stood over his work to inhale the evocative scent of fresh turned soil, a scent he preferred even to the forthcoming redolent flowers for which his labor was focused. Removing his gloves, he aimed his wheelbarrow for the garden shed that by day's end inevitably resulted in a state of complete disarray. He needed to hurry if he hoped to return the garden tools to their proper place, re-stack the crates he had earlier disassembled in search of his favorite trowel, and still find time to wash and change before Silas arrived.

Entering the house through a side door, he left his soiled shoes upon an old mat, hung his work coat upon its hook and climbed the back stairs. By the time he had made use of the washbasin on the stand and replaced his soiled clothes with garments suited for the city, he could hear the clatter of Mercy Tubbs and her carriage coming up the path.

To be prudent, Bernhart reserved the five mile trek into the city for the week's end, staying throughout the week in the main house perched at the crest of Bartram's Garden. On Fridays, Silas crossed the Market Street bridge to fetch him and they rode back to the city together. He now hurried out, closing the heavy door with a tug and stepping across the rock-strewn lane to find Silas gazing out over the grounds that softly fell away toward the river.

"Smells like spring, wouldn't you say?" Silas asked, his horse drinking from the trough against the shed.

"Indeed, a lovely scent, especially at this hour with the day dwindling and the evening chill setting back in."

"I see you turned your beds. Is something due up soon?"

"In due time. I like the idea of all that happens at the very beginning, underground, to ensure that a shoot will, well, shoot forth. Have you noticed some of the trees have buds? That one there," he pointed to a large tree at the mouth of a walking path, "is one of my favorites. The sweet gum tree with its star-like leaves and then of course its audaciously large spiked fruit, which one might argue, when it dries, resembles a different kind of star."

"You can turn an ankle on one a them prickly things," Silas said. "Done it before."

"Indeed," laughed Bernhart. "Do you know what I enjoy the most, Silas? The seed collecting. I have been searching along the paths for those species neglected during the autumn collection. And now that the seeds are dry, there is the fascinating process of classifying and arranging them." He had been assigned the task of helping put together Bartrum Boxes. Small crates, with individual compartments to hold a variety of uncommon and desirable seeds that were shipped all over the country, even as far as Europe. The boxes themselves, were handcrafted especially for Bartram's Garden.

"Can you imagine receiving one on your doorstep? Nearly as thrilling as being the one to send it off." Bernhart added, "That reminds me, our supply of boxes is dwindling and we have yet to find a new carpenter. Our boxes are of a very particular and specialized design. Any chance you would happen to know of a skilled carpenter, Silas?"

The sun was lowering toward the tops of the bare trees. Without the leaves and from the height at which they stood, the men could catch a glimpse of the moving river and the murmuring of it fell against their thoughts.

Now it was Silas's turn to chuckle, "Well Bernhart, I'm gonna have to admit I do. In fact, I do. I know a carpenter that could make you any kind a box you could ever need."

"Wonderful news. I shall have to meet him."

"I think we better set out 'for we lose the sun altogether. I'll tell you about him on the way." Silas went to his horse and gave her a pat, shielding his smile from Bernhart but shining it all over Mercy Tubbs.

As the two men mounted the carriage, coming to sit next to each other on the bench, Silas clucked his tongue to signal for the horse to move, then added, "Sure is enough to do to keep a man busy out here, but I bet your thoughts still drift to Miss Agnes when you're working the day long."

"Yes, admittedly they do," sighed Bernhart. "But I hope to see her one day soon, perhaps come summer." He adjusted the hat upon his head before continuing, "I do not believe I could have dissuaded her from her pursuits, even had I tried. And as she never deterred me from mine—apart, I suppose, from the dusting powder—I felt it only fair to encourage her to go."

The carriage bumped along as they ticked past the trees on both sides of the path like the seconds on a clock. "Moreover, I have found fulfillment here in the garden. I can see now that my studies will take me further into the subject of botany, void of any pressure to invent anything at all, let alone some new species." He grinned, then added, "I trust Agnes and I shall be together one day. Funny thing I've noticed of late, the bittersweet ache that comes from being apart reminds me of spring. No of winter turning to spring. Like a slice of a season, an in between season, all my own."

After a stretch of silence, Silas informed his companion that they had received a letter from Canada. Zeb had found lodging with a family who was building their own house amidst a growing town.

"Excellent. And how about for you, Silas? Any trouble of late?"

Silas shook his head. "No more than we can handle. They ain't about to set us off course. We plan to continue to do what we aim to do. I come to think, once you're certain you doing what's right, don't matter much what happens after that. Once you know it's right," his voice had become as murmurous as the wind slipping through the saplings, "don't matter so much after that."

They were expected for dinner at the boarding house, where Erzsebet would be waiting. They rambled eastward, away from the glowing sun dancing between the tree trunks behind them.

꙳

Larkspur ran her hand over a bolt of fabric. She was in need of a new dress and although warm weather was on its way, by habit she found herself planted in front of an arrangement of dark wools at the dry goods store.

"You can't be supposin' to tailor a new dress from somethin' as scratchy as that, eh. What's gotten into you, lass?" Penny admonished. "You spend each workin' day in the drab black one, but you need a pick-me-up for tea parties and such." Penny turned Lakspur by the elbow toward a series of brighter bolts, a few with floral prints.

"Tea parties?" Larkspur frowned.

"Oh, don't give me such a right look. You never know when you might get invited. Pretty as you are, a miracle could happen."

They exchanged smiles. Larkspur would not consider a dress full of flowers, she had never worn anything of the kind. Even a bright hue would be a departure. Her eyes moved over a bolt of indigo, a heather gray, and then landed on one that brought to mind a vibrant clump of bright green sorrel stumbled upon in the woods. She stretched her hand to it, the lemony taste of the herb suddenly on her tongue.

When there was no longer the possibility of reuniting with Ignatius, her spirits had dimmed. Missing was the sense of purpose that had both grounded and inspired her. So for the remainder of the winter months she turned to her daily tasks, ordinary and predictable, to keep her mind from wandering towards the future.

Now, as she moved her fingertips over the green fabric, which seemed the exact color of spring, she felt a stab of excitement for what lay ahead.

"Yes?" asked Penny, nodding at the green one.

"Yes, but not today. Next time," she promised. She wanted to imagine herself wearing a dress of such fine hue before having to sew it.

"Good enough. Let's be off then as Mr. Hommes will be makin' his wonted stop for saturday tea. I'd hoped to offer him my famous bread and butter puddin'. That is, if there's ample time to stir it up and toss it in the oven."

She noticed a little spark in the younger woman's eyes so she hooked her arm as they left the store and turned toward home.

Penny had worried over the likelihood of Larkspur's continued employment with the Trossens. She found the matter troubling her in the middle of the night, so that she would often reach for a matchstick, lighting a candle in order to properly mull over the issue. Despite the diminished workload due to Agnes's departure, Penny vowed to make certain Larkspur would have the opportunity to retain her position. After all, the house had not shrunk and the garden had doubled. She knew well how to steer Mrs. Trossen toward a certain decision. Yet the possibility that Larkspur might choose to venture forth on her own accord, abandon passing and live within her own community, or even move further north, was what kept her up watching the candle turn into a pool of wax upon the bedside table.

Over the granite pavement their shoes now tapped a rhythm, while the sun shown brightly and warmed their faces. A yellow goldfinch swooped down before them and began pecking at the dirt of a small tree. Larkspur stopped.

"The birds have come back for spring," she stated, then spoke to the bird directly. "How come you're not in the meadow searching through the thistle for your meal, little one? Where's your flock?"

"A pretty yellow thing, ain't she?" asked Penny.

"*He.* The male has the bright coat." As she said this the bird let out a series of soft twitters, turning its head in their direction. Larkspur remembered her blustery meeting with the old woman at the dock and how the black bird, in the middle of winter, had sat on the branch overhead.

"Seems as though you have something to say, pretty bird," she whispered. The bird suddenly lifted up, dodging the branches above and taking flight. As it left it sang out, holding a long note at the end of its musical warble. Larkspur drew her hand to the key around her neck, something she hadn't done of late. In fact, last month she had slipped her charm bag into the small drawer of her bedside table, and pushed at the stiff drawer until she heard the tiny sound of disappointment when it finally slid shut.

She now let her hand fall to her side, wishing she had the velvet pouch to clutch.

" 'Tis a beautiful day," murmured Penny. "Reminds me o' days spent with my granddad. Sundays, in particular, when there was a rest from toilin' in our small plot."

Larkspur thought back to her own Sundays. Perhaps it was the fading gift of the bird's departing note, or the caress of the mild sunshine, or just the familiar presence of the woman beside her, but after a moment she began to reminisce.

"Sunday was the only day we had any time to ourselves. The only day we could hope to meet. After the preaching ended, I waited near an old fencepost between the two farms until Ignatius made his way over, after the others drifted away. Sometimes one thing or another would come up and he wouldn't get the chance to stay. But when he did," she giggled, "my nerves would get to jumping so that I'd start rambling on over silly things that didn't much matter. I made him laugh." She paused. When she began again her voice had dropped.

"The last few times though, the talk turned grave. By then we had heard word that the farm was to be sold. There was a frantic sound to my voice, I know, and he did well to calm me. There was something in his touch, in his skin that worked like medicine against mine. So he held me for a long while, not saying a word. Then he said we needed a plan. He said he'd been meaning to run and now he knew the time was right." She stopped walking but continued looking straight ahead.

"When nearly every last thing gets taken from you, you try to grab ahold of something. So we decided to try to hold onto each other, made a promise out of it. I had Aunt Celena, but I don't think he had anybody but me in this whole world." She swallowed. "I know now that a promise is a tricky thing. For there's no way of knowing if it can be kept, if you should spend up all your hope on it, without knowing what lies up the road?" Turning, she added, "I suppose sometimes the magic of a promise comes in making it, more so than in trying to keep it."

A breeze swept up the sidewalk towards them, fluttering the ribbons of their bonnets and tugging at the ends of their shawls. Penny smiled.

"'Tis a blessin' to have someone care what happens to you. No, 'tis more than a blessin', 'tis the very thing, the very thing that shuttles the blood through the veins and keeps the heart beatin'."

As they continued to walk, settling into a silence, Larkspur listened for the bird's song even after they had entered the

NIGHT SHADE | 221

kitchen, removed their bonnets and shawls, and pressed the door closed behind them.

ॐ

After the fires had been banked in the hearths, a cloth draped over what remained of the bread and butter pudding, the dandelion greens from Bernhart left to dry upon the window sill for Larkspur to employ as remedy for constipation, and the lamp in the kitchen extinguished, Penny sat upon the bed in her small room. She dabbed a bit of comfrey balm into the broken skin around her knuckles. Beginning to sing the lyrics of an old song of her mother's, she slipped her hands into a pair of socks so the ointment would not stain her bedcovers.

When Larkspur overheard the song, having come down for a drink of water carrying a candle in order to see her way through the dark house, this time she knocked gently against the half-open door. Stepping into the room, she said, "I've been meaning to pay you a compliment. Your voice, it's real pretty."

"Why thank you, lass. I must say it comes from my dear mam. She could sing a tune as fine as anyone in the hamlet." After a quiet moment, she added, "What is it you're needin' at this hour? Don't fool me into thinkin' there's more work to do. I'm plum through."

"I came only for the music," replied Larkspur. "But your song got me thinking." A rare, sly look crept upon her face and the words that followed mimicked Penny's accent. "Have you no lad to pay you a visit? With a pretty face like yers, a miracle could happen?"

Penny's eyes danced and a bubbling laugh spilled out. "Oh, so now there's two smart alecs in the house to go at each other." After a moment she sighed and her voice grew more sober. "Perhaps a day will arrive when a poor soul comes along that I find tolerable, but 'til then I'll take my chances with the knot o' folks who treat me kindly and care for me when I'm sick. I lost my kin to the famine in Old Ireland, so I know," she looked down at her hands, gently removing her socks, "that sometimes friends will have to do."

"Penny," Larkspur whispered. "I been meaning to tell you something. I decided to go away for awhile." The older woman's eyes shot up, while the younger continued, "There is a man I've come to learn about. His proper name is James Still but he goes by the Doctor of the Pines. They say he was never given the opportunity for real schooling, but he's known for helping folks with their ailments. He lives in New Jersey, in a country town called Medford, not too far after you cross the river on the ferry."

"Are you sick, lass?"

"Oh no, it's nothing such as that. See, he works with plants, the roots and leaves, just like I do." Penny noticed how her words suddenly zipped along, in a way they had never done before. "I'm eager to learn his ways, to work alongside him. I been asked to come out for the summer, to serve as his apprentice."

"Well how did you come to hear o' him? You can't be sidlin' up to just any fellow simply because he knows better than to grab a handful o' stinging nettles, like some."

Larkspur laughed. "He is the brother of a man I know already. A well-respected man that Mr. Clemons calls a friend." It was quiet while Penny took it in. The flickering light of the candle in Larkspur's hand and the glow from the lamp against the wall softly filled the space between the two women.

Finally, Penny rose from the bed and announced, "My mam always declared, each of us is made to shine. Her last words to me, as I recall, were ones urgin' me to be bright and round, shiny like the name she bestowed upon me. 'Tis only right I tell you to do the same, though to say it, breaks my heart a bit. I suppose as it did hers when she set me upon the boat."

Walking over to the wardrobe, she fiddled with the knob before calling over her shoulder, "But I won't be hearin' of you not coming back regular to share a pot o' tea and givin' me a hand on how to tame the garden." Before any tears gathered in her eyes, she continued, "And I shall keep the garrett for you. When the cold winds return and there's no more scamperin' about in the woods, you may need a warm bed. That is if the urchin who tried to steal Mr. Clemons's horse n' wagon hasn't pilfered the mattress by then. Lately, he's been arrivin' most days before the cock crows askin' to perform a chore or two in exchange for a hot meal. I shall set him to carryin' the ash pots after you've gone."

For a moment the room filled with sadness, until Penny stomped back over to her bed. "Now, when did you say you were plannin' to leave?"

"Not for a bit longer." Relieved by Penny's reaction, Larkspur let out an imperceptible sigh. "A few more weeks at least." Then reaching into the pocket of her apron, she withdrew a pencil and a brown scrap of butcher paper. "There's another matter. I was hoping to ask a favor. I was hoping you might help me learn to write my name."

Penny broke into a smile. "Just the thing I've been meanin' to tell you. Would you care to hear the tale of how my granddad taught me to read and write? He was a kind old gem, who worked wonders with a stick in the dirt." Waving off the scrap of paper in Larkspur's hand, she withdrew a sheet of white paper from the drawer and set it upon the table, under the lamp's glow. "Pull up the chair, lass. Shall we start, then, with L for Larkspur?"

The young traveler who had arrived nearly a year ago, with an odd name, a hidden bag of charms, and an enigmatic identity, had succeeded in shirking the most ill-fitted disguise of all, slavery. While her Nate had been proud to claim that he would not die a slave, she had since concluded that neither had he been born one. Nor had she, for she understood that she had been born something much different. She had been born a healer. So, as she eased into the chair beside Penny, wrapping her shawl around her shoulders, she spoke assuredly.

"If you don't mind Penny, since I was given the name Delphinium I believe it best to start with D. My mama gave me the name of a flower, and she meant for me to use it."

Outside, at the edge of the Trossen woodpile, the opossum began to nose his way out into the yard, while across the grassy lane Mercy Tubbs eased down upon her fresh strewn hay. The birds had gone silent. The cool night air crept along the stepping stones of the garden path, wrapping around the young stems of the spring ephemerals and burrowing back into the soil abandoned by the day's departure. The plants that preferred the night to day, stretched forth, whispering to each other. Overhead, stars flung light across the dark canvas of sky.

Acknowledgements

Upon moving to New Jersey (just across the bridge from Philadelphia) twenty years ago, I was awakened to the rich history of the area. I met a young man who was not only my plumber but who introduced me to the story of his relative, William Still and the book he published in 1872 entitled *The Underground Railroad*, which chronicled his work as the clerk of the Pennsylvania Society for the Abolition of Slavery. I also met a man whose grandmother was friends with Walt Whitman and whose church was a stop on the Underground Railroad. While visiting a handful of historic sites in New Jersey that were connected to the Underground Railroad, including The Peter Mott House in Lawnside, I found myself longing to know the people that once filled the rooms. And when my children enrolled in a Quaker school in Philadelphia, founded in 1689 by William Penn, not only did I gain a deeper understanding of how the Quakers assisted the black community of Philadelphia in the abolitionist movement, but I began to walk the narrow, cobbled streets of the city, sit under the london plane trees in the squares, visit the one-room meeting houses and find myself summoned through the wrought iron gates of the city's old graveyards. The worn-thin headstones, names lost to weather and time, held like empty pages waiting for a story, pulling me back through the delicate fabric of time.

Thank you to Forty Press, to Catherine Knaeble, Elizabeth Knaeble, and to Keith, Mason and Carmen Williams.

CPSIA information can be obtained
at www.ICGtesting.com
Printed in the USA
FFHW021845020919
54638722-60330FF